MUSICIANS

on

MUSIC

ENCORE MUSIC EDITIONS

Reprints of outstanding works on music

edited by F. Bonavia

MUSICIANS
on
MUSIC

HYPERION PRESS, INC.
Westport, Connecticut

Published in 1957 by R. M. McBride, New York
Hyperion reprint edition 1979
Library of Congress Catalog Number 78-66892
ISBN 0-88355-725-8
Printed in the United States of America

Library of Congress Cataloging in Publication Data
Bonavia, Ferruccio, 1877-1950, ed.
  Musicians on music.

  (Encore music editions)
  Reprint of the 1957 ed. published by R. M. McBride, New
York.
  1. Music—Addresses, essays, lectures. I. Title.
[ML55.B65 1979]   780'.8   78-66892
ISBN 0-88355-725-8

CONTENTS

v

GERMANY

ITALY

POLAND

RUSSIA

ACKNOWLEDGEMENTS

WE ARE INDEBTED to the following for their courtesy in permitting us to reproduce extracts from the works named: Messrs Felix Alcan, Paris, for an extract from *César Franck* by Vincent d'Indy: Messrs Edward Arnold & Co. for an extract from *The Letters of Clara Schumann and Johannes Brahms*: Messrs Augustea, Rome, for an extract from *21 plus 26* by Alfredo Casella: Messrs Arti Grafiche Majella de Aldo Chicca for an extract from *Rossini* by Radiciotti: Messrs Constable & Co. Ltd. for an extract from *Studies and Memories* by Sir Charles Stanford: Messrs J. M. Dent & Sons Ltd. for an extract from *Beethoven's Letters*: Messrs Elek Books Ltd. for an extract from *Mendelssohn's Letters*: Messrs Aldo Garzanti Editore già Fratelli Treves for an extract from *Contemporary Musicians* by Ildebrando Pizzetti: Messrs Desmond Harmsworth Ltd.: Messrs John Lane the Bodley Head Ltd. for an extract from *The Life of Tchaikowsky* by Rosa Newmarch: Messrs Albert de Lange, Amsterdam, for an extract from *Erzinerungen* by Alma Mahler: Messrs Longmans, Green and Co. Ltd. for an extract from *Farewell My Youth* by Sir Arnold Bax: Messrs Putnam and Co. Ltd. for an extract from *Bach* by Sir Hubert Parry: Messrs Martin Secker and Warburg Ltd. for extracts from *My Musical Life* by Rimsky-Korsakov and from the correspondence between Richard Strauss and von Hofmannstahl: Messrs Williams and Norgate Ltd. for an extract from *Monsieur Croche* by Claude Debussy: Mrs C. Elgar Blake, and the Editor of the *Daily Telegraph*, for *A Visit to Delius* by Sir Edward Elgar.

Acknowledgement and thanks are due to Mr Frank Howes for his assistance in preparing this posthumous volume for publication.

CHIEF SOURCES FOR THE PASSAGES IN THIS BOOK

Sir Hubert Parry: *Johann Sebastian Bach*, Putnam, 1909

Sir Charles Stanford: *Studies and Memories*, Constable, 1908

Ralph Vaughan Williams: Royal College of Music Magazines, Easter 1945

Sir Edward Elgar: the *Daily Telegraph*

Sir Arnold Bax: *Farewell my Youth*, Longmans, 1943

Sir George Dyson, Royal College of Music Magazines, Christmas 1944 and Christmas 1945; *The New Music*, Oxford University Press, 1926

Hector Berlioz: *Memoirs*: *The Life of Hector Berlioz* [Calmann-Lévy] 1896–7

Camille Saint-Saëns: *Outspoken Essays*, Kegan Paul, 1922

Claude Debussy: *Antidilettante*, Williams & Norgate

Vincent d'Indy: *César Franck: A Study*, Bodley Head, 1909

Wolfgang Amadeus Mozart: *Letters*, ed. Emily Anderson, 1938, McMillan & Co.

Ludwig van Beethoven: *Beethoven's Letters*, Dent, 1926

Louis Spohr: *Autobiography*, Longmans, 1864

Felix Mendelssohn: *Mendelssohn's Letters*, Elek, 1947

Robert Schumann: *Schumann's Letters*, Dobson, 1947

Ashton Ellis: *Richard Wagner's Prose Works*, Kegan Paul, 1893–97

Hans von Bülow: *Early Correspondence of von Bülow*, Fisher Unwin, 1896

Johannes Brahms: *Letters of Brahms and Clara Schumann*, Arnold, 1927

13

Alma Mahler: *Recollections and Letters of Gustav Mahler*, A. de Lange (Amsterdam)

Richard Strauss: *Correspondence between Strauss and von Hofmannsthal*, Secker 1928

A. Godignola: *Paganini*, Municipio di Einora, 1935

Radiciotti: *Rossini*, Tivoli, 1928

F. Bonavia: *Verdi*, 1930. Oxford University Press, 1947

Giuseppe Verdi: *I Copialettere* (Milan)

Arrigo Boito: *Lettere di A. Boito*, Novissima, Rome, 1932

Giacomo Puccini: *Letters of Giacomo Puccini*, ed. Adami, Harrap, 1931

Ferruccio Busoni: *Briefe an seine Frau*, ed. Schnapp, 1937 (paraphrased in E. J. Dent's *Ferruccio Busoni: A Biography* 1933)

Ildebrando Pizzetti: *Musicisti Contemporanei*, Treves, Milan, 1914

Alfredo Casella: *21 plus 26*, Augustea, Rome, 1931

F. Niecks: *Chopin as a Man and Musician*, Novello

Frédéric François Chopin: *Chopin's Letters*, ed. Opienski, Harmsworth, 1932

Nicholai Andreievich Rimsky-Korsakov: *My Musical Life*, Secker, 1924

Peter Ilitch Tchaikovsky: *The Life and Letters of Peter Ilitch Tchaikovsky*, ed. Rose Newmarch, John Lane, 1906

Introduction

THE WRITINGS OF great musicians do not teach us how to compose fine symphonies. That art, in so far as it can be taught at all, must be learnt in the discipline of the schools. The present collection of essays and letters is no substitute for a text-book on harmony. Its aim is rather to allow composers to tell their own tale unaided—or unhampered—by critic and historian and provide for us the means for understanding their thought. It is derived from many sources, the authors being men whose work is the mainstay of the concert and opera repertory.

Most of these excerpts have a direct bearing on the art of music; all connect somehow the artist and the man. To prove that such a connection exists is difficult; it is impossible to assume that it does not exist at all. The psychology of genius cannot be defined by syllogisms. One can but record facts that are often contradictory, exhibiting comedy and tragedy, nobility and vanity, generosity and prejudice side by side. Literary qualities cannot be claimed for these writings but they lack neither artistic nor human interest. Men are seldom dull when they discuss a subject they have at heart. And even when not concerned with artistic matters in their comments and observations the writers must needs lay bare their character.

Mendelssohn's description of his visit to Queen Victoria and Prince Albert for instance conveys a very clear picture of the brilliant artist who was also the accomplished man of the world as much at ease in court as in the concert room. Others might have felt flattered by the invitation and possibly a little shy—not Mendelssohn. Nowhere in England, he says, is he so much at home as in Buckingham Palace. We associate genius with a Grub Street garret or a Buckinghamshire cottage: Mendelssohn is the first great artist to claim a royal palace as his spiritual home. He was a born courtier. He told Prince Albert that he wanted to hear him play the organ so that he could boast about it in Germany; he told Queen Victoria that he had come to England solely to ask permission to dedicate to her his Scottish symphony. He was also a good Victorian. Poor sister Fanny had a pretty talent for musical composition but she was not encouraged to publish because woman's place was the home. The world was the best of all possible worlds for Felix Mendelssohn; he never knew the sorrow, the anger, the pain and ecstasy that give depth to the music of Beethoven.

Much has been written in sober prose and in purple patches about Beethoven's tragedy. His music alone can tell us all the passion that agitated his great soul. We gather something of what this master of music felt when, at thirty-two, he realized that he would never hear sound again, in the 'Heiligenstadt' testament. Others laboured to create while suffering pain and physical disability—Leopardi, Milton, Alexander Pope. But Milton could at least express his grief in *Samson* and Alexander Pope vented anger and ill-humour in satire. Beethoven never allowed pain and bitterness to cloud his inner vision and the man whose manners were ridiculed by the Viennese ended his career expressing an ideal that is, even now, too exalted and too lofty for humanity. Bettina Brentano was not wrong when she described him to Goethe as 'a man far ahead of modern civilization'.

Out of the many letters we have of Mozart a few have been chosen written when he was engaged to Constanze—pathetic documents showing the young composer torn between love for a father who strongly objected to the union and attachment to Constanze, a noble nature humbled by a passion it cannot resist. Paganini's letter to a Parisian daily on the other hand is included simply as an historical page illustrating the effect that transcendental virtuosity had on the public of the day. At the present time anyone suggesting that even the greatest skill is supernatural would be suspected of unsound mind. Paganini's contemporaries held different views. A wiser generation would have objected that Paganini as a keen man of business was quite unlikely to barter his soul for the bombastic fustian of his D major concerto. But the romantic age had a weakness for the supernatural and even great men like Shelley and Walter Scott began writing in the manner of Mrs Radcliffe.

The longest and most important extract in the collection is Richard Wagner's essay on conducting now translated by Dr

Mosco Carner. Dr Carner has overcome the difficulties of the tortuous prose very ably but this is not reading for an idle half-hour. Thoughts crowd into the writer's mind and he sets them down with little regard for method, but the essay repays close study. It describes German musical life with extra-ordinary candour; it lays down the laws of a sound interpreta-tion; it provides a touchstone by which we can distinguish the responsible from the irresponsible. At the time, it served to found the new school of conductors, the chief exponents of which were Bülow, Richter, Liszt; it remains today an invaluable guide to all serious music-lovers, who would know something of the problems of the conscientious interpreter (and all musicians are interpreters) when he performs the works of other men.

The composers of the last century have written less about their art or system than our contemporaries. If the men of today are not so well represented it is because we are too near to see them objectively and because the general public is inevitably more interested in their music than in their writing. If music fails to please and interest, the most logical argument will not make it attractive. The future alone can show how much in the treatises of recent date will stand the test of time. The great majority of the composers included in the collection are either well known to the public or else have something to say that the public may care to know. These writings can be no substitute for expert knowledge; they may however take us a little nearer to the mind and heart of the creative musician.

F. B.

ENGLAND

Sir Hubert Parry

BACH'S ORGAN AT MÜHLHAUSEN

THE MUSICAL TRADITIONS at Mühlhausen were of a high order. But the organ at St Blasius seems to have been in very bad order and one of the most interesting documents drawn up by John Sebastian himself which remains to the world is his scheme of suggestions for making good its defects. The main trouble must be inferred from this document to have been that the bellows were insufficient for the work they had to perform, and John Sebastian made some simple and practical suggestions about them. Most of the other suggestions refer to new stops, and in these are some noteworthy features. It seems surprising to modern ears that he recommended the addition of no less than six new harmonic stops to the choir organ and only one soft stop of eight-foot tone. This, together with the strange constitution of the choir organ at Arnstadt, suggests that musicians of the time had a liking for this quality of tone, comprising the least possible foundation and a crowd of harmonics, and that Bach, either from association or individual taste, endorsed it. Another feature, which chimes with what everybody must feel who knows his music, is the number of suggestions he makes with regard to the pedal organ, in which he wanted a better supply of wind, a thirty-two-foot stop, and a complete set of new and larger pipes to the bass posaune, which would add weight and fullness. The most surprising of the suggestions, when coming from a composer of Bach's disposition, is that a set of twenty-six bells, . which the parishioners had already procured and paid for, should be attached to the pedal organ. However, there seems no need to infer that Bach used the bells in the pedal parts of his fugues and toccatas. It was not at all an unusual thing in the Middle Ages to have peals of bells connected with mechanical appliances like organ keys or pedals, which were played upon by an individual performer; and elaborate music was written for such contrivances, and musical reputations, like that of Mathias van den Gheyn, were even founded on such compositions and performances. And, moreover, whatever artistic purists might say about it, the sound of carillon and bells mixed up with a hurly-burly of singing and organ and other instruments had a strangely exhilarating effect on brilliant festive occasions; and for such occasions these bells may well have been reserved.

The suggestions for these extensive alterations seem to have been taken in good part, and the work decided on. But so short was Bach's stay in Mühlhausen that the reconstruction was not completed before he had moved elsewhere.

BACH'S VIOLIN STYLE

It must be admitted that the style of violin music was quite overwhelmed in him by the pre-eminent influences of the organ style; but for that there seems sufficient reason in the fact that in his boyhood the style of violin music was but slightly differentiated. The violin had been cultivated throughout the seventeenth century, but it was only by very slow degrees that its technical resources were evolved, that the particular passages suited for it were devised, and that its powers of expression in cantabile passages and its capacity for rapid passages were so far realized as to serve as the basis of the admirable exposition of its true capabilities which is shown in the works of Vitali, Bassani, Corelli and Vivaldi, and the Italian violinists who succeeded them. Though it is true that some of Corelli's works were written early enough for Bach to have heard them in his boyhood, it is probable that most of the violin music which came under his notice was the product of an earlier generation, presenting but few traits of distinctive style, and that organ music, which was the one and only branch of instrumental music of which the style was decisively differentiated, was the only one upon which his developing sensibilities could be decisively nurtured.

Thus organ style became in all things the most persistent influence in determining Bach's procedure, even when he was writing for an instrument so radically and uncompromisingly different as the violin. The violin is primarily a melodic instrument, the organ is most emphatically not so; the violin has an infinite capacity for expressive variation of tone, like a voice, the organ has none except such as is arrived at by mechanical devices; the violin is a single-part instrument, the organ essentially and necessarily a many-part instrument. Without entering further into their oppositions, the contrast between them is summed up in the analogy which their natures suggest. The organ has often been called 'the king of instruments', and if justly so the violin may fairly be called 'the queen'.

But of these radical differences of nature Bach was neither unaware nor inapt to take advantage. No composer ever had a finer sense of the free and sensitively expressive type of melody, which the violin has a pre-eminent capacity for presenting, than John Sebastian. He shows the type in many of the arioso recitatives for solo voices in cantatas and other great works of the kind. The melody of the violin, moreover, being free from words, left him more untrammelled both by association and by the constraint of submission to actual syllables to soar away from conventions and formulas into the region of introspective emotionalism which was dear to his Teutonic nature. Moreover, no composer ever had a happier sense of vivacious, merry, sparkling dance measures such as the violin is so ideally fitted to present and for which the organ is so utterly ill suited. So the aspects in which the organ style is discernible in his violin music are, after all, confined to such as do not seriously affect its real appositeness; consisting mainly in the use of types of passages which were familiar in the organ music but also capable of being rendered on the violin, and in the use of contrapuntal texture, and the suggestion of suspensions and large progressions of harmony, to which the attitude of a mind nurtured in organ music preferably resorted. The extraordinary difficulties which his solo music presents impelled violinists ultimately to develop a special phase of technique to conquer them, because the music is in itself so supremely great and noble that high-minded performers could not rest satisfied till they found the way to master it. And hence it has come about ultimately that these solo works are regarded as among the most convincing proofs of the powers of interpretation of the foremost violinists of later times.

THE ORCHESTRA IN 1724

IN CONSIDERING SUCH a work as the *Johannes-Passion* Bach's use of his instrumental resources calls for some notice. The resources which he had at his disposal were, without doubt, the same as he would have had for any of his cantatas, among which three trumpets and drums and horns had frequently been prominent.

But the attitude of composers of that time to the orchestra was altogether different from that of later times. It was usual then to choose particular groups of instruments for particular movements, and to spread the tone colour over wide spaces, when in modern music there would have been a constant shimmer of variety. A composer who really gave his mind to his work would choose the particular instruments which were most appropriate to the sentiment of the words and the character of the movement. This is obviously shown in the manner in which Bach, as well as other composers, reserved the trumpets for brilliant occasions, and for movements in which there is exuberance of rejoicing or praise. It is also illustrated by the fact that Bach omits them, as well as the horns, altogether from the score of the *Johannes-Passion*. It was natural that for a function the object of which was the devout contemplation of the central mystery and tragedy of religion he should choose instruments of more subdued tone, and he distributes them with evident consideration for the enhancement of the sentiment.

For the ordinary full accompaniments of the choruses and chorales, flutes and hautboys join with the strings and organ, sometimes having separate parts, sometimes merely doubling the voices, and sometimes doubling the strings. Bach's habit in that respect must be admitted to be puzzling. It can only be inferred that he accepted the usual course in this matter, and it is strange that its many anomalies should not have arrested his attention. The flutes are often too weak for the work they have to perform when they wrestle in the polyphony on equal terms with the strings, while the flutes, hautboys, and strings, being doubled or even trebled in unison, only spoil one another's tone, and the persistent sound of the piercing hautboy becomes positively distressing. But the distribution of the solo instruments in accompanying the arias is evidently carefully considered, both with the view of aptness to the sentiment and to the general plan of the work. Thus the first aria, which is a tender, sad strain, is accompanied by two hautboys and figured bass; the second, in a bright and loving vein, is accompanied by the flutes doubled in unison passages. The third aria, in which much use is made of slow, expressive polyphony, is happily allotted to the strings; the solemnly pathetic arioso 'Betrachte, meine Seel', is accompanied by the unique and suggestive combination of two viole d'amore and lute, which must have had a sense of twilight stillness and quietude, truly admirable for the contemplation suggested by the words; the aria which follows is connected with the arioso by continuing the use of the viole d'amore, but the use of the lute is restricted to the arioso. In the aria relating to the crucifixion, 'Es ist volbracht', the viola da gamba is employed; in the arioso 'Mein Herz', following the reference to the earthquake and the veil of the temple being rent, the natural expedient is employed of strings tremolandi and rushing in rapid unison passages below chords for the flutes and oboi da caccia, and in the last aria 'Zerfliesse, mein Herze', the two oboi da caccia are combined with flutes and the throbbing bass of the lower instruments. Thus each aria is accompanied by a different group of instruments not only inducing contrasts in wide spaces, but, as it were, allocating a special colour to each reflective sentiment. The system presupposes long continuance in one vein of feeling, which is not altogether natural to modern audiences, and requires some revival, at least in imagination, of the conditions in which the work was produced.

Sir Charles Stanford

MUSIC IN CATHEDRALS

THE CHURCH IS in a unique position as regards music. Music is, of all the arts, the one which is in the closest daily relationship with her. She is not dependent upon it for monetary profit and, therefore, has a free hand in advancing what is best without regard to what will pay; a consideration which, in the circles of music itself, is unfortunately at all times a pressing problem. I take it that no one will deny that, amongst the many duties of the Church, education, refinement and improvement in the matters of taste are not, or should not, be absent and therefore I hold that in respect of music it is not only possible but imperative that the Church should educate, refine and improve its members in that particular branch of it which is especially devoted to herself. She should lead taste and not follow it. She should uncompromisingly adopt what is best, irrespective of popularity, and eschew the second-rate, even if it is momentarily attractive. I am thus brought face to face with the question whether the Church, through her cathedrals and in 'quires and places where they sing' is doing her duty in this respect: and study of her recent musical records obliges me to answer the question with a decided negative.

Cathedral music in England has a great history. We have to thank the cathedrals for keeping alive, in artistically dark times, much of the half-buried talents of this country. They were the nurseries of such men as Tallis, Byrd, Gibbons, Farrant, and, greatest of all, Henry Purcell. The traditions of these men and many more are not lightly to be brushed aside. They represented not merely learning, but luminous fancy; their works were English to the backbone, solid in foundation; sometimes, perhaps, severe to a new acquaintance but, once understood, always growing in sympathetic feeling and constant in the affection they inspired. They have an atmosphere about them which affects every man who from his childhood has known an English cathedral. In this respect they occupy the same position in the English Church that Heinrich Schütz and the Bachs did in the Lutheran, and Palestrina and his contemporaries in the Roman.

At the present time, in the Roman Church, we find all the signs pointing in the direction of the renaissance of Palestrina and his school. . . . In the Lutheran Church the influence of Bach has never been superseded. In the English Church alone do we find our own great masters being more and more systematically neglected and a new conglomerate style introduced in their place. . . . In the time of Samuel Wesley it was not so; his son, Samuel Sebastian Wesley, though he had a touch of the reformer in him, never led or hinted at revolution. Thomas Attwood Walmisley, one of the most gifted of our Church composers, never left the path of the genuine school; Sterndale Bennett, though owing so much to German training and influence, never ceased to belong to the British school in his church music.

What is the cause of this condition of affairs? Partly, perhaps, a lack of veneration of our traditions . . . partly the fact that music has become so popular that the supply has not been limited to the works of those who have something to say and know how to say it. But the real root of the mischief is, I am convinced, the trammelled position of the man who is responsible for the performance of the music, the organist. In most cases the responsibility for the choice of music is not centred in him, the expert, but either altogether in the hands of one of the clergy or divided between a precentor and the organist. There are instances where this disastrous policy does not hold but they are unfortunately exceptions, not rules.

The organist is the learned and cultivated musician, and the clerical official has not (save in a very few instances) qualified either by study or research for a task demanding exceptional musical skill and routine. But he retains a power for which he has in the lapse of time lost the necessary equipment and the result is a far-spread amateurishness of taste which, if it is permitted to rule, will inevitably destroy the best traditions of English Church music.

The advice I would venture to give is best expressed in the

words of two great composers of this century. As Wagner says in *Meistersinger*, 'Ehrt eure deutschen Meister', so let me adapt it, 'Honour your English Masters', and as Verdi said not long ago, 'Torniamo all'antico'—make the mainstay of your music the great works of the past without ceasing to encourage all that is best in contemporary music.

WHY BRAHMS DID NOT VISIT ENGLAND

IN 1877 CAMBRIDGE UNIVERSITY offered Brahms (together with Joachim) an honorary degree. Mr Mason in his book *From Grieg to Brahms* has a remark about this which is erroneous, and is really a confusion between two wholly distinct events. He says that 'when the university of Cambridge offered him a degree, suggesting that he should write a new work for the occasion, he replied that if any of his old works seemed good enough to them, he should be happy to receive the honour, but he was too busy to write one!' The actual facts are these: Brahms hesitated long about visiting Cambridge and, being much pressed to do so by both Joachim and Frau Schumann, was almost on the point of accepting, when unfortunately the authorities of the Crystal Palace got wind of the possible visit and announced in *The Times* that he would be invited to conduct at one of their Saturday concerts. This piece of over-zeal wrecked the visit. The university did not ask him to write a new work for the occasion, but although he would not come, and could not be given a degree 'in absentia', he entrusted the manuscript score and parts of his first symphony in C minor (which had then only once been played in Karlsruhe) to Joachim, and it was performed together with the 'Schick-salslied' at the concert of the University Musical Society, at which his presence was so desired. The incident to which Mr Mason refers was probably an invitation in 1887 to write a new work for the Leeds festival, an institution which had hitherto wholly neglected his compositions, and which was conducted by Sullivan, who made no secret of his lack of sympathy with them. To this he replied: 'I cannot well decide to promise you a new work for your festival. Should you consider one or other of my existing works worthy the honour of a performance, it would give me great pleasure. But if this, as it appears, is not the case, how could I hope to succeed this time? If, however, the charm of novelty is a "sine qua non", forgive me if I admit that I neither rightly understand nor greatly sympathise with such a distinction.' A very pretty riposte and a thoroughly dignified specimen of epistolary satire. . . .

I made two attempts to induce him to visit England after this. First in 1889, when his *Requiem* was given at the Leeds Festival. I wrote and told him that if he would come to Cambridge via Harwich I would go to Leeds and back with him and conceal his identity from every one; but he was not to be stirred. Last, in 1893, when Cambridge University Musical Society was about to celebrate its fiftieth birthday, we wrote once more and offered him, with Verdi, an honorary degree. He was this time sorely tempted and much touched by the request, but he turned it off by saying how old he would seem beside the everlasting youth of Verdi. . . .

VERDI'S 'FALSTAFF'

THE DANGERS OF indiscreet prophecy are proverbial, and instances of it are many and occasionally amusing. Perhaps no more striking example could be found than one short sentence which occurs at the close of the article 'Verdi', in Grove's *Dictionary of Music and Musicians* (First Edition), which was written, before the production of *Otello*, by a warm admirer and enthusiastic compatriot of the great composer. It runs as follows: 'For the musical critic, *Otello*, whatever it may be, can neither add to nor detract from the merits of its author. From *Oberto Conte di S. Bonifacio* to the *Messa di Requiem*, we can watch the progressive and full development of Verdi's genius, and though we have a right to expect from him a new masterpiece, still nothing leads us to believe that the new work may be the product of a "nuova maniera".' After the experience of *Otello* in February 1887, and of *Falstaff* in February 1893, these remarks can scarcely fail to raise a smile. But their author may be forgiven for failing to foresee that the seven-leagued boots which carried Verdi from *Nabucco* to *Aïda*, would prove capable of taking another stride, and a longer one.

Mazzucato left two important factors out of his calculations—
the influence of Boito and the perennial youthfulness of the
composer. It is scarcely necessary to insist that Verdi has
developed a 'nuova maniera', a third style as distinct from his
two earlier methods as is that of Beethoven; but differing
from the Bonn master in that the latest manner is of the nature
rather of a radical change than of a natural development of the
earlier growth. To lay down roughly the landmarks of Verdi's
three styles is not a matter of great difficulty. The first may be
said to extend from *Oberto* to the *Forza del Destino*, the second
from *Don Carlos* to the *Requiem*, and the third from *Otello*
to ————, here we may happily leave a blank. I am loth to
follow the example of the 'Dictionary', and to put a full stop
to the catalogue. The musical world may yet be startled by a
new opera as far in advance of *Falstaff* as *Otello* is of *Aïda*. To a
man of such strength and health, such brains and wealth of
imagination, nothing is impossible. His is not the nature of
a Rossini, who, after a series of successes made in the full
vigour of manhood, sat down and spent the rest of his witty
existence chewing the cud of memory; but rather that of a
Titian, whose work ceased only with the breath of life. There
is a curious parallel between these two great artists; the painter
who worked without apparent loss of power to the age of
ninety-nine, and only died by the accident of the plague; and
the composer who produced his best and most mature work at
the age of seventy-nine, and is to all appearance capable of as
much more, both good and new. In such hale veterans this
century has happily been rich, and Italy can claim her share.
In Verdi she has a source of pride which she is not slow to
appreciate or backward in acclaiming. Those who lately witnessed the triumph of his last opera could not fail to be deeply
impressed, on the one hand, by the touching affection which
leavened the enthusiasm of the country—an affection felt and
expressed alike by king and by peasant—and on the other, by
the modesty and dignity with which it was accepted by the
great composer. So devoid was he of all self-assertion, that he
even expressed his regret that so vast a concourse of strangers
should have taken the trouble to come from all parts of Europe
for the 'première', and declared that he preferred the days of

his earlier career, when his operas were accepted or rejected on their merits alone, and when the test was independent of any considerations of personal popularity. A glance at his honest eyes was enough to satisfy the hearer that these were his true convictions and no affections of humility. Such men are at all times rare; but living as Verdi does at a moment when the younger Italian school, which he has so long fostered almost single-handed, is rapidly coming to the fore, and is reaching an important crisis of its development, his influence for good cannot possibly be over-rated, nor can it fail to be productive of the highest results.

It is interesting to turn for a moment to the earlier works of Verdi's long career, and to notice the points of difference between them and the works of his maturity, as well as the threads of similarity which connect them. At all times vivid and poetical, the earlier operas have undoubtedly been defaced by a certain lack of refinement, and by a neglect of the balance which should exist between orchestra and singers. The very superabundance of melodic gift which seems almost to inundate them interferes with the dramatic cohesion and cloys rather than satisfies the ear. The orchestral treatment, although more important than it had been in the hands of Donizetti and Bellini, was more influenced by their methods than by the sounder traditions of Cherubini. Many instances of this bald handling of the orchestra will be found in page after page of the *Trovatore* and the *Traviata*, where the most tragic and highly wrought passages of vocal declamation are supported by an ordinary waltz rhythm in the accompaniment, which indeed seems to be doing its best to belie the drift of the words sung. Sometimes traces of the most unqualified banality occur, as witness the music assigned to the stage-band at the opening of *Rigoletto*, a passage which it is almost impossible to listen to without a feeling of aversion. But even these worst moments possess in the very outspokenness of their vulgarity a certain genuine ring, a spontaneity of expression, which cannot fail to bring home to the listener that the composer is an honest man doing his best according to his lights. It is this honesty of purpose, coupled with an immense fertility of imagination and adaptability of temperament, which has permeated Verdi's life-work, and resulted in this his latest, his most powerful, and his most beautiful composition. It is precisely this genuineness to which Meyerbeer, with all his astuteness, was unable to attain. Verdi's was an unpolished metal, Meyerbeer's a stage tinsel. Verdi's was a natural genius, Meyerbeer's a cultivated ingenuity. The natural process was in the one case a power of taking the highest burnish and polish, in the other a gradual thinning of the veneer, and the eventual exposure of the inferior material which underlay it. Some similarity of workmanship at one time undoubtedly existed between these two men; but their ways divided as sharply and trended as differently as those of Meyerbeer and his contemporary Weber. Between Verdi and his great German colleague Wagner there is a far closer relationship of method. But only of method, and not of workmanship based on the method. The styles of these two composers vary so completely that it seems impossible to assert that the Italian learned from the German. It would be fairer to say, as perhaps posterity will say, that the immense development of opera in the latter half of the nineteenth century was rather the result of a natural process than the work of any one man; that *Tristan, Carmen,* and *Otello* are only so many landmarks on the road of progress which each country was making in its own way. In one respect Wagner had the advantage (if a questionable one) of his brethren. He had a pen for words as well as notes, for criticism and essay as well as for poetry and music; his conception of the relations of music and drama was therefore laid before the unmusical as well as the musical public, and that with much fire and fury, and with quips and thrusts which directed the eyes of all Europe to his polemical genius. With these methods Verdi has had nothing to do. He has contented himself with working out his own ideas on music paper, and trusting his fame to the application of theories alone, while abstaining from their discussion. He has therefore, by the mere fact of making no ferocious enemies, created no cult of aggressive friends. But his best work will not suffer on that account, and the Italian may be counted, at any rate, the happier man. The very dissimilarity of the natures of Wagner and Verdi accentuates the identity of their principles, and goes to prove that solid truth was at the bottom of the well from which each drew his inspiration.

The principles were harder to apply in Italy than in Germany. Wagner found the way prepared for him by Weber and by Spontini, who though of Italian birth identified himself with Germany. There the orchestra was already raised to the position of a participator in the drama, vocal effect had already begun to give way to truth of expression. Not so in Italy. The latest work of Rossini was rather a French than an Italian opera, and the threadbare productions of Donizetti and Bellini were all that intervened between the school of the *Barbiere* and the beginnings of Verdi. It would not have been surprising if, under these circumstances, he had turned from his sources of inspiration to the works of other countries; but this is precisely what Verdi did not do. He had the consciousness of the strength he derived from contact with his native soil, and determined for good or ill to work upon it alone. *Otello* and *Falstaff*, both as uncompromising in their fidelity to dramatic truth of expression as *Tristan* and the *Meistersinger*, are both unmistakably Italian operas, in warmth of feeling, in force of declamation, and in wealth of purely vocal melody. In one respect at least Verdi's later works are more satisfactory in their effect upon the public than those of Wagner, namely in concentration. The very fact that Wagner was his own librettist was necessarily detrimental to his sense of proportion. Immense as was the advantage which he gained by uniting all the elements of construction of a music-drama in his own person, they were undoubtedly counterbalanced by the disadvantages arising from the lack of discussion and of criticism. There was no independent composer to curb the redundancies of the librettist, no independent librettist to warn the composer of undue lengthiness. The result is that, except under the special conditions of Bayreuth, it may safely be said no work of Wagner's is given in any opera house without many and extensive cuts;[1] cuts moreover that from the point of view of actual physical comfort are necessary to the average theatre-goer, be he ever

---

[1] *This was in 1893: but what was true of the past may yet be true of the future.*

such a devotee of the master. In the case of Verdi this is wholly different. In Arrigo Boito he has found a fellow-worker who is at once a poet and a dramatist of the highest rank, and in addition is gifted with the keenest musical perception. Conference, discussion, and mutual criticism have done their work and eliminated all the *longueurs* both in acting and in music; as a consequence it is hard to lay one's finger on one single scene either in *Otello* or in *Falstaff* where a cut would not absolutely injure the construction or mutilate the piece. Both operas are therefore of reasonable length and fatigue neither audience nor performers. If on the one hand it is impossible to credit Verdi with the possession of the immense power which created the Death March in the *Dusk of the Gods*, we are equally unable to credit Wagner with the power of exquisite vocal writing which is the glory of the Italian master. It may be urged that such comparisons are odious, but to the mind of the unprejudiced admirer of both these giants they are not so. They are only instructive. Neither creator could, even if he would, change his nature; the fact that each was true to his own is the highest testimony to the value of their respective creations.

I have said that *Falstaff* is written upon the same principle as the *Meistersinger*. It is curious, however, to note how each master uses these principles in his own way. In the *Meistersinger* the orchestra is the pivot of the whole, and asserts itself markedly to be so. In *Falstaff* it plays the same part, but in such a way as to call no attention to its importance. It is rather felt than heard, much as in *Don Juan* and the *Marriage of Figaro*. In the *Meistersinger* the voice parts go entirely by the natural declamation of the words without regard as to whether the result is melodic and vocal or the reverse. In *Falstaff* the declamation is so perfect as to be (in the words of Boito) a physiological study, and yet the notes sung never cease to be melodious and grateful to the singer. A most happy instance of this is the phrase sung by Mrs Quickly at her entrance in Act II to the word 'Reverenza'. In the *Meistersinger* there are no full closes, save at the fall of the curtain, and the music runs continuously on from beginning to end. In *Falstaff* there are numerous full closes, which are, however, so artfully conceived that they give the impression of continuity without sacrificing the relief to the ear. In the *Meistersinger* there are definite phrases associated with definite personalities and situations; in *Falstaff* the same result is produced by orchestral colouring and by the use and interchange of certain definite rhythms. In the *Meistersinger* there are two or three complete lyrical passages, songs, if they may be so termed without offence, which can be performed separately from the work without much sacrifice of effect or of value. In *Falstaff* there are none, nor is it possible to repeat any passage without wholly spoiling the scene. The encores, which, though few, were insisted on at the Scala, amply proved how fatal any break, however short, in the play was to its unity of purpose.

It will thus be seen that *Falstaff* is as modern in construction as its German predecessor; and, if it is impossible to assign it quite so high a position in the catalogue of masterpieces, that is only because it is not so rich in human interest, and fails to touch so deeply the emotions. This is, however, the character of the play. There is no creation in it so sympathetic as the figure of Hans Sachs, no element of rest so satisfying as the moment where the watchman walks up the deserted street in the moonlight; no set melody so riveting as the 'Preislied'. In these points, and in these alone, it falls short of the high-water mark of the *Meistersinger*. The charm, the vivacity, the wit of the Italian are in every page. To expect more would be to expect Verdi to belie his nationality. We do not the less admire a Giovanni Bellini because we may prefer a Dürer; nor do we expect from the Venetian the qualities of the Nürnberger. The preference will be according to the temperament and race of the hearer. A Teuton will prefer the *Meistersinger* and a Latin will prefer *Falstaff*. It is enough for us that we possess both.

No criticism upon the later works of Verdi would be complete without a reference to the important share in their production held by Arrigo Boito. To the brilliant composer of *Mefistofele* is to be traced the force which impelled Verdi to start afresh upon operatic work. It can hardly be denied that his influence has had a powerful effect on the direction of the older composer's mind. It is not for the first time in history that such a bond has united the elder and the younger generation. Blow and Henry Purcell obviously had common interest and sympathies of a similar sort, and to a still more striking extent Haydn and Mozart. Nor was Wagner himself uninfluenced by younger men, as witness the effect of Cornelius's *Barber of Baghdad* upon the *Meistersinger*. So it is with Verdi and Boito. Certainly the composer never before had librettos so worthy of his genius, or so suggestive to his imagination, as the poems of *Otello* and *Falstaff*.

The construction of *Falstaff* is extremely clear and concise. There are three acts almost equal in length, each subdivided into two scenes also more or less of equal length. The persons of the Shakespeare play are reduced in number. The character of Slender is merged in that of Dr Caius, a proceeding which cannot fail to cause regret; for the latter remains a somewhat colourless and troublesome figure, while the well-known thin and sentimental Slender would have made an admirable foil to the fire and jealousy of Ford and the fat and humorous hero. Without Slender there is no pendant to Falstaff. This and this only is the weak point of the casting of the play. The alternations of scenes are admirably conceived, and happily contrasted. The poetry is no whit inferior to the construction; many passages, both of translation and of original matter, are well worthy of a separate existence. As examples of excellent and almost literal reproduction of Shakespeare may be mentioned the monologue upon Honour, which has been ingeniously worked into the first scene, and the speech of Ford at the close of the first scene of the second act. The original passages are naturally of greater interest, chief among them a sonnet sung by Fenton at the beginning of the scene in Windsor Forest, a perfect specimen of its kind. The Italian is often difficult, even to the natives; for Boito has adopted a number of fifteenth-century methods of expression which give an archaic flavour to his text; these are not always easy to follow, and the series of epithets which are flung about from mouth to mouth in the final scene almost require an annotated edition to elucidate them. Notwithstanding this occasionally obscure diction, the poet's knowledge of early Italian literature is so profound, and his use of it apparently so natural, that the pedantry which in less skilled hands might so easily have asserted itself is wholly absent.

The difficulty of adapting the plot of the *Merry Wives of Windsor* for operatic purposes has always lain in the fact that the discomfitures of the fat knight are too numerous, and one of them (his escape in the guise of the old woman of Brentford) most difficult to manage with any semblance of reality. Moreover, it has a trace of vulgarity which is only too easily accentuated by the least carelessness in acting or dress. This scene Boito has with great judgment suppressed, reducing the attempts and failures of *Falstaff* to two, and gaining a greatly enhanced effect by this concentration. Moreover, he has vastly strengthened the 'dénouement' of the scene of the buck-basket by introducing a double interest. He conceals Fenton and Anne Page behind the screen (which replaces Shakespeare's arras) when Falstaff is covered up in the basket and this gives occasion for a complication of the most humorous kind; so laughter-provoking indeed did it prove that at the first performance the music became almost inaudible owing to the unrestrained mirth of the audience. A word of praise must also be given to the 'ensemble' verses, sometimes as many as nine in number, mostly written in the most complicated rhythms, but all fitting together without strain, while giving the composer every opportunity for varied treatment. Nor has Verdi failed to reach the standard of excellence attained by the poet. His subtlety of characterization is as keen as it was in the days of the quartet in *Rigoletto*, and the matter with which he has clothed his manner is superior in refinement, in force, and in delicacy to the earlier work. He writes for nine voices with such consummate ease that no sensation of undue complication is felt for an instant. In this respect the 'ensembles' in *Falstaff* are superior to those in *Otello*, where, as in the finale of the second act, it is impossible not to plead guilty to a certain sense of bewilderment.

To criticize separate portions of the music is almost as impossible as to select fragments for concert use. The work is so evenly balanced that hardly any scene is superior to the rest. Audiences, however, will have their favourite phrases and passages, and as such may be mentioned the monologue on Honour, the short love-duet between Fenton and Anne Page (the most fascinating and charming number in the score), the duet between Mrs Quickly and Falstaff, and the whole scene between Ford and the Knight; the short scherzo, 'Quando era un paggio', the song of the fairies in Windsor Forest, and last, but not by any means least, the final fugue. But many equally interesting though more unassuming passages will strike the hearer as he becomes more and more familiar with the work. There is hardly a page without a gem, and not a trace of ugliness from cover to cover. Moreover, there are virtues of omission as well as of commission; for Falstaff is happily devoid of those awkward moments which used to be called stage-waits, but have lately been dignified with the name of 'intermezzi.' Perhaps younger Italy, always on the look out for novelty, and apt to imitate innovations, will amuse itself by trying to write final fugues to its operas. If it takes this healthy exercise, it assuredly will do itself no harm, even if the fugues are dull, which Verdi's are not, and have to be cut out in performance, which his never will be.

But it is not merely the music itself which is new in style, the orchestration is also strikingly fresh and original. The composer has hit the happy mean between superabundance and poverty. The instruments are always at work upon something which repays attention, but never interfere with the voice, or with the enunciation of an important sentence or a witty phrase. The consequence is that attention is never diverted from the stage, while the band is almost unconsciously helping to elucidate the situation. Many of the effects, such as the now famous mountain of shakes, where Falstaff swallows his 'quart of sack with a toast in it', are almost overpowering in force and directness. Played as they were by the admirable orchestra of the Scala, all such points told to the full. The delicacy of the fairy music, so different in style and conception from that of Weber and Mendelssohn, was realized in a manner which must have rejoiced the master himself as much as it did his audience. In a word, the orchestra, which Mascheroni directed with consummate skill, understood to the full the art of accompanying without loss of tone or monotony of detail. Unnoticed by the mass of the audience (and that is the greatest meed of praise which it is possible to bestow), it reached a level of perfection far superior to that attained by the vocalists.

Ralph Vaughan Williams

FILM MUSIC

SOME YEARS AGO I happened to say to Arthur Benjamin that I should like to have a shot at writing for the films. He seemed surprised and shocked that I should wish to attempt anything which required so much skill and gained so little artistic reward. However, he mentioned my curious wish to Muir Mathieson, whom, at that time, I hardly knew, though we have since become firm friends. The result was that, one Saturday evening, I had a telephone call asking me to write some film music. When I asked how long I could have, the answer was 'till Wednesday'.

This is one of the bad sides of film writing—the time limit. Not, indeed, that it hurts anyone to try to write quickly; the feeling of urgency is often a stimulus. When the hand is lazy the mind often gets lazy as well, but the composer wants to have the opportunity, when all is approaching completion, to remember emotion in tranquillity, to sit down quietly and make sure that he has achieved the *mot juste* at every point. That is where the time-limit inhibits the final perfection of inspiration.

On the other hand, film composing is a splendid discipline, and I recommend a course of it to all composition teachers whose pupils are apt to be dawdling in their ideas, or whose every bar is sacred and must not be cut or altered.

When the film composer comes down to brass tacks he finds himself confronted with a rigid timesheet. The producer says, 'I want forty seconds of music here.' This means forty, not thirty-nine or forty-one. The picture rolls on relentlessly, like fate. If the music is too short it will stop dead just before the culminating kiss; if it is too long it will still be registering intense emotion while the screen is already showing the comic man putting on his mother-in-law's breeches.

A film producer would make short work of Mahler's interminable codas or Dvořak's five endings to each movement.

I believe that film music is capable of becoming, and to a

certain extent already is, a fine art, but it is applied art, and a specialized art at that; it must fit the action and dialogue; often it becomes simply a background. Its form must depend on the form of the drama, so the composer must be prepared to write music which is capable of almost unlimited extension or compression; it must be able to 'fade-out' and 'fade-in' again without loss of continuity. A composer must be prepared to face losing his head or his tail or even his inside without demur, and must be prepared to make a workmanlike job of it; in fact, he must shape his ends in spite of the producer's rough hewings.

It may be questioned, is any art possible in these conditions? I say, emphatically, 'Yes, if we go the right way to work.' It is extraordinary how, under the pressure of necessity, a dozen or so bars in the middle of a movement are discovered to be redundant, how a fortissimo climax really ought to be a pianissimo fade-out.

There are two ways of viewing film music; one, in which every action, word, gesture or incident is punctuated in sound. This requires great skill and orchestral knowledge and a vivid specialized imagination, but often leads to a mere scrappy succession of sounds of no musical value in itself. On this the question arises: Should film music have any value outside its particular function? By value I do not mean necessarily that it must sound equally well played as a concert piece, but I do believe that no artistic result can come from this complex entity, the film, unless each element, acting, photography, script and music are each in themselves and by themselves intrinsically good.

The other method of writing film music, which personally I favour, partly because I am quite incapable of doing the former, is to ignore the details and to intensify the spirit of the whole situation by a continuous stream of music. This stream can be modified (often at rehearsal!), by points of colour superimposed on the flow. For example, your music is illustrating Columbus's voyage and you have a sombre tune symbolizing the weariness of the voyage, the depression of the crew and the doubts of Columbus. But the producer says, 'I want a little bit of sunshine music for that flash on the waves.'

Now, don't say, 'O well, the music does not provide for that, I must take it home and write something quite new.' If you are wise, you will send the orchestra away for five minutes (which will delight them). You look at the score to find out what instruments are unemployed—say the harp and two muted trumpets. If possible, you will call Muir Mathieson in to assist you. You write in your flash at the appropriate second, you re-call the orchestra and the producer, who marvels at your skill in writing what appears to him to be an entirely new piece of music in so short a time.

On the other hand, you must not be horrified if you find that a passage which you intended to portray the villain's mad revenge has been used by the musical director to illustrate the cats being driven out of the dairy. The truth is that, within limits, any music can be made to fit any situation. An ingenious and sympathetic musical director can skilfully manoeuvre a musical phrase so that it exactly synchronizes with a situation which was never in the composer's mind.

I am only a novice at this art of film music, and some of my more practised colleagues assure me that when I have had all their experience my youthful exuberance will disappear, and I shall look upon film composing not as an art, but as a business. At present I still feel a morning blush in my art, and it has not yet paled into the light of common day. I still believe that the film contains potentialities for the combination of all the arts such as Wagner never dreamt of.

I would therefore urge those distinguished musicians who have entered into the world of the cinema, Bax, Bliss, Walton, Benjamin and others, to realize their responsibility in helping to take the film out of the realm of hack-work and make it a subject worthy of a real composer.

If, however, the composer is to take his side of the bargain seriously, the other partners in the transaction must come out to meet him. The arts must combine from the very inception of the idea. There is a story of a millionaire who built a house and showed it to a friend when it was near completion. The friend commented on the bare and barrack-like look of the building. 'But you see,' said the millionaire, 'we haven't added the architecture yet.' This seems to be the idea of music held by too many film producers. When the photography is finished, when the dialogue and the barking dogs and the whistling trains and the screeching taxis have been pasted on to the sound-track (I expect this is an entirely unscientific way of expressing it), then, thinks the producer, 'let us have a little music to add a final frill'. So the music only comes in when all the photography is done and the actors dispersed to their homes or to their next job. Perhaps the composer has (unwisely from the practical point of view) already read the script and devised music for certain situations as he has imagined them before seeing the pictures, but what can he do about it? The photograph is already there, the timing is rigidly fixed, and if the composer's musical ideas are too long or too short they must be cut or repeated, or, worse still, hurried or slowed down, because, the photograph once taken, there can be no re-timing.

What is the remedy for all this? Surely the author, producer, photographer and composer should work together from the beginning. Film producers pay lip service to this idea; they tell you that they want the ideal combination of the arts, but when all is finished one finds that much of the music has been cut out or faded down to a vague murmur, or distorted so that its own father would not know it, and this without so much as 'by your leave' to the unhappy musician.

I repeat, then, the various elements should work together from the start. I can imagine the author showing a rough draft to the composer; the composer would suggest places where, in his opinion, music was necessary, and the author would, of course, do the same to the composer. The composer could even sketch some of the music and, if it was mutually approved of, the scenes could be timed so as to give the music free play. Let us suppose, for example, that the film contains a scene in which the hero is escaping from his enemies and arrives at a shepherd's hut in the mountains. The composer finds he wants a long theme to 'establish' the mountain scenery, but the producer says, 'that will never do; it would hold up the action'. And so they fight it out. Perhaps the producer wins and the composer has to alter or modify his music, or the producer is so pleased with the composer's tune that he risks the extra length. My point is that all this should be done before the photographs are taken.

This would not prevent further modifications in the final stages.

An outsider would probably consider this procedure obvious, but, so far as my limited experience goes, it has never occurred as a possibility to the author, or the producer, and certainly not to the composer.

Again, when music is to accompany dialogue or action, surely the actors should hear the music before they start rehearsing, and at rehearsal act to the music, both from the point of view of timing and of emotional reaction.

I need hardly say that the same give and take would be necessary here; that is, that the composer must be ready occasionally to modify his music to fit the action and dialogue.

It is objected that this is unpractical; one could not have a symphony orchestra day after day in the studio accompanying a long-drawn-out rehearsal for each scene. The expense, it is said, would be impossible. When I hear of the hundreds of thousands of pounds which are spent on a film production, it seems to be rather queer to cavil at the few extra hundreds which this would involve—but let that pass. If an orchestra is impossible, how about the pianoforte? The trouble would be to eliminate the pianoforte sounds and substitute an orchestral equivalent which would absolutely synchronize. I am told that no method has yet been devised that can do this. I know nothing about the mechanics of film making; the skill of the whole thing fills me with awe, so I cannot believe that the engineers, if they really wished, could not devise a method—where there's a will there's a way. At present, where film music is concerned, there is not the will.

A third method would be to rehearse with the music played, I presume, on the pianoforte, and then, having registered the exact timing and the exact emotional reaction of the actors to the music, to act it all over again in exactly the same way without the music. I cannot help feeling that the result would be intolerably mechanical.

Of these methods, the pianoforte accompaniment (afterwards to be eliminated) seems to be the best solution of the problem. Does it really pass the wit of those marvellous engineers of the film to devise some method by which it can be achieved?

I believe that this and many other problems could be solved by those who have had much experience, if the composer insisted. As long as music is content to be the maid-of-all-work, until the musicians rise to their responsibilities, we shall achieve nothing.

Perhaps one day a great film will be built up on the basis of music. The music will be written first and the film devised to accompany it, or the film will be written to music already composed. Walt Disney has pointed the way in his 'Fantasia'. But must it always be a cartoon film? Could not the same idea be applied to the photographic film? Can music only suggest the fantastic and grotesque creations of an artist's pencil? May it not also shed its light on real people?

I have to confess to a desire to see a film built up on Bach's *St Matthew Passion*. Of course, it must be done by the right people; but then, does not that apply to every work of art? And when I say the 'right people' I naturally mean the people that I should choose for it. 'Orthodoxy is my doxy, heterodoxy is other people's doxy.'

What a wonderful *via crucis* could be devised from the opening chorus, the daughter of Sion summoning all women to weep with her; then the sudden call 'See Him, the bridegroom,' and the culmination in the choral 'O Lamb of God most holy'.

Then could not the opening narrative be illustrated by a realization of Da Vinci's 'Cenacolo', and at the choral we should switch over, as only a film can, to St Thomas at Leipzig and the huge congregation singing 'O blessed Jesus, how hast Thou offended'. But I could go on for ever with these vague imaginings, and this is only one example of how music can initiate the drama.

Does what I have written sound like the uninstructed grouse of an ignorant tyro? I hope not, indeed. I venture to believe that my very inexperience may have enabled me to see the wood where the expert can only see the trees.

I have often talked over these difficulties with authors, pro-

ducers and musical directors, and they have been inclined in
theory to agree with me. I acknowledge with gratitude that
when I have worked with them they have, within their scheme,
stretched every possible point to give my ignorantly composed
music its chance; but they have not yet been able to break
down the essentially wrong system by which the various arts
are segregated and only reassembled at the last moment, instead
of coming together from the beginning. It is only when this is
achieved that the film will come into its own as one of the
finest of the fine arts.

(1945)

Sir Edward Elgar

A VISIT TO DELIUS

SIR EDWARD ELGAR *celebrated his seventy-sixth birthday by flying to France, having been invited to conduct his violin concerto in Paris, where it was played, to his great satisfaction, by Yehudi Menuhin. The visit was in every way most successful. Elgar was congratulated by the President of the Republic, M. Lebrun, whom he later accompanied to a concert of French music. But the crowning event was the visit he paid to Frederick Delius, at his retreat at Grez-sur-Loing.*

The two were old friends. Distance had prevented close intercourse; but they had much in common beside the bond of nationality and the affection in which they were held by their countrymen. They were drawn together by comradeship and an understanding of each other's aims and mentality. Exaggerated rumours of Delius's impaired state of health made it advisable to inquire beforehand whether a visit would be welcome. Delius answered at once:

'Your kind letter gave me the greatest pleasure, and I should like nothing better than to welcome you here at Grez. . . . In spite of my infirmities, I manage to get something out of life, and I should love to see you.'

I found Delius, as the energetic, bold writing of his letter had led me to hope, a very different being from the invalid of some portraits. It is true that illness has robbed him of strength and set a limit to his activities, but the infirmities of the body have not in the least dimmed the brilliance of his mind—the mind of a poet and a visionary.

Delius takes a keen interest in all that goes on. He is very much amongst us; little escapes his alert intelligence of what is of interest or value in contemporary art—music, painting, literature. And he is still writing.

Just now he has finished a composition for soprano, baritone and orchestra to words by Walt Whitman which he is to call 'Romance'. Delius is a man with a future.

A short conversation shows that he is conversant with the literature of all countries. He had Hergesheimer's last volume, although he shares my belief that there is, among modern novelists, no one great outstanding name.

Delius has been re-reading Dickens, and remarked on his rich humanity and uncertain art; this led to a discussion of the comparative merits of his novels. Apart from the *Tale of Two Cities* and *Barnaby Rudge* (which are historical), and *The Pickwick Papers*, which stands apart, I have always held *Bleak House* the best of his writings. Delius thought *David Copperfield* might claim the first place, but agreed that the picture of Dora was, to say the least, overdrawn.

Then the talk went round to older writers, and I mentioned Montaigne, whose translation by Florio Delius does not know. He became at once tremendously interested. 'Elgar has new ideas,' he said to his wife, and, throwing up his left arm outstretched (his characteristic gesture when making a decision), 'we'll read Montaigne,' he declared. I inquired what prospects there were of seeing him in London. There is nothing Delius would like better, and he is anxious to be present when his opera is performed. But the journey, the going from train to steamer and from steamer to train, is, for him, too arduous an undertaking. Having flown from Croydon to Paris, I suggested the pleasant alternative, and pointed out how after motoring to Le Bourget he could reach London by aeroplane in less than two hours.

The prospect attracted him. 'What is flying like?' he asked.

'Well,' I answered, 'to put it poetically, it is not unlike your life and my life. The rising from the ground was a little difficult; you cannot tell exactly how you are going to stand it. When once you have reached the heights it is very different. There is a delightful feeling of elation in sailing through gold and silver clouds. It is, Delius, rather like your music—a little intangible sometimes, but always very beautiful. I should have liked to stay there for ever. The descent is like our old age—peaceful, even serene.'

My description must have pleased Delius. Up went the left hand; 'I will fly,' he said determinedly.

I told how the spell of being amongst clouds was suddenly broken by the smell of whisky ordered by a passenger and carried past me—the horrible smell brought my mind to earth.

'Whisky!' said Delius, 'the worst smell on earth! But, Elgar, you have not become a teetotaller?'

With vivacity I denied the impeachment.

'Let us then drink a glass of wine together,' said Delius. This seemed rather an astonishing proposition; but Mrs Delius, to whom I looked questioningly, interposed: 'Oh, Frederic will join you.'

Champagne was brought, and as we drank in the sunshine my old friend talked of present and past friends, of Granville Bantock ('the best of fellows,' said Delius) and Percy Pitt, for whose musicianship Delius professed great admiration.

The time passed all too quickly, and the moment of parting arrived. We took an affectionate farewell of each other, Delius holding both my hands. I left him in the house surrounded by roses, and I left with a feeling of cheerfulness. To me he seemed like the poet who, seeing the sun again after his pilgrimage, had found complete harmony between will and desire.

In passing through the pine-scented forest of Fontainebleau on the way to see Delius, I had come to a turn of the road leading to Barbizon. The scent recalled a romance of 1880, and I nearly—very nearly—turned to Barbizon. In that far-off time little did I dream that one day I should sit at the side of the President of the Republic. After my visit to Grez I decided to go to Barbizon, but when I passed the cross-roads the longing had passed away. That belonged to the romance of 1880, now dead. My mind was now full of another romance—the romance of Frederick Delius.

(1933)

Sir Arnold Bax

MACKENZIE—PARRY—STANFORD

OUR PRINCIPAL (at the R.A.M.) was Sir Alexander Mackenzie, a man with a notable gift of frenzy. The students' orchestra which he conducted on Tuesdays and Fridays presented a surprisingly stolid front to his strident shouts and bawlings, even though his Edinburgh accent became keyed up to tones of excoriating menace, or though, as on one occasion, he hurled his baton back into the auditorium. Those boys and girls never looked either amused or alarmed; their attitude was indifferent as that of a herd of cattle in a thunder-storm.

In his more mellow moods Sir Alexander could call upon a pretty store of wit. The story goes that when Elgar first entered the Savile Club as a new member, Mackenzie ran across him in the smoking-room, looking rather bewildered and embarrassed. Though there was little love lost between them, Mackenzie, prompted by a kindly thought to put the younger man more at his ease, proposed that they should lunch together. It was a somewhat constrained and uncomfortable meal, but things were beginning to go tolerably when the cheese course was reached. Here Elgar appealed: 'You know the ropes of this place, Mackenzie. What cheese do you advise?' 'I think I know your taste' was the other's instant reply. 'Why not try a little port salut d'amour?'

Reflecting upon the three precursors of Elgar and the modern English school (a misnomer—we are all individualists, and no such school exists), I conclude that Parry was too ingrainedly the conventional Englishman. He was educated at Eton (where those playing fields still are); he proceeded to Oxford where he continued to participate in manly English sports; he settled down as a well-to-do Gloucestershire squire, and I should not be surprised to learn that he was even in the position to present livings to vicars. He read and set Milton and the safer and more demure Elizabethans, and in Edwin Evans' phrase in another connection, 'became an admirable

SIR ARNOLD BAX   51

"prop to the pyramids".' I can see him dining hugely with his spiritual progenitor, Handel, or hunting with enormous view-hallos in the company of Trollope, but I cannot divine any possibility in him of the 'chaos at heart which gives birth to a dancing star'. Such conservatism as Parry's does not propagate works of searching imagination.

If Parry was too robustly English, Stanford was not Irish enough. An Irishman by birth, he belonged to that class, abominated in Ireland, the 'West Briton'. There are intimations in some of his work that he started not without a certain spark of authentic musical imagination, but quite early he went a-whoring after foreign gods and that original flicker was smothered in the outer darkness of Brahms.

Mackenzie, who began life as a comparatively poor man, obliged to struggle upwards, first by fiddling in inferior Scottish bands and later as a rank-and-file violinist in the orchestra at Sondershausen, probably was more musically gifted by nature than either of the others. But he had no literary taste and little general culture of any kind. . . .

Parry, Stanford, Mackenzie—they were all three solid, reputable citizens and ratepayers of the United Kingdom, model husbands and fathers without a doubt, respected members of the most irreproachably Conservative clubs, and, in Yeats's phrase, had no 'strange friend'. Of this I am sure.

So pure was their moral tone that they regarded sensuous beauty of orchestral sound as something not quite nice (here I am paraphrasing an actual dictum of Parry's). But unhappily all this array of social and aesthetic virtue was not enough and it was left to the cranky and contradictory Elgar to prove to the outside world that even the despised Englishman could be a musical genius.

ATONALISM

IN THE VANITY and arrogance of youth we boast that no new development in our art could ever perplex us . . . but after the thirty-fifth year myopia sets in and we are apt to make ourselves as ridiculous in the opinions of the next generation as our fathers and grandfathers seemed to us. To me, for example, and to most of my contemporaries, atonalism appears to be a cul-de-sac cluttered up with the morbid growths emanating from the brains rather than from the imagination of a few decadent Central European Jews. It is true that this idiom is now thirty years old and has never yet found favour with any save the actual personal disciples of its prophet, but who shall say with any certainty that the thing is worthless?

Sir George Dyson

MUSIC AND SCIENCE

PROFESSOR DINGLE IS one of the growing number of scientists who never forget that what we call the scientific approach to the world is an abstraction and, sometimes, a very narrow abstraction. He gives a striking example by quoting the first lines of Omar Khayyám:

> Awake, for Morning in the Bowl of Night
> Has flung the Stone that puts the Stars to Flight
> And Lo! the Hunter of the East has caught
> The Sultan's Turret in a Noose of Light.

Science, he says, challenged to express such a thought, would have to discuss the wave-theory of light, the analysis of prismatic colours, and produce terrifying mathematical formulae of wave-lengths and heaven knows what. In this process the actual experience to be described, which is sunrise and all that sunrise means to our minds and imaginations, completely disappears.

You can apply the process to music. The three or four chords or the turn of a melody which we call music can only be described scientifically in a forbidding complication of vibrations and harmonics and all the paraphernalia of mathematical acoustics. And when you have done all this, the music, as music, is no longer there at all. The very process of abstraction is only possible by ignoring the actual fact, namely the musical experience itself, which you are trying to explain. There is a wide field in the world for scientific analysis and all that it implies. No one would challenge that. But it does not and cannot yet touch the world of aesthetic values in which painters and musicians and poets must live. It is important to stress the fact today. There has been far too much intellectualization of the arts in recent years. Too many of the fashions and systems and 'isms' of various kinds which have infected so many aberrations of the arts have been founded on some theory or abstraction which ingenuity has spun out of its own head. People play music and write about music and even compose music who do not seem to feel music at all. Yet music is fundamentally an aesthetic experience, not a scientific one. The intellect is there to discipline and control, but it can never be of itself the basis of an art.

We are concerned with certain fundamental artistic values. They are values of experience. They are actual, real. They are not to be expressed in any other terms than those of music itself. Only those of us who have a faculty for intense musical experience, and who can convey something of that quality into the music which we ourselves play or sing or write can hope to preserve and maintain the heritage on which all true musicianship must be built.

MUSIC IN AN AGE OF MACHINES

WE WERE ALL born into an age of machines and these machines are now unalterably the first necessities of our organized life. We live today as we fight today by mass-production, mass-communication, mass-suggestion. None of these things in itself is either good or evil but all of them as we know only too well can be directed to good or evil ends. All of them tend to regard the individual as a mere cog in a vast and uncomprehended mechanism. More and more the growth of an individual character, of an individual talent, must take place, if at all, outside the routine of the factory or office. Man has not lost his creative and enterprising spirit but he cannot exercise it adequately in nine out of ten of the occupations which are open to him.

By virtue of these same tendencies we shall find ourselves with more and more leisure. With the help of the machines and the organization which the machines make possible we can satisfy most of our material wants in shorter working hours than ever before. What are we going to do with the rest of our time?

We are among the greatly favoured for we have a profession which is absorbing, creative and lifelong. Somehow we must persuade or encourage our fellow-men to find this or some other interest of a creative and satisfying kind to fill their leisure hours and stimulate their leisure thoughts. This is really our mission, as I see it, whether our province be to create music, to interpret music or to teach music. It is a duty we share with all artists, all craftsmen of every nation and every age. There is no peace in idleness, there is no peace in stagnation, there is no peace in suppression. Peace, whether in the individual or the nation, is a very delicate balance between a satisfying use of our own lives and a sympathetic conscious-ness of the lives of others. We must have a religion of values, human and individual as well as national and social, and we must find expression for these values both singly as men and women and corporately as societies. Is not this precisely the purpose which the arts should serve and especially our own art of music?

(1944)

THE EXAMPLE OF JENNY LIND

THE MOST INTERESTING and in some respects the greatest of the nineteenth century singers was Jenny Lind. . . . Jenny Lind was a Swedish girl who at a very early age was put into the school of the Royal Theatre Stockholm and became while still very young a very accomplished actress. This training gave her remarkable dramatic power as an opera singer but she sang too hard and too young. After a year or two of great success her voice was practically broken when she was twenty. She went to Garcia in Paris, the greatest teacher of the age, who said: 'It would be useless to teach you. You have no voice left!'

She was so completely crushed that Garcia so far relented as to tell her to go away for six weeks, not to sing a note or even talk more than she must and he would then see her again. He did and then set to work for nearly a year to bring back her voice slowly, carefully, almost one note at a time. Garcia succeeded but to the end of her life Jenny was never completely reassured. She worked, she wept, she took incredible pains and care. Any difficult word, in any language, she would practise by the hour on every note of her compass until she could both sing and pronounce it with ease. She never sang without days of quiet practice at every detail of her part. She was conscien-tious to a fault. In a famous sleep-walking scene where the heroine has to walk over a rickety stage bridge it was usual to dress up one of the chorus to do this for fear of accidents. Jenny would have none of this. 'I should be ashamed,' she said, 'to pretend that I had crossed the bridge if I had not really done it.'

For about seven years, to 1849, she sang with overwhelming success in European opera, made a large fortune which she devoted mainly to endowing schools for children in Sweden and then to the consternation of everyone she retired from the stage. She was twenty-nine. She said she just could not bear the nervous strain any longer. The adulation itself was excessive and distasteful to her. She would sing songs and oratorio but not opera any more. And she kept her word. Of her voice Chopin wrote in 1848: 'Her singing is infallibly pure and true. The charm of her piano passages is indescribable.' Mendelssohn who afterwards wrote the soprano solos in *Elijah* for her wrote from Vienna: 'Such a voice I have never heard in all my life, nor have I met with so genial, so womanly, so musical a nature. It is the mastery wielded by an inspired soul which works the magic.'

Jenny Lind continued to sing with this unfailing magic. . . . She settled in England following simple country pursuits at her home near Malvern and in the last years teaching at the Royal College of Music. She died in 1887. I have known many old people who knew her and in their memory of her there was a unique and universal fragrance. Her character was as great as her art.

(1945)

FUTURISM A CONTRADICTION IN TERMS

FUTURISM INVITED THE graphic arts to develop a comparable technique of their own, a technique in which the graphic adventures of lines, spaces, masses and colours should be themselves the vehicle of an intrinsic beauty, a beauty no more bound to natural objects than is the beauty that music evolves from sound. Theoretically this is a truly aesthetic ideal. The graphic arts have always found their most intimate forms of expression in those elements which, transformed by the vision and hand of the artist, have thus escaped the mechanism of representation. . . . But this same futuristic school when it touched music became a farrago of nonsense. In music it was to desert just that formal purity which the graphic arts were said to lack and to indulge in all kinds of infantile realisms, using the complicated apparatus of the orchestra, for example, to manufacture effects of incredible silliness. The futuristic art of the pencil was to be pure design; the futuristic art of music was to be the noise of the farmyard. This is perhaps an extreme instance of aesthetic confusion but analogous contradictions of principle are to be found in the internal handling of many contemporary artistic problems. Yet there can be no coherent work, either creative or appreciative, without reasoned convictions or stable intuitions of some kind, be they no more than principles of selection. Futurism as a whole was a contradiction in terms.

ON MELODY

IT IS NO use attempting to disguise the fact that melody is quite literally song. The more difficult it is to sing a phrase either actually or imaginatively the less it partakes of the essential nature of melody, or, as some would say, of music. Our ears and our aesthetic reactions are in this matter not instrumentally but vocally attuned. Two or three generations are a trifle in the evolutions of faculties as inbred as these. The normal ear recognizes as music only that which it can to some degree assimilate and as the first primitive endowment of this faculty was vocal so have the accumulated impressions it has since gathered been consistently related to the origin. We are all singers, whether we know it or not, and singers we shall for some long time yet remain.

Now it is sometimes urged that vocal melody having any claim to originality must become, by the mere cumulative exhaustion of possibilities, increasingly difficult to write. This may be true though it is, to say the least, by no means certain that the more we know the less there is to know. Take, for example, the whole body of the Fugue subjects of Bach, than which there is not in music a more amazing array of significant melodic ideas. Are we to say that Bach has in any sense narrowed the field of discovery? Is it not more inherently probable that where one mind was able to extract so many crystals of melodic thought there must be a vast remainder could we but find them? There is in this type of argument a radical fallacy on both sides. Bach did not invent his phrases. Every one of them had, in detail, been used hundreds of times before. It was the imaginative relations in which he placed them that made them seem new. English poetry was not exhausted because Shakespeare covered almost the whole vocabulary of it. It is literally with those elements of an art that are most familiar that genius produces its most marvellous effects. We neglect vocal melody not because there is no more to be discovered, but because our interests and our talents lie elsewhere.

FRANCE

Hector Berlioz

BELLINI'S OPERA 'ROMEO AND JULIET'

IN THE COURSE of conversation I learnt that a new opera of Bellini was going to be performed; people were praising the music and also the libretto—to my great surprise as the Italians put up with anything in the nature of a libretto. Here, I said, is something new. At long last I am going to hear a real Romeo worthy of the genius of Shakespeare. What a subject! It seems specially written for music. The ball in Capulet's palace with its array of beauties where Montagu meets for the first time sweet Juliet . . . then the furious fighting in the streets of Verona with Tybald as the genius of angry vengeance . . . that balcony scene with the lovers whispering their passion . . . the biting jests of Mercutio, grave Father Lawrence . . . the appalling catastrophe . . . love's sighs turned to gasps of agony. . . . I ran to the Pergola theatre.

The choristers who filled the stage seemed good enough. Their voices were rich and about a dozen boys of fourteen or fifteen sang alto with excellent effect. But the principal characters were out of tune with the exception of two women. Of these one, tall and massive, sang Juliet, while the other, small and slender, sang Romeo. Heavens above! Is it then inevitable that Juliet's lover must appear without the characteristics of virility? Is it then a child whose sword pierces the heart of Tybald and having forced the doors of his mistress's tomb scorns and kills Paris? His despair when he is exiled, his terrible grief on learning that Juliet is dead, his delirious ravings after taking poison—are these volcanic emotions the emotions of the eunuch?

Is it suggested that feminine voices are more effective? If so, what is the use of tenors, basses, baritones? Let all parts be sung by women. Moses or Othello sung by women will not sound more odd than Romeo.

What a disappointment! In this libretto there is no Capulet ball, no Mercutio, no gossipy nurse, no grave and calm Father

Lawrence, no balcony scene, no sublime monologue for Juliet when she receives the monk's phial, no dialogue between banished Romeo and the monk—no Shakespeare—a complete failure. And yet the poet who wrote this libretto is Felice Romani who has been forced by the deplorable customs of the Italian lyrical stage to tear into tatters Shakespeare's masterpiece. The composer has found a way to give one scene a striking and beautiful effect. At the end of the act where the two lovers are forced apart by their angry parents, they leave saying 'We shall meet in heaven'. Bellini has added to the words expressing these sentiments a phrase alive with passion and tense with emotion which Romeo and Juliet sing in unison. The two voices vibrating like one, a symbol of perfect union, give to the music extraordinary force, and I was deeply moved possibly by the setting of the melody, by the unexpected unison or by the melodic phrase itself. Since that day composers have not only used, but abused the effects of unison.

ON PALESTRINA

A GERMAN CRITIC—a very worthy fellow—has lately taken upon himself to defend the policy of the Sistine Chapel. 'The greater part of the travellers,' he says, 'on entering the chapel expect to hear music of a livelier and even more amusing character than that of the operas which pleased them at home. Instead of that the singers of the Pope offer them secular plain-song—simple, religious, devoid of accompaniment. These disappointed amateurs on their return assert that the Sistine Chapel has nothing of musical interest to offer and that the accounts of beautiful performances are mere travellers' tales.'

We shall not follow the example of these superficial observers mentioned by the German writer. On the contrary the harmonies of ancient days which have reached our times without modification of style or form have for the musician an interest similar to that which the frescoes of Pompeii have for the painter. We are far from regretting the absence of the big drum and trumpets fashionable with Italian composers without which singers and dancers fear that their efforts will not be applauded as they deserve to be. Indeed, the Sistine Chapel is the only place in Italy which has not been invaded by this deplorable abuse and where one finds a happy refuge against the artillery of the cavatina-merchants. We agree with the German critic when he says that the thirty-two singers of the Pope, incapable of making themselves heard in the largest church of the world, are all that is needed for the performance of the works of Palestrina within the limits of the Papal chapel, and that pure and restful harmony creates a dreamy mood that is not without charm. But the charm is in the harmony—not in the pretended genius of the composer—if one can call composer the man who passed his life writing successions of chords like those of Palestrina's 'Improperia'.

In these four-part psalmodies, in which neither rhythm nor melody have a share, and where harmony consists of common chords with a few suspensions, it is possible to see how the musician was guided by taste and a certain scientific knowledge. But genius! That is surely a jest.

Moreover, those who sincerely believe that Palestrina deliberately adopted that style in order to get nearer to ideal piety are in error. No doubt they have never seen frivolous and worldly madrigals set to music closely resembling that of the religious works. The truth is that Palestrina did not know how to write any other music. So far was he from seeking a new and purer art that one finds in his writings many examples of the contrapuntal tricks made fashionable by the very predecessors against whom he was supposed to have revolted. His *Missa ad fugam* proves it. Now how can these contrapuntal problems—no matter how cleverly solved—contribute to religious emotion, how can the patient weaving of chords reveal a true concern with the object of his work? It cannot. For instance, the fact that a composition is written in the form of an infinite canon does not make its expression either more powerful or more real. . . . The difficulty that the composer has overcome does not add to the beauty or the truth any more than if while writing he had been worried by physical pain or by a material obstacle. If Palestrina had lost the use of his hands and had written his music with his toes, his works would not have gained worth thereby, and would not have been either more or less religious.

The German critic does not hesitate to describe as sublime the 'Improperia' of Palestrina. 'All the ceremony,' he says, 'its subject, the presence of the Pope with his cardinals, the value of the performance by singers who declaim with admirable precision and intelligence—all this constitutes one of the most touching and imposing events of Holy Week.' We agree; but all that does not make the music a work of inspired genius.

HOW 'LA CAPTIVE' CAME TO BE WRITTEN

ONE DAY I was with my friend Lefebvre, the architect, in the hotel at Subiaco, where we were both staying, when a movement of his elbow sent to the floor a book that had been on the table where he was making designs. I picked it up. It was Victor Hugo's *Orientales* and was open at the page of 'La Captive'. I read that delightful poem, and turning towards Lefebvre said, 'I *feel* that poem so that if I had a piece of paper with ledger-lines I could set it to music now.' 'Don't let that stop you,' said Lefebvre, 'I will give you some.' Taking a ruler and a piece of paper he quickly traced a few lines; I then wrote the melody and the bass of the little aria and put the MS in my portfolio without giving it another thought. A fortnight later when I was back in Rome we were music-making in the apartment of our director, when I said to Mlle Vernet: 'I must show you a little aria I improvised in Subiaco; I should like to know what it sounds like. At present I haven't a notion.' The piano accompaniment sketched in in haste was enough to allow us to go through it creditably. It became so much of a favourite that a few weeks later M. Vernet said to me: 'When next you go to the mountains I hope you will not return with another song like your "Captive" which is making my life a misery. I cannot go about the house or the garden, the woods or the corridors, without hearing somebody singing or growling your melody. It's enough to make one lose one's reason. I am sending away one of the servants tomorrow, and I will only take on another on condition that he does not sing "La Captive."'

I have since developed the melody and scored it for orchestra. I believe it is one of the most warm-hearted things I have done.

HOW I BECAME A CRITIC

AFTER MY RETURN from Italy, I wrote some articles for many newspapers and magazines which, short and not particularly important, did not contribute to the improvement of my exchequer. One day, hardly knowing what to do next to earn a few francs, I wrote a sort of tale which was published by the *Gazette Musicale*. I was sad and despondent when writing, but the story was gay to the point of extravagance. It was reproduced by the *Journal des Débats* with an introduction in which flattering reference was made to the author. I called on M. Bertin to thank him when he suggested that I should join his paper as music critic in place of M. Castil-Blaze who had retired. My first duty was to report on concerts and new compositions. . . . My dislike for work of this kind is intense. I can never read an announcement of a new production without feeling a discomfort that becomes acute and vanishes only after I have written my notice. This task that never ends now poisons my life. Yet, apart from the fee it brings me, I cannot give it up without finding myself unarmed against the fury and hatred my writings have evoked. . . . And yet what miserable compromises have I been forced to accept! How many circumlocutions have I not used to avoid the plain truth! I have made concessions to social relations and even to public opinion, holding back my rage and shame. They speak of me as being fanatical, severe, contemptuous. If I were to say what I really think it would soon be found that the bed of nettles which, it is said, I have made for my victims is a bed of roses in comparison with the grid on which I would have them roasted.

In justice to myself, I must say that on no consideration whatever have I been deterred from expressing admiration or enthusiasm for men who could inspire those sentiments. I have given warm praise to those who had hurt me and with whom I was not on speaking terms. The only compensation I derive from my press work is that it gives me an opening for the expression of my aspirations towards things great, true and beautiful. To praise an enemy who deserves it is a pleasure as well as the honest critic's duty. On the other hand, it is very painful to have to write of a friend who has no talent. As all

critics know, the outcome is the same; the man who hates
you will hate you all the more for the credit you gain by doing
justice to his merit, while the man who loves you will love
less for the little praise you are able to give him. We must not
forget the suffering caused to one who has the misfortune to
be both artist and critic by the thousand plots and intrigues of
those who are in need of him. It amuses me to watch the
subterranean labours of those who hope to secure a favourable
notice of the work they intend to do. Nothing is so laughable
as their spade-work except perhaps the patience with which
they prepare their mine and built their tunnel; till the exasperated critic undoes it all, destroying the preparation and
sometimes the labourer as well.

In his admirable *Comédie Humaine* Balzac has said many
excellent things about contemporary criticism. But while
noting errors and wrongs committed by critics, he has not
laid enough stress on the value of those who are honourable,
nor has he taken into account their secret sorrows.

A CRITIC'S LIFE

AT THIS TIME my existence held nothing of musical interest.
I lived in Paris: my time was taken up almost entirely not by
criticism but journalism—a very different thing. The critic—
the honest and intelligent critic—writes only when he has ideas,
when he intends to clear an issue, fight a system, give praise or
blame. He has an incentive for his view, for praising or con-
demning. The unfortunate journalist, obliged to write on anything that happens, only desires to reach the end of a task that
has been forced upon him. Often he has nothing to say about
a subject which may arouse neither interest, anger nor admiration—the subject, as far as he is concerned, simply does not
exist. And yet one must give the impression of being interested,
of having an opinion, a reason why the attention has been
aroused. The majority of my colleagues get over the difficulty
without much trouble, often even with most admirable ease.
I myself could only do it after long and painful effort. Once
I sat three days in a room to write an article on the Opéra-
Comique without being able to make a start. I have forgotten

the particular work I was to discuss (a week after hearing it I had completely forgotten the very title) but I well remember the tortures I had to endure during those three days before putting down the first three lines. . . . Sometimes I sat at the table holding my head, sometimes I marched up and down the room like a sentry. Looking out of the window I could see the gardens, the top of Montmartre, the setting sun and my thoughts flew miles away from that cursed opéra-comique. When, turning round, I saw the title at the top of the page waiting for the lines that were to follow, I was seized by despair. I put my foot through a guitar that was resting against the table. Over the mantelpiece two pistols seemed to be looking at me. . . . I hit my head with my fists. Finally I cried like a schoolboy who cannot do his homework, tearing my hair. Those tears relieved me. I turned the barrels of the pistols against the wall. I had pity on the poor guitar, and taking it in hand, struck a few chords. It was the evening of the third day. Next day I succeeded—somehow—in writing I know not what or what about.

That was fifteen years ago and my tortures go on.

IMPRESSIONS OF WAGNER

THE DRESDEN COMPANY, once conducted by the Italian Morlacchi and the illustrious composer of *Freischütz*, is now directed by Messrs. Reissiger and Richard Wagner. Of Reissiger we in Paris know only the gentle and sad waltz, 'Last thoughts of Weber'. . . . Of the young Kapellmeister, Richard Wagner, who lived sometime in Paris and is known to the public only as the author of a few articles published in the *Gazette Musicale*, I first realized the worth when he helped me with my rehearsals which he did cordially and zealously. He had only taken up his work the day after my arrival in Dresden, and I found him in a most happy mood. After experiencing in France the pains and privations that fall to the lot of obscure men, Richard Wagner returned to his native Saxony where he had the courage to undertake and the good fortune to compose both the words and the music of a five-act opera, *Rienzi*. This opera had a striking success in Dresden. Shortly afterwards he wrote *The*

Flying Dutchman, an opera in three acts, writing again both words and music. Whatever opinion one may have of these works it must be granted that not many men are capable of accomplishing what Wagner has done and writing the literary as well as the musical text of two operas—a task that is quite sufficient to attract attention to his abilities. The King of Saxony realized as much; when he gave to his first Kapellmeister Richard Wagner as a colleague, the friends of art must have said to His Majesty what Jean Bart said to Louis XIV when he named him Commander of the Fleet: 'Sire, you have done well.'

Rienzi exceeds the usual length allowed to German opera, and is now not given in its entirety; one evening is devoted to the first and second acts; the other three are performed the next night. I have only been able to hear the last part and, having heard it but once, I cannot express a considered opinion of its merits. I remember a fine prayer sung by Rienzi, a well-shaped triumphal march based on—but without servile imitation—the magnificent march of *Olympie*. The score of *The Flying Dutchman* seemed to me remarkable for its dark colouring and certain stormy effects perfectly in keeping with the subject. But I noted also a tendency to abuse tremolo—it was also evident in *Rienzi*—a tendency which points to a certain spiritual laziness on the part of the composer who will have to guard against it. Of all the orchestral effects nothing tires the ear sooner than a sustained tremolo; it needs no power of invention in the composer unless it is accompanied by some striking idea above or below. However this may be, tribute must be paid to a king who, by giving him work and protection, has saved a young artist endowed with rare gifts.

THE FAILURE OF 'BENVENUTO CELLINI'

THE DIRECTOR OF the Opéra was then M. Duponchel who looked upon me as a sort of madman whose music could be nothing more than a tissue of absurdities. He accepted the opera to oblige the *Journal des Débats*[1] and after reading declared himself pleased. But he went everywhere saying that what he

---

[1] *Berlioz was music critic to the Journal.*

liked was not the music which he knew to be ridiculous, but the action which he found charming. Rehearsal practice began, and I shall never forget the tortures I endured during those three months of preparation. The evident slackness—not to say disgust—of the singers attending rehearsal; the bad temper of Habeneck; the gossip that went round the theatre; the stupid remarks about a libretto that differed from the flat, rhythmic prose of the Scribe school made by a company of illiterates—all that revealed a hostility against which I was powerless and which I had to pretend to ignore.

When we came to the orchestral rehearsals the musicians, seeing the bored looks of Habeneck, held aloof. But they did their duty while Habeneck did not do his duty. He was never able to catch the lively lilt of the saltarello danced and sung in the middle of the second act. The dancers, unable to adjust their steps to his dragging tempo, came to me to complain and I would urge him: 'Quicker, quicker, go faster.' Habeneck grew angry, beat the desk and broke fifty bows (the violin bow was used in conducting). After seeing him pretend to be angry, I turned to him with a calm that exasperated him and said: 'Good Heavens, breaking fifty bows will not prevent your pace from being twice as slow as it should be. This is a saltarello.'

That day Habeneck stopped the orchestra and addressed them thus: 'Since I have not the good fortune to please M. Berlioz, we shall stop for today. Gentlemen, you may go home.' The rehearsal was over.

In spite of the reserve of the orchestral players who did not wish to antagonize my opponents, some of them praised various pieces and even went so far as to declare that my score was one of the most original they had ever heard. Their words were reported to Duponchel and I heard him say: 'Has there ever been such a change of opinion? They are finding the music of Berlioz charming and our idiotic musicians sing its praises.' Others, however, were very far from siding with me. I caught two one evening who instead of doing their part in the finale of the second act, were playing the tune of 'J'ai du bon tabac' hoping, no doubt, to please their conductor. It was the same on the stage. In that very finale which represents a night scene in Piazza Colonna with a masquerade, the male dancers amused

themselves by pinching the ladies whose cries mingled with the
voices of the singers and upset them. When I called the director
to stop the unseemly disorder, Duponchel was not to be found.
It was beneath his dignity to be present at rehearsal.

The opera was produced. There was exaggerated applause
for the overture; everything else was hissed with energy and
unanimity. Many years have passed. I have since read again my
poor score and I still find in it a wealth of ideas, a lively verve,
a richness of musical colour such as I may never be able to find
again and which deserved better fortune.

A CHILDREN'S FESTIVAL IN ST PAUL'S

A PIECE OF paper which fell into my hands informed me that
there was going to be an Anniversary meeting of Charity
children in St Paul's Cathedral. I tried to get a ticket, and
after many enquiries and letters, I secured an invitation thanks
to the courtesy of M. Goss, the organist of the Cathedral.
The crowd gathered in the neighbourhood at six in the morning and I had some difficulty in reaching the place. Having
climbed to the organ loft reserved for the seventy members of
the choir (men and boys) I was presented with a score of the
bass and with a surplice so that my dark suit should not break
the harmonious effect of the white garments of the choir.
Disguised as a churchman, I then awaited what was to come
with some emotion caused by my surroundings. . . . As the
children entered, nave and aisles began to fill. Imagine the
magnificent church of St Paul's—the largest of all churches
except St Peter—and everywhere order, quiet, calm. Nothing
in the theatre can equal that scene which now seems a dream.
I could hear the English people near me say: 'What a lovely
scene,' and my emotions were deeply stirred when the five
thousand little singers began the first psalm of the day:

All people that on earth do dwell

It is hopeless to attempt to give you a notion of what the effect
was. To compare the very best masses with that singing is like
comparing the Cathedral of St Paul with a village church. It
must be added that the choral part with its striking character

and long sustained notes was supported by the magnificent harmonies from the organ which never overpowered the singers. It pleased me to learn that this psalm which has long been attributed to Luther is the work of a Frenchman, Claude Goudimel, organist at Lyons in the sixteenth century.

In spite of the violence of the emotion I felt (I was trembling all over) I managed to conquer my feelings enough to sing my part in the psalms which formed the second item in the programme. A 'Te Deum' of Boyce dating from 1760, a composition devoid of character, made me completely master of myself again. When the Royal Anthem was sung with the children joining in, 'God save the King! The King for ever! Amen! Hallelujah!' my agitation began once more. I began to count rests in spite of the kind offices of neighbours who, believing that I had lost my place, showed me the point they had reached in the score. During a psalm of J. Ganthaumy, an English master of the eighteenth century, sung by the whole mass with organ, trumpets and timpani—the tremendous sonority of a hymn with grand harmony, warm, inspired, touching, overcame me completely, and nature reasserted her rights. I had to use the music as Agamemnon used his toga—to hide my countenance. During the sermon of the Archbishop of Canterbury, which I was too far away to hear, one of the ushers led me (still in tears) to other parts of the church to witness from different points the spectacle that could not be seen in its entirety from any one place. When he left me among the great congregation the last psalm began, and I realized that the volume of sound was now twice as great. Coming out I met old Cramer who, in his enthusiasm, forgetting his French, addressed me in Italian: 'Cosa stupenda, stupenda! La gloria dell'Inghilterra.'

After Cramer, I saw Duprez who in his brilliant career has stirred the emotions of so many audiences. I have never seen him so moved. He wept; he could hardly speak at all. The Turkish Ambassador and a handsome young Indian passed by cold and as sad as if they had heard their dervishes screaming in one of their mosques. O sons of the East! You lack one of our senses: will you ever acquire it?

Before describing the music of the Chinese, of the Indians

and the Highlanders which I heard in London, I must tell you
that in the last few years (on the Continent the fact is unknown)
England has founded societies of great importance where music
is not an object of speculation as it is in the theatre, but is
cultivated on a large scale with great care, ingenuity and true
affection. Such are the Sacred Harmonic Society, the London
Sacred Harmonic Society and the Philharmonic societies of
Liverpool and Manchester. I cannot say anything about the
Liverpool society which I have not heard. But the Manchester
society, conducted by Charles Hallé is, according to impartial
judges, even better than the London societies.

(1851)

ON STYLE

I NOTICE THAT I have said nothing so far of my technique
and my way of composing and perhaps you would like to hear
something about it.

As a general rule my style is very bold but there is not the
slightest tendency to do away with any element that is part of
the art of music. On the contrary, I take pains to add to the
number of those elements. I have never dreamt of writing
music without melody as has been foolishly suggested in
France. A school which intends to abolish melody exists now
in Germany and it horrifies me. It is not difficult to prove that
without choosing short melodies for my themes—as has often
been done by the great masters—I have taken care to make my
compositions extremely melodic. It is possible to question the
value of my melodies—their distinction, novelty, charm. To
deny their existence implies either bad faith or ineptitude. My
melodies are often of uncommon length and childish, short-
sighted people do not clearly see their shape; or they are
blended with other melodies of secondary importance which
veil their outline and puzzle foolish people; or they are so
different from the trivialities which the lower musical classes
call melody that they cannot apply the same name to them.

The salient characteristics of my music are passionate expression, inner warmth, rhythmic impetus and unexpectedness.
When I say passionate expression I mean expresssion that
corresponds to the intimate sense of the subject even if that

subject is one of profound calm, sweet, tender, the reverse of passionate. Such is the type of expression found in *L'Enfance du Christ* and, above all, in the scene 'In Heaven' of my *Damnation de Faust*, and in the Sanctus of my *Requiem*.

Some of the problems I set myself to solve are exceptional in that they require an extraordinary apparatus. For example, in the *Requiem* I have four brass bands set in different parts of the hall which carry on a dialogue round the orchestra and the massed choir. In the *Te Deum* it is the organ which at one end of the church carries on a conversation with the orchestra, and two choirs placed at the other end, while a third choir singing in unison represents the mass of the people taking part, from time to time, in this vast religious concert. But it is the shape of these compositions, the breadth of the style, the formidable gravity of certain progressions whose purpose is not to be guessed, that give these works their strange and gigantic aspect. It is the vastness of the form that causes people either to understand nothing at all or to be overwhelmed by tremendous emotion. Many times during performance of my *Requiem* there have been listeners who trembled with a sensation that shook their very souls, side by side with others who opened large ears without hearing or understanding anything.

Works of mine which critics have described as 'architectural', are my *Symphonie Funèbre et Triomphale* for two orchestras and choir; the *Te Deum* whose finale (Judex Crederis) is undoubtedly the most grandiose thing I have done; my cantata for two choirs *L'Impériale*, performed at the concerts of the Palais de l'Industrie in 1855 and, above all, my *Requiem*.

As for my compositions which demand no more than the usual means, conceived in accordance with common notions of proportion, it has been their inner warmth, their expression and the originality of their rhythms that, demanding special understanding in the interpreters, have been their bane. In order to render them well, the executants and especially the conductor, must feel as I myself feel. They demand extreme precision together with irresistible zest, controlled impetuosity, dreamy sensibility and a nostalgic expression that might almost be called morbid. Without this the main features of my works will be either distorted or disappear completely. That is why it is so painful for me to hear my compositions conducted by others than myself. I very nearly had a stroke when I heard in Prague my *King Lear* overture conducted by a musician who was yet a man of unquestionable talent. It was nearly right—but in this instance a 'nearly' was enough to turn sense into nonsense.

If you now ask which of my works I prefer I answer that I concur with the majority of artists in giving preference to the adagio (love scene) of *Romeo and Juliet*. One day at Hanover I felt somebody plucking my coat. On turning I saw the musicians near me kissing the hem of my jacket. I would not play that piece on any account in some halls or before some audiences.

'LES TROYENS'. LETTER TO NAPOLEON

WHEN AT WEIMAR I visited the Princess of Wittgenstein (a woman of heart and spirit, devoted friend of Liszt and a great comfort to me in my bitterest hour) and happening to talk about Virgil, I mentioned my idea of writing an opera on the third and fourth books of *Aeneid* in imitation of a Shakespearean drama. I added that I well knew the pain and worry such a work would cost me. 'Your passion for Shakespeare, together with your love for the old poet'—said the Princess—'should result in something new and magnificent. You must write your opera and your libretto. Do as you like; but you start and finish the job.' I was about to raise objections when the Princess went on: 'If you are afraid of the trouble that the work will give you, if you are so weak that you do not dare everything for Dido and Cassandra, don't come to me again. I shall refuse to see you.' I needed nothing more to spur me on and as soon as I got back to Paris I set about writing verses for *Les Troyens*. I began the music later and after three and a half years of changing and correcting, the work was done. While I was polishing and re-polishing the score, listening to the advice of various people, I had the idea of writing to the Emperor the following letter:

Sire,

I have finished an opera for which I have written words

and music. In spite of the boldness and variety of the means I employ, the resources of Paris are adequate to its performance. Will Your Majesty allow me first to read the poem and to solicit your patronage (if I should have the happiness to deserve it)? The Opera House is at this moment directed by an old friend of mine who has some odd notions about my style which he has never studied and does not know; the two leaders working under him are hostile to me. As the Italian proverb says, I can save myself from my enemies, but only Providence can save me from my friends. If Your Majesty, after hearing the poem, should not think it worthy of performance, I shall accept your decision with profound respect, but I cannot submit my work to the judgment of people whose understanding is bounded by prejudice and whose opinions are, in consequence, worthless as far as I am concerned. They might easily reject the opera, giving as a reason an inadequate libretto.

I was tempted to solicit the privilege of reading the libretto to Your Majesty while Your Majesty was at Plombières, but the music was not finished then, and I feared that, if the libretto should not please, I might feel discouraged and give up all thought of finishing the work. I did want to write the great score, to write it fully with an ardour, care and love that never grew cold. Now it exists and neither grief nor discouragement can alter the fact. It is a great and strong opera and, in spite of the complexity of the means, perfectly simple. Unfortunately it is not vulgar, but this is one of the faults Your Majesty forgives; the Parisian public begins to understand that trickery of sound is not the highest of all aims. May I then say as one of the characters of the old era of my subject said: 'Arma citi properate viro.'

I am with the greatest respect and devotion
Your Majesty's most humble, obedient servant,
Hector Berlioz

The Emperor never read my letter. M. de Morny persuaded me not to send it because he thought the Emperor would find it inopportune. When *Les Troyens* was somehow performed, His Majesty did not consider the event worth a visit.

One evening at the Tuileries I had a brief talk with the
Emperor who authorized me to send him the poem of *Les
Troyens* and assured me that he would read it as soon as he had
an idle hour. Can one have an idle hour when one is Emperor
of France? I sent the MSS to the Emperor who did not read it
and returned it to the bureau of theatrical management. There
my work was condemned; treated as absurd and senseless; they
said it would last eight hours; that two full companies were
necessary; that I wanted three hundred extra choristers etc.
A year later Alphonse Royer told me that the Minister had
ordered that my opera should be rehearsed at the Opéra, and
was anxious that I should be completely satisfied. From that
moment I heard nothing more. That promise, like so many
others, came to nothing.

That is why after waiting a long time for no purpose, tired
of being affronted, I listened to M. Carvalho and consented to
his running the risk of producing *Les Troyens à Carthage* at the
Théatre Lyrique, although it was obviously impossible to make
a good job of it. He had just secured from the government a
yearly subsidy of 100,000 francs. The venture was too much
for his resources. His theatre was not large enough, his singers
had not enough skill, neither his choir nor his orchestra were
sufficiently numerous. He made important sacrifices; I, too,
had to sacrifice much. I paid out of my own pocket for extra
performers in the orchestra; I even mutilated my score in many
places so as to bring it into line with the available performers.
Madame Charton-Demeur (the only singer capable of playing
the part of Dido) acted like a generous friend and accepted the
engagement offered by M. Carvalho, refusing a much better
offer from Madrid. In spite of everything the performance was
—and could not help being—inadequate. Madame Charton-
Demeur had great moments; Monjanze, who sang Aeneas, had
warmth and passion; but the mise-en-scène, which Carvalho
insisted on, was very different from what I had meant it to be,
in places even absurd or ridiculous. At the first performance
the engineer nearly caused a fiasco by his clumsiness in the
scene of the hunt in the storm. This scene which at the Opéra
would have produced a great effect through its wild beauty,
seemed mean here; an interval of fifty-five minutes was neces-

sary to allow the scenery to be changed. The outcome was that next night hunt, storm and the scene were omitted. In order to be able to organize properly the production of an opera of that importance, I must be absolute master of the theatre, just as I am sole arbiter at the rehearsing of a symphony. It is necessary to secure the willing co-operation of everyone; all must obey without questioning. Otherwise my energy after a few days is exhausted in fighting opinions that are opposed to mine. . . . I ended by resigning and consigning the whole thing to the devil. Carvalho, protesting that he meant to conform to my instructions and do what I wanted, made me suffer much to secure the cuts he thought necessary. When he did not dare to ask himself, he asked some common friend to intervene. One man told me that a certain passage was dangerous; another wrote to beg me to suppress another. Their criticism of details drove me mad.

'Your rhapsodist holding a lyre with four strings. That is, of course, the explanation of the four notes of the harp—a bit of archaeology.'

'Well?'

'It's dangerous. People will laugh.'

'You have a word in the prologue that makes me afraid.'

'What word?'

'Triomphaux.'

'Why does it frighten you?'

'It's a word one never hears.'

'Will you do me a favour?'

'What can I do?'

'Let us do away with Mercury. His winged heels will make people laugh. Wings are for the shoulders.'

Will anybody realize what anxieties those idiotic questions caused me? Carvalho, in order to aid the production he had devised, never hesitated to ask me to play faster or slower, or to add half a dozen bars or cut three or two bars out. In his opinion the staging of an opera is not an adjunct to music; it is the music that exists to serve the stage manager. . . . The first performance of *Les Troyens à Carthage* took place on November 4th, 1863, as Carvalho had announced. As the opera still needed another three or four full rehearsals, nothing went smoothly, especially on the stage. But the director was at the end of a repertory that no longer attracted the public and was anxious to try something different. Directors thus placed are fierce. We expected a stormy evening with hostile manifestations—nothing happened. My enemies did not show themselves with the exception of one individual who hissed at a certain moment and later, accompanied by a collaborator, returned to hiss again in the same place at the tenth performance. In the corridors I was discussed with comical violence, people saying that the performance of such music should not be allowed. Five papers criticized me in terms that could wound most deeply. On the other hand, during the next fortnight, more than fifty articles appeared showing such enthusiasm and an intelligence that gave me a joy I had not felt for a long time.

Camille Saint-Saëns

ART IS FORM

M D'INDY, LIKE Tolstoi, M. Barres and many other thinkers, seems to see nothing in art but expression and passion. I cannot share this opinion. To me art is form above all else.

It is perfectly clear that art in general, and especially music, lends itself wonderfully to expression and that is all that the amateur expects. It is quite different with the artist. The artist who does not feel thoroughly satisfied with elegant lines, harmonious colours, or a fine series of chords, does not understand art.

When beautiful forms accompany powerful expression we are filled with admiration and rightly so. In such a case what is it that happens? Our craving after art and emotion is equally satisfied. At the same time we cannot therefore say that we have reached the summit of art since art can exist apart from passion or emotion.

This is proved, speaking of music, by the fact that during the whole of the sixteenth century admirable works were produced entirely devoid of emotion (apart from a few exceptions such as Palestrina's *Stabat Mater*). Their true purpose is defeated when an attempt is made to render them expressive. Wherein does the Kyrie of the famous mass *Papae Marcelli* express supplication? Here is form and nothing else. On the other hand see to what a low level music descends when it neglects form and sets emotion in the forefront!

In the introduction of his book M. d'Indy says fine things about the artistic consciousness, the necessity of acquiring talent as the result of hard work and not relying solely on one's natural endowments. Horace said the same thing long ago; but it cannot be repeated too often at a time like the present when so many reject all rules and restrictions and declare that they mean to be 'laws unto themselves', replying to the most just criticism by the peremptory argument that they 'will do as they please'. Assuredly art is the home of freedom but freedom is not anarchy and it is anarchy that is now fashionable, both in literature and in the arts. Why do poets not see that in throwing down barriers they give free access to mediocrities and that their vaunted progress is but a reversion to barbarism? Fétis had foreseen the coming of the 'omnitonic' system. 'Beyond that I see nothing,' he said. He could not predict the birth of cacophony, of pure *charivari*. Berlioz speaks somewhere of atrocious modulations which introduce a new key in one section of the orchestra while another section continues in the former key.

At the present time as many as three different tonalities can be heard simultaneously. . . . The dissonance of yesterday, we are also told, will be the consonance of tomorrow; one can grow accustomed to anything. Still, there are such things in life as bad habits and those who get accustomed to crime come to a bad end. . . .

HUMAN VOICE THE FINEST INSTRUMENT

THE MASTERPIECES OF the three great classics (Haydn, Mozart and Beethoven) have made us forget too readily that the human voice is the finest instrument of all. It is the only inimitable instrument—living, divine, even miraculous; for no one can understand how the two ligaments called the vocal chords and the resonator called the larynx are capable of producing it. Those who in recent times have been affecting the most profound scorn for ornamental singing, trills, *vocalises*—though these were utilized by all the great composers of the past—ought rather to express wonder and amazement thereat. Berlioz ridiculed singers who succeed in playing on the larynx as one plays on the flute. Where is the harm? Not Handel nor Sebastian Bach nor Mozart nor Beethoven nor Weber had any objection to florid singing. A curious thing is that Berlioz in his lyrical comedies also uses *vocalises*, although he treats them in a singularly clumsy manner. . . .

There is no need to conceal from ourselves the fact that, with the exception of a few special and comparatively restricted circles, the public prefers vocal to instrumental music. The cause of this is not to be found in more or less explainable reasons; it is nature herself that insists upon it because the voice is the only natural instrument. It is even the one eternal instrument so far as human things can be eternal. Instruments pass and have their day; the instrumental music of the sixteenth century is, for the most part, impossible of execution today. But the human voice remains.

THE REWARDS OF OPERA

M. D'INDY INSINUATES that the love of gain may have something to do with the preference for opera shown by certain composers. As the public has always shown a marked preference for this form it is not to be wondered at if musicians instinctively turn to a kind of music that will enable them to earn a living; not everyone has the good fortune to be born with a silver spoon in his mouth. At the same time there must be another reason, for almost all composers have written for the theatre or have tried to do so.

Love of gain was not the incentive which made Richard Wagner embark upon his colossal work, the *Ring of the Nibelungen,* under conditions of so exceptional a nature that he did not know if it could ever be produced. Meyerbeer was possessed of a great fortune, the major part of which was swallowed up by his musical works. Duprez in his memoirs artlessly tells how the gifted composer made every possible sacrifice to ensure the execution of his operas and how he—the famous singer—profited thereby.

Haydn wrote Italian operas in his youth. During his stay in London, when producing his finest symphonies for the Salomon concerts, he began an *Orfeo* which he never finished owing to the fact that the theatre where it was to have been given went bankrupt. Mozart would still be Mozart even if there remained nothing but his theatrical works. The reason why Beethoven confined himself to the symphony and did not devote himself to the theatre is that the Vienna Opera would not accept his offer of giving them a new work each year for five years.

No one can tell what would have happened if Beethoven's offer had been accepted and he had acquired that theatrical experience which is not to be found outside the theatre, and which is evident in the second version of *Fidelio* when compared with the first *Leonora*. Certain parts of *Fidelio* are not inferior to any of his works: the famous 'pistol scene' resembles nothing that had been done before. Had Beethoven been able to realize his desire, the direction in which the lyrical theatre was going would have been probably quite different.

Both Mendelssohn and Schumann tried the theatre. The failure of Schumann's *Genoveva*—interesting from the musical point of view though anything but adapted for the theatre—was the cause of his hostility to Meyerbeer; he could not understand how Meyerbeer's music could be regarded as *music*, though he must have realized that the theatre has to accept art forms that would be inadmissible elsewhere. Painting of stage scenery is different from painting on an easel. Wagner placed the purely musical, symphonic interest in the foreground; but success was achieved only as the result of pressure upon the public, the duration and intensity of which were such that nothing like it had been seen up to that time or probably ever will be again.

Berlioz after writing the following terrible sentence: 'Theatres are the disorderly houses of music and the chaste Muse one drags therein cannot enter without shuddering' treated thus his own Muse and certainly the results were not always satisfactory. Nevertheless *Les Troyens* is a superior work though it was not smiled upon by Fortune, the implacable queen who rules over battles and operas alike. . . .

Richard Strauss after becoming known to the public by symphonic poems has revolutionized the musical world by extraordinary operas upon which I will not dwell to avoid giving offence to his admirers. . . .

GERMAN INFLUENCE

NOTHING COULD BE better than to go to Germany for masterpieces but to go there for theories. . . . Even Richard Wagner's theories are often pernicious; his works would not be what they are if he had always conformed to them; the harm they have done is incalculable. M. Debussy has been highly praised for avoiding them. True, his music resembles in no way that of the author of *Tristan*, but he has none the less applied as completely as he could the Wagnerian system which consists in diverting interest from the singer to the orchestra.

CÉSAR FRANCK

I WAS ONE OF the first to give a hearing to the works of Franck at my own risk and at a time when the public still disregarded them. Further, Jules Simon, then Minister of Education, consulted me on the choice of a professor of the organ for the Conservatoire, and I strongly recommended Franck to him so that Franck, with the salary granted by the state, should not find himself compelled to waste, in giving pianoforte lessons, the time he could employ more profitably in composition. Yet, though I highly esteem his works and endeavoured to get them appreciated at their true worth, I have never gone so far as to set them on a level with those of the great masters of music. They lack too many qualities for that distinction. Berlioz was more of an artist than a musician; Franck was more of a musician than an artist: he was no poet. In his works we do not find that latent warmth, that irresistible charm which makes us forget everything and transports us into unknown and supernal realms. The sense of the picturesque seems absent from them. At one moment we come across an ill-timed modulation—as in the sonata for pianoforte and violin where we are suddenly transported from E major to B flat minor, the latter key thus acquiring, as it were, an unpleasant bitterness; at another moment we have a construction in which something is lacking as in the *Prélude, Chorale et Fugue*, a *morceau* anything but pleasant or convenient to play, where the chorale is not a chorale, nor the fugue a fugue, for it speedily falls all to pieces and continues in interminable digressions which no more resemble a fugue than a zoophyte resembles a mammal. These digressions are scarcely atoned for by the brilliant ending. Assuredly it is not in this way that we shall, even at the present time, understand the possibilities of the time-honoured, venerable fugue. César Franck made frequent use—even too frequent—of canons; but his canons are always either in unison or in octaves, thus presenting no difficulty of any kind. His much-vaunted work, *Les Béatitudes* is very unequal in merit. Occasionally we meet with something quite insignificant; nor is the declamation invariably free from reproach. Speaking generally, we are more likely to find in him a violent and meritorious aspiration towards beauty rather than beauty itself. His efforts remind us of Victor Hugo's act of faith in God: 'Il est, il est, il est éperdument.'

His emotion is seldom communicative; I say 'seldom' not 'never'. It is a pleasure for me to cite the beautiful soprano aria in *The Redemption* illuminating and cheering this austere landscape, as the sun does, with genial beams.

At times a gloomy sadness hangs over his work, so that in listening to it we are conscious of a pleasure which may be compared with that afforded by the Psalms of David in the Church Service. But this is neither the tragic and splendid sadness of Mozart (in the Fantasia in C minor) nor that of Beethoven in his celebrated sonata in C sharp minor. . . .

Franck's religious music, though eminently deserving of respect, calls to mind the austerities of the cloister rather than the perfumed splendours of the sanctuary.

LISZT AS PIANIST

THE HOUR OF justice struck when the centenary of Liszt's birth came round and his works were performed on a grand scale. No longer was it possible to affirm that the author of *Christus,* of the *Legend of Saint Elizabeth,* of the symphonies *Dante* and *Faust*, was simply a writer of 'pianists' music'. 'Pianists' music!' Well, Mozart was the greatest pianist of his day, Beethoven was a pianist of the highest rank and Sebastian Bach, that mighty genius, was an unrivalled organist and clavecinist. Unfortunately for Liszt—an extraordinary performer who extracted from his instrument the strangest effects, completely transforming it as Paganini transformed the violin—he was fated to emphasize his virtuosity. At the same time it was not virtuosity, however amazing, but rather his own admirable musical nature that showed his true worth. Though accused of attaching undue importance to the pianoforte at the expense of music, it was the contrary that really happened; his aim was to introduce the orchestra into the pianoforte. With wonderful ingenuity, substituting the free for the literal (and, therefore, unfaithful) translation, he actually succeeded in expressing through his instrument the sonorous measures of Beethoven's symphonies and Berlioz's *Symphonie Fantastique*. Into his lesser pianoforte pieces (even the Fantasias on opera motives) there enters the idea of the orchestra, giving an aesthetic character to apparently most futile things.

As most of his inventions have ceased to be copyright, in these days we are no longer aware of the radical transformations he wrought, of the many novel resources he introduced in pianoforte technique. A veritable revolution was effected; the sonority of the instrument appeared to have doubled in volume. . . .

Certain of Liszt's compositions, which were once regarded as impossible of execution, are now the everyday task of young pupils. On the pianoforte, as on all other instruments, virtuosity has made gigantic strides all along the line. What hard things have been said against virtuosity! How fiercely it has been attacked in the name of Art with a capital A! To think of implacable, impious war declared on the concertos of Beethoven and Mozart! It would have been impossible to be more completely wrong. In the first place—the fact must be proclaimed from the house-tops—in art a difficulty overcome is a thing of beauty. This truth has been affirmed by Théophile Gautier in immortal verse and after such testimony there is nothing further to be said. In the second place, virtuosity is a powerful aid to music, whose scope it extends enormously. It is because instrumentalists have become virtuosi that Richard Wagner was able to display so lavishly that wealth of sound of which a good deal would have been impossible but for the virtuosity we affect to despise. Beauty, however, comes into existence only when the difficulty is overcome to such a degree that the listener is unaware of its existence.

We thus enter that realm of superior execution wherein Liszt was enthroned as a king, performing with the ease and the assurance of a god; power, delicacy, charm, along with a rightly-accented rhythm, were his, in addition to unusual warmth of feeling, impeccable precision and that gift of suggestion which creates the great orator, the leader of the masses.

When interpreting the classics he did not substitute his own personality for the author's, as do so many performers; he seemed rather to endeavour to get at the heart of the music and find out its real meaning—a result sometimes missed even by the best players. This, moreover, was the plan he adopted in his transcriptions. His Fantasia on 'Don Juan' sheds new light upon the deeper meanings of Mozart's masterpiece.

Why have I not the art of word-painting? As I write I picture myself once again in the home of Gustave Doré, gazing upon that pallid face and those eyes that fascinated all listeners, whilst beneath his apparently indifferent hands, in a wonderful variety of nuances there moaned and wailed, murmured and roared, the waves of the 'Légende de Saint François de Paule marchant sur les flots'.

Never again will be seen or heard anything to equal it.

CHOPIN

'CHOPIN!' WHEN THE good King Louis Philippe was alive you should have heard with what a dainty accent and eager expression women uttered the two syllables. The artist's elegant manners and the ease with which his name was pronounced certainly contributed largely to the huge success he attained. Besides, he was consumptive at a time when to be healthy was unfashionable and women, on sitting at table, would thrust their gloves into their glass and only nibble a few dainty morsels at the end of the meal. It was considered a mark of *bon ton* for the young to look pale; then Princess Belgiojoso appeared on the boulevards dressed in black and silver white, looking as wan and ghastly as Death himself.

Chopin's illness, though real enough, was regarded as an attitude he had assumed. This 'jeune malade à pas lentes', a foreigner with a French name, the son of an unhappy country whose fate was pitied and whose resurrection was desired by all in France, was in every way calculated to please the public of the day; indeed, this served him better than his musical talent which, as a matter of fact, this same public did not understand.

Proof of this lack of comprehension is to be found in the

popularity of a certain Grand Waltz in E flat strummed then on every piano to the exclusion of other works that were really much more characteristic of his genius.

He had few admirers worthy of the name—Liszt, Ambroise Thomas, Princess Czartoriska, his best pupil, Mme Viardot and George Sand, who extolled him to the skies in her Memoirs, proclaiming him the greatest of all composers, 'approached by Mozart alone', a childish exaggeration, though at the time a useful counterpoise to the general opinion which saw in Chopin merely an agreeable pianist and looked upon Liszt merely as possessed of amazing powers of execution.

Times have changed. After years of barren strife the great compositions of Liszt have taken their rightful place. The Waltz in E flat is forgotten and all the dream-land flowers that appeared in the garden of the marvellous artist, proclaimed by both France and Poland, now blossom in perfect freedom scattering their fragrance around. We admire and love, but—do we understand them?

Chopin's musical studies had been so incomplete that he was forbidden to write great vocal and instrumental compositions and had to confine himself to the piano where he discovered an entirely new world. This is particularly apt to lead judgment astray. When interpreting his works, we think too much of the piano, of the instrument as an end in itself—we forget both the poet and the musician. For Chopin is above all a poet who may be compared with Alfred de Musset. Like Musset he sings of love and women.

Above all, Chopin was sincere. His music, without being in accordance with any particular programme, is invariably a tone picture: he did not 'make' music, he simply followed his inspiration. He expressed the most varied human feelings; he also gave musical form to the impressions produced on him by the sights of nature. But whereas in others, in Beethoven for instance, these impressions may be pure and unalloyed, in Chopin's music (with the exception of a few polonaises that voice his patriotism) woman is ever present; everything is referred to her and it is this standpoint we must adopt if we would give his music its rightful character. His work thrills with a passion, now overflowing, now latent and restrained, that gives it an inner warmth of feeling replaced by some interpreters with an affected, jerky performance, and contortions, utterly opposed to the real Chopin style, which is both touching and simple. To speak of simplicity in connection with music that bristles with accidentals, complicated harmonies and arabesques may seem surprising. But we must not, as is generally done, lay too much stress on details. Fundamentally, the music is simple; it betokens great simplicity of heart and it is this that must be expressed when we play it—under penalty of completely falsifying the intentions of the composer. Chopin distrusted himself; he invited, and sometimes followed pernicious advice, unaware that he himself, guided by instinctive genius, was more clear-sighted than all the savants around him who were devoid of genius of any kind.

His marvellous works are threatened with a great peril. Under pretext of popularizing them there have appeared editions bristling with erroneous fingering. That indeed is in itself a small matter, but alas, they have also been 'improved'— which means that alien intentions may gradually replace those of the composer. It is high time someone thought of bringing out an edition, if not of all his works, at least of those that deserve to be handed down to posterity, going back to the fountain head and showing the master's thought in all its purity. Before it is too late, may a really intelligent editor raise to Chopin's memory the imperishable monument that will have nothing in common with the 'Kritik-Ausgaben' with which the musical world today is invaded as by some destructive phylloxera.

Claude Debussy

NIKISCH

O N SUNDAY THE Berlin Philharmonic Orchestra conducted by Nikisch gave its first concert. All the
well-known and attentive ears that Paris boasts were
there, and particularly the dear, wonderful ladies! This is the
best kind of audience for one who knows how to make use of
it. Almost all that is required to rouse its enthusiasm is a
graceful attitude or a romantically waved lock of hair. Nikisch
has the pose and the lock but, fortunately, he has also more
solid qualities. Moreover, he has his orchestra marvellously in
hand and one seems to be in the presence of men whose sole
aim is the serious production of music; they are poised and
unaffected like the figures in a primitive fresco—quite a touching novelty.

Nikisch is a unique virtuoso, so much so that his virtuosity
seems to make him forget the claims of good taste! I would
take as an example his performance of the *Tannhaüser* overture,
in which he forces the trombones to a portamento suitable at
best to the stout lady responsible for sentimental ditties in the
Casino de Suresnes, and in which he stresses the horns at
points where there is no particular reason for bringing them
into prominence. These are effects without any appreciable
causes, amazing in a musician as experienced as Nikisch shows
himself to be at other times. Earlier, he had given evidence of
unique gifts in Richard Strauss's *The Merry pranks of Till Eulen-
spiegel*. This piece might be called 'An hour of original music
in a lunatic asylum'. The clarinets leap in frenzied curves, the
trumpets everlastingly choke, and the horns, forestalling a
latent sneeze, hasten to rejoin: 'God bless you!' while a big
drum goes boom, boom! apparently emphasizing the antics of
the clowns. One wants to shout with laughter or else to shriek
with pain. Then follows the startling discovery that everything is in the right place; for, if the double-basses blew down
their bow or the trombones fiddled on their brass tubes with an
imaginary bow, or if Nikisch perched himself on the knee of a
programme seller, it would not be in the least surprising.

Meanwhile there is no gainsaying that genius is shown at times in this work, above all in the amazing orchestral assurance, the mad rhythm that sweeps us along from beginning to end and forces us to share in all the hero's merry pranks. Nikisch conducted this orchestral tumult with outstanding coolness and the ovation which greeted both his orchestra and himself was eminently justified.

During the performance of Schubert's Unfinished Symphony a flock of sparrows fluttered to the windows and twittered pleasantly. Nikisch had the grace not to demand the expulsion of these impertinent melomaniacs who were probably drunk with the ether or perhaps were merely innocent critics of a symphony which cannot decide once and for all to remain unfinished.

RICHTER

IT IS NOT for me to say precisely in what the superiority of the Anglo-Saxons consists but, among other things, they have Covent Garden Theatre. This theatre possesses the peculiar characteristic of making music seem at home there. More attention is given to perfect acoustics than to sumptuous decorations and the orchestra is numerous and well disciplined. Besides this, André Messager assumes his artistic responsibilities with the perfect and unerring taste which everyone expects from him. You see how astonishing all this is, for they actually think that a musician can manage an Opera House successfully! They really must be mad—or else they are systematic! In any case I shall institute no comparisons; they would demonstrate completely the poverty of our own methods and our national pride might suffer. Only let us avoid false notes in blowing the trumpets of fame on behalf of the glory of our own Opéra; or, at least, let us use a mute.

Recently I attended the performances of The Rhinegold and The Valkyrie. It seems to me impossible to achieve greater perfection. Although the scenery and certain lighting effects were open to criticism, the artistic care shown throughout compelled admiration.

Richter conducted the first performance of The Ring at Bayreuth in 1876. At that time his hair and beard were red-gold; now his hair has gone, but behind his gold spectacles his eyes still flash magnificently. They are the eyes of a prophet; and he is in fact a prophet and only ceases to be, at least as far as the Wagnerian cult is concerned, through Mme Cosima Wagner's decision to replace him by Siegfried Wagner, her estimable but mediocre son—a splendid arrangement from the point of view of domestic economy, but deplorable for the fame of Wagner. Such a man as Wagner needs musicians like Richter, Levy or Mottl—they are part of the splendid adventure which, at a given time, brought Wagner into touch with a king—not to mention Liszt whom he conscientiously plagiarized and who met him with nothing but kindly smiles of acquiescence. There is something miraculous in Wagner; his impunity as a despot almost excuses his imperturbable vanity.

If Richter looks like a prophet, when he conducts the orchestra he is the Almighty: and you may be sure that God Himself would have asked Richter for some hints before embarking on such an adventure. While his right hand, armed with a small, unpretentious baton, secures precision of rhythm, his left hand, multiplied a hundredfold, directs the performance of each individual. This left hand is 'undulating and diverse', its suppleness unbelievable! Then, when it seems that there is really no possibility of obtaining a greater wealth of sound, up go his two arms, and the orchestra leaps through the music with so furious an onset as to sweep the most stubborn indifference before it like a straw. Yet all this pantomime is unobtrusive and never distracts the attention unpleasantly or comes between the music and the audience.

I tried in vain to meet this marvellous man. He is a sage who shrinks in wild alarm from interviews. I caught sight of him for a moment as he rehearsed Fafner, the unfortunate dragon on whom that heroic little simpleton, Siegfried, was just about to test the virtue of his sword. It is easy to understand my emotion as I watched the conscientious old man bent over the piano while he performed the duties of a mere producer. Could I interrupt so excellent a man on the futile pretext of extracting confidences from him? Would it not be as outrageous as a presumptuous offer suddenly to extract one of his teeth?

WEINGARTNER

WEINGARTNER CONDUCTED THE Pastoral Symphony with the care of a conscientious gardener. He tidied it so neatly as to produce the illusion of a meticulously finished landscape in which the gently undulating hills are made of plush at ten francs the yard and the foliage is crimped with curling-tongs.

The popularity of the Pastoral Symphony is due to the widespread misunderstanding that exists between Man and Nature. Consider the scene on the banks of the stream: the stream to which, it appears, oxen come to drink, so at least the bassoons would have us suppose; to say nothing of the wooden nightingale and the Swiss cuckoo-clock, more representative of the artistry of M. de Vaucanson than of genuine Nature. It is unnecessarily imitative and the interpretation is entirely arbitrary. How much more profound an interpretation of the beauty of the landscape we find in other passages in the great Master, where, instead of an exact imitation, there is emotional interpretation of what is invisible in Nature. Can the mystery of a forest be expressed by measuring the height of the trees? Is it not its fathomless depth that stirs the imagination?

Weingartner conducted an orchestral fantasy by Chevillard in which the most extraordinary orchestration lends itself to a highly personal method of developing ideas. A gentleman who was extremely fond of music furiously expressed his dislike of the fantasy by whistling on a key. This was excessively stupid. Could anyone tell me whether the said gentleman was criticizing Weingartner's manner of conducting or the composer's music? One reason is that the key is not an instrument of warfare but a domestic article. Monsieur Croche always preferred the butcher-boys' elegant method of whistling with their fingers: it is louder. Perhaps the gentleman is still young enough to learn this art.

Weingartner recovered ground by conducting Liszt's *Mazeppa* magnificently. This symphonic poem is full of the worst faults, occasionally descending even to the commonplace; yet the stormy passion that rages through it captures us at last so completely that we are content to accept it without further questioning. We may affect an air of contempt on leaving; that is pleasant but sheer hypocrisy. The undeniable beauty of Liszt's work arises, I believe, from the fact that his love of music excluded every other kind of emotion. Liszt's genius is often disorderly and feverish, but that is better than rigid perfection, even in white gloves.

Weingartner's personal appearance suggests at first glance a new knife. His gestures have a kind of angular grace; then suddenly the imperious movement of his arms seems to compel the trombones to bellow and to drive the cymbals to frenzy. It is most impressive and verges on the miraculous; the enthusiasm of the audience knew no bounds.

MUSSORGSKY

MUSSORGSKY WAS BORN in 1839 and died in 1881. He had not much time in which to develop his genius, but he did all that was needed in the short time he had, for he will leave an indelible impression on the mind of those who love him or will love him in the future. No one has given utterance to the best within us in tones more gentle or profound: he is unique and will remain so because his art is spontaneous and free from arid formulas. Never has a more refined sensibility been conveyed by such simple means; it is like the art of an enquiring savage discovering music step by step through his emotions. Nor is there ever a question of any particular form; at all events the form is so varied that by no possibility whatsoever can it be related to any established, one might say official, form since it depends on and is made up of successive, minute touches mysteriously linked together by means of an instinctive clairvoyance.

Sometimes, too, Mussorgsky conveys shadowy sensations of trembling anxiety which move and wring the heart. In the *Nursery Suite* there is the prayer of a little girl before she falls asleep which conveys the thoughts and the sensitive emotions of a child, the delightful ways of little girls pretending to be grown-up; all with a sort of feverish truth of interpretation only to be found here. The 'Doll's Lullaby' would seem to have been conceived word by word, through an amazing power of sympathetic interpretation and of visualizing the realms of the special fairyland peculiar to the mind of the child. The end of the lullaby is so gently drowsy that the little singer falls asleep over her own fancies. Here too is the dreadful little boy astride a stick turning the room into a battlefield, now smashing the arms and now the legs of poor, defenceless chairs. He cannot do this without hurting himself too. Then we hear tears and screams; happiness vanishes. It is nothing serious; a moment on his mother's lap, a healing kiss, the battle starts afresh and the chairs do not know where to hide.

All these little dramas are set down with the utmost simplicity; Mussorgsky was content with a construction that would have seemed paltry to Mr—— (I forget his name) or so instinctive a modulation that it would be quite beyond the range of Mr—— (the same fellow).

RICHARD WAGNER

DID THE *Société des Grandes Auditions* intend to punish me for my Wagnerian iconoclasm by depriving me of *Parsifal*? I do not know, but I should prefer to think that these private performances are designed for people whose nobility or position in high society entitles them to attend such little entertainments with a well-bred indifference to what is played. The unimpeachable distinction of the name on the programme frees them from the need of any other illumination and makes it possible to listen attentively to the latest scandal or to watch those pretty movements of the heads of women who are not listening to music! But let the *Société des Grandes Auditions* beware. They will turn Wagner's music into a fashionable 'at home'. After all, that phase of Wagnerian art which originally imposed on his votaries costly pilgrimages and mysterious rites is irritating. I am well aware that this Religion of Art was one of Wagner's favourite ideas; and he was right; such a formula is excellent for capturing and holding the imagination of an audience; but it has miscarried and becomes a kind of Religion of Luxury, excluding perforce many people who are richer in enthusiasm than in cash. The *Société des Grandes Auditions,* by carrying on these traditions of exclusiveness, seems to me doomed to end in that most detestable thing, the art of fashionable society.

When Wagner was in a good humour he liked to maintain
that he would never be so well understood as in France. Was
he referring to aristocratic performances only? I do not think
so. King Louis II of Bavaria was already annoying him with
questions of arbitrary etiquette; and Wagner's proud sensitive-
ness was too acute to miss the fact that true fame comes solely
from the masses and not from a more or less gilded and
exclusive public. It is to be feared that these performances,
directed avowedly to the diffusion of Wagnerian art, may serve
only to alienate the sympathy of the masses; a cunning trick to
make it unpopular. I do not mean that the performance will
hasten a final eclipse; for Wagner's art can never completely
die. It will suffer that inevitable decay, the cruel brand of time
on all beautiful things; yet noble ruins they must remain, in
the shadow of which our grandchildren will brood over the
past splendour of this man who, had he been a little more
human, would have been altogether great.

In *Parsifal*, the final effort of a genius which compels our
homage, Wagner tried to drive his music on a looser rein and
let it breathe more freely. We have no longer the distraught
breathlessness that characterizes Tristan's morbid passion or
Isolde's wild screams of frenzy; nor yet the grandiloquent
commentary on the inhumanity of Wotan.

Nowhere in Wagner's music is a more serene beauty attained
than in the prelude to the third act of *Parsifal* and in the entire
Good Friday episode; although it must be admitted that
Wagner's peculiar conception of human nature is also shown
in the attitude of certain characters of this drama. Look at
Amfortas, that melancholy Knight of the Grail, who whines
like a shop girl and whimpers like a baby. Good Heavens! A
Knight of the Grail, a king's son, would plunge his spear into
his own body rather than parade a guilty wound in doleful
melodies during three acts. As for Kundry, that ancient rose of
hell, she has furnished much copy for Wagnerian literature;
I confess I have but little affection for such a sentimental
draggle-tail. Klingsor is the finest character in *Parsifal*: a
quondam Knight of the Grail, sent packing from the Holy Place
because of his too pronounced views on chastity. His bitter
hatred is amazing; he knows the worth of men and scornfully

weighs the strength of their vows of chastity in the balance. From this it is quite obvious that this crafty magician, this gaol-bird, is not merely the human character but the moral character in a drama in which the falsest moral and religious ideas are set forth, ideas of which the youthful Parsifal is the heroic and insipid champion.

Here, in short, is a Christian drama in which nobody is willing to sacrifice himself, though sacrifice is one of the highest Christian virtues! If Parsifal recovers his miraculous spear, it is thanks to old Kundry, the only creature actually sacrificed in the story: a victim twice over, once of the diabolical intrigues of Klingsor and again of the sacred spleen of a Knight of the Grail. The atmosphere is certainly religious, but why have the incidental children's voices such sinister harmonies? Think for a moment of the child-like candour that would have been conveyed if the spirit of Palestrina had been able to dictate its expression.

The above remarks only apply to the poet whom we are accustomed to admire in Wagner and have nothing to do with the musical beauty of the opera, which is supreme. It is incomparable and bewildering, splendid and strong. *Parsifal* is one of the loveliest monuments of sound ever raised to the serene glory of music.

Vincent d'Indy

CÉSAR FRANCK

ONE OF THE most striking characteristics of Franck was his power of working. Winter and summer he rose at 5.30 in the morning, devoting as a rule the first two hours of the day to composition. At 7.30, after a frugal breakfast, he left home to run all over the town to teach. To the end of his life this great man had to give most of his time to the training of young pianists, some of them amateurs, and to teach in various schools and colleges. Thus he spent the day going from one end of the town to another, returning home in the evening in time for the evening meal. There, tired after the labours of the day, he still found a few moments for copying or scoring and receiving organ and composition pupils to whom he was prodigal of valuable and disinterested advice. It is thus that his most valuable works were written in the early morning hours or during the few weeks holiday allowed by the Conservatoire. Nevertheless he found time to keep in touch with all current artistic manifestations and specially with works of literature. In the summer he used to rent a little house at Quincy where he gave up some hours every day to reading. One day he was reading in the garden and his little sons, seeing him smile to himself, asked him: 'What are you reading that amuses you so much?' The answer was: 'A work of Kant, the *Critique of Pure Reason.*' Is it not permitted to see in these words of the musician, a believer and a Frenchman, the best possible criticism of the heavy and indigestible volume of the German philosopher?

He was a great worker, but not because he sought the rewards of work—fame, wealth, success. He only wanted to express by means of his art his own thoughts and sentiments, for at heart he was modest. He never knew the fever which torments so many artists' lives as they race to win honours and reputation. He never thought of intriguing to secure the nomination to the Institute, not because like Dégas and Puvis he scorned nomination, but because he naïvely believed he had not done enough to deserve it.

97

This modesty did not prevent a confidence in himself, the confidence that is so important in the creative artist when it is backed by sound judgement and not inspired by vanity. . . . Steadfastness in work, modesty, artistic integrity—these were the outstanding qualities of Franck's character. But he possessed also another, a very rare one—a kindly and indulgent benevolence.

I shall not be contradicted when I say that no modern musician was, in his work and in his life, more honest, more sincere than César Franck. No one possessed in a higher degree the artistic conscience—that touchstone of true genius. We see it in many of his works, as the artist worthy of the name expresses well only that which he himself has felt, experiencing great difficulty in giving artistic expression to anything that is alien to his nature. Because he could not even envisage evil, Franck could not express effectively in his music such things as hatred, injustice—in one word, evil. To see it we have but to look at the choirs of rebels of the unjust and tyrants in the fifth and seventh Beatitude or to the part of Satan where the spirit of evil adopts the pompous declamatory style of a demon of Cornelius or Wiertz.

GERMANY

Wolfgang Amadeus Mozart

COURTSHIP AND MARRIAGE

To his father

YOU ASK ME to explain the words added at the end of my last letter. Most gladly would I have opened my heart to you long ago, but for the fact that you might have thought I had chosen the wrong time to make a confession. My one desire is to have an assured income; with that and a few extras one could live well and get married. Does the thought of marriage frighten you? I do beg you, best of fathers, to listen to me. Nature urges me to take a wife. I cannot live as the majority of men do here. I am deeply religious and too honest to take advantage of an innocent girl. I am too careful of my health to risk horrible, loathsome diseases. I can swear to you that I have never had anything to do with women of the streets. If I had, I would say it, since it is human to err and to err once would be nothing more than weakness. . . . I know that this is not sufficient reason; but my temperament inclines me more to a homely than to a roistering life. I have never been accustomed to look after my things and my linen; a woman would be very useful for that. I am convinced that two can live on what I earn as comfortably as one. Many of my present expenses would be unnecessary and as for new expenses, we know what they would be and can make our plans accordingly. To my thinking a bachelor is only half alive. I have thought, I have reflected and always think of this.

Now, who is the object of my affection? Please do not be frightened. Is it a member of the Weber family? It is—but not Josepha nor Sophia. It is Constanze, the third girl. Nowhere else have I seen such difference in the characters of three sisters. The eldest is lazy, ill-mannered, untrustworthy, cunning. Her sister is too young to be anything—a good soul but frivolous. Heaven keep temptation from her! The third instead, my good and dear Constanze, is the martyr of the family, and the most tender-hearted, most amiable—the best. She does all the house-work, getting no thanks from anyone.

Oh my dear father! I would have to fill many sheets to tell you all that has happened in this house. If you wish, I will do so in my next letter. Before I finish I must say something more about my Constanze. She is neither ugly nor beautiful. All her beauty is in two little black eyes and a fine figure. She is not witty but has all the intelligence required for the duties of a good wife and mother. It is not true that she likes luxuries; on the contrary, she has been used to shabby clothes because her mother gives everything to the others and nothing to Constanze. Of course she would rather dress decently, but she does everything herself. She dresses her own hair, she is economical and has the best heart in the world. I love her and she loves me. Could I have wished for a better woman? I tell you candidly that when I first knew the family I did not feel in the least attracted to her. Affection began when I experienced her kindness and her care of me.

I only wish to have a small, steady income (I have good reason to hope for that) and I will never cease to ask you to help us and make us all happy. Are you as happy as I am? Half my income will be for you, my dearest father. I have now opened my heart to you. Do open yours to me. Have pity on your son.

15 December 1781

I am still furiously angry on account of the shameless lies of the arch-scoundrel Winter. Yet I am cool and calm because they cannot affect me and also happy with my dearest, incomparable, excellent father. I expected nothing less from your intelligence, your affection and your goodness. You have read the letter in which I confessed my love and you will guess my intentions. At twenty-six I am not likely to be such a fool as to marry without an income of some sort. The reasons why I wish to marry as soon as possible are sound; you will have seen from the description I gave you that the girl suits me perfectly. She is exactly as I described her—nothing more nor less. I will also make full confession of my marriage contract, being convinced that you will forgive me for taking such a step since, had you been in my place, you would have done the same. I only beg you to forgive me for not having told you before. I have already said why I did not write and I hope for your forgiveness; no man could have been more worried about it than I was. Even if you had not given me occasion to speak about it in your last letter I would have told you all; I could no longer be silent.

Now as regards the marriage contract (or rather declaration of my intentions) you know that after the death of the father—most unfortunately for the family, for myself and Constanze—a guardian was appointed. This gentleman does not know me at all and zealous busybodies like Mr Winter must have told him all kinds of silly things about me—that he must be very careful; that I have no job; that I have been too friendly; that I might desert the girl and make her very unhappy. The mother, who knew me, never said a word to him. In any case our relation consisted only in my living in the same house, and later, in calling on them every day. I never went anywhere with Constanze. Her mother, having been told all sorts of things about me, came and begged me to see him. We met, I spoke to him but apparently did not express myself clearly because the outcome was that he forbade me to visit the Webers again till I had declared my intentions in writing. Her mother said that our relation was that of friends, that she was grateful to me and could not think of forbidding me the house. But he then ordered her to stop all intercourse unless I did as he wanted. What was I to do? I had either to write or give up all thought of Constanze. Can anyone who loves truly and sincerely forsake his beloved? What would her mother, what would Constanze herself have thought of me? That was my position. I then wrote the document binding myself to marry Constanze; if through unforeseen obstacles I should change my mind, I was to pay her 300 florins a year. It was easy enough to promise it as I shall never leave her. If I were so unfortunate as to change my mind I should be only too happy to be free at the cost of three hundred florins and I know Constanze would be much too proud to be bought and sold. But what do you think does this divine girl do as soon as the guardian had left? She took the declaration from her mother's hands and, saying to me: 'Dear Mozart, I have no need of written documents. I believe your word', tore up the paper. This made her dearer than ever to me. As the guardian had promised not to say anything about the matter to anybody I felt much more tranquil about you, my dear father. The girl has everything one could wish—except money—and I felt sure of your approval. I know your way of looking at things. Will you now forgive me? I hope and indeed have no doubt. . . .

Dearest father, everything will improve you will see. What is the use of making a fuss? Sudden strokes of good fortune do not last. 'Chi va piano va sano.' We must cut the coat according to our cloth. Of all the rascally things Winter has said, nothing angers me more than his saying that my Constanze is a——. I have described her to you. . . . If you wish to know more about her, write to the Auerhammers where she has visited and dined or to Baroness Waldstatten where she lived for a month while the lady was sick. . . . Heaven send that I can marry her soon. I must add that Winter said to me: 'If you marry her, you are not a wise man. You are earning enough and you can do it; why not keep a mistress instead—what prevents you . . . religion?' Let him think what he likes.

December 22, 1781

I cannot understand how it is that I am still without news from you. Are you angry with me? If you are angry because I did not tell you about it before, I can understand. But if you have read my explanation you will forgive me. You cannot be angry because I am going to marry; you know my religious sentiments too well and my way of thinking. I could say much but it is my custom not to speak or talk of what does not concern me. That is how I am made and I am ashamed when I have to defend myself against calumny; I believe that truth will come to light in the end. I can write no more as I have had no reply to my last letter. No news. Keep well. I beg you once more to forgive me and give me your sympathy. I could never be happy or satisfied without my Constanze; but if you are not happy, I could only be partially happy. Will you not make me completely happy, my dear, best of fathers? I do beg you.

January 9, 1782

I wrote in a hurry. It is 10.30 at night but I must ask you urgently to do something for me which I hope you will not take amiss. Will you please send me *Idomeneo* with the German text or with the translation? I lent my copy to Countess Thun who has now moved to another house and cannot find it. . . .

I must conclude, but if I want to sleep peacefully I must add this: do not think ill of my Constanze. I could not love her if she were what you suppose. She and I know perfectly well what her mother means. But the old lady is very much mistaken if she thinks we are going to lodge with her. It would never do either for myself or for Constanze. She means not to see much of her mother after we are married and I will do all I can to help her keep her resolution. We know the old lady too well. Most dear and excellent father, we want to get together as soon as possible so that you can see Constanze and love her. I know you love kind hearts.

January 30, 1782

To Constanze

Dear and excellent friend,

May I so call you or do you hate me so much that you will no longer let me be your friend or you mine? Even if this is so you cannot prevent me from thinking well of you as I did in the past. Remember what you said to me in spite of my pleading. Three times you turned your back and told me you would have nothing more to do with me. I cannot resign one I love as easily as you; I am not so impulsive or so thoughtless. I love you too much to accept my dismissal. I beg you hence to give some thought to the cause of my anxiety. You were so bold as to tell your sisters in my presence that you allowed your calf to be measured. This is what no young woman who cares about her good name will allow to happen. To do as your neighbours do is a good maxim but other things have to be considered—whether they are friends and whether you are a child or a grown woman (especially if you are engaged to be married) and whether the people are below or above you in the social scale—and particularly if they are noble. That the baroness should allow it is another matter. She is a woman of middle age who rather likes certain things. I hope you will not take her as an example even if you do not marry me. If you could not avoid doing what the others did, then you should have taken the ribbon in your hands and measured your calf yourself as all the respectable women of my acquaintance do. You should not have allowed another to do it. I myself would never have dared to do it before company. It was still worse to allow one you don't know, a complete stranger, to do it. Now it's all over; a little word of repentance from you would settle everything and, if you will not take offence at my saying it, can still end it all. You can see from this how fond I am of you. I don't bluster as you do; I think, reflect and feel. Listen to your better self and I am sure that if you do I shall be able to say this very day that Constanze is virtuous, judicious, has a regard for her honour and is faithful to her honest and true Mozart.

April 29, 1782

To his father
I must beg you, dearest father, for everybody's sake to give your consent to my marriage with Constanze. It is not only that I want to get married. If it were only that, I could wait quite patiently; but it is my honour that is in question—and Constanze's; my head, my heart and my health suffer. How can I work when my heart is in a continuous flutter and my brain in a whirl. . . . . Most people believe that we are already married; her mother is angry and leads us both a dreadful dance. The remedy is so easy. Believe me, if Vienna is dear, people who practise economy find it possible to live here as cheaply as anywhere else. Bachelors do not know it, but anyone lucky enough to have a wife like mine is indeed lucky. We shall live in peace, quiet and content. Do not let the possibility of my falling ill upset you. I am sure that the first nobles of the land would help me, particularly after I am married. I am quite confident of it. I know what Prince Kaunitz said to the Emperor and to the Grand Duke Maximilian about me. My excellent father, I wait for your consent most anxiously. I need

it because of my good name and my honour. Do not delay the joy of embracing your son and his wife.

27 July 1782

I mean well; but I cannot do the impossible. I do not intend to write down anything that comes into my head and I must wait for the next post-day before sending you the whole symphony. I could send the last movement, but I would rather send the complete work and save the expense. What I have sent already cost me three florins.

Today I received your letter of the 26th—a cold, indifferent letter such as I could never have anticipated after the news I gave you of the success of my opera. I imagined you too anxious to open a parcel that held your son's opera which in Vienna has met with such a reception that people go to hear nothing else. The theatre is packed night after night. We had the fourth performance yesterday and it will be given again on Friday. But you had no time. . . . Meanwhile you will have my last letter and I am sure you will now give your consent. You cannot oppose it. The girl is honest, kind, of good family; I can keep her, we love one another. What you have written or anything you can write can only be by the way of advice— good no doubt—but of no use to us. There is no reason for delay. It will be much better to put our house in order at once now and be honest about it.

July 31, 1782

Mozart and Constanze Weber were married, against Leopold's wishes, on August 7.

Ludwig van Beethoven

HIS SAD LIFE

To Carl Amenda

MY DEAR, my good Amenda, my heartily beloved friend,

With deep emotion, with mixed pain and pleasure did I receive and read your last letter. To what can I compare your fidelity, your attachment to me? Oh! how pleasant it is that you have always remained so kind to me; yes, I also know that you, of all men, are the most trustworthy. You are no 'Viennese friend', no, you are one of those such as my native country produces. How often do I wish you were with me, for your Beethoven is most unhappy, and at strife with nature and Creator. The latter I have often cursed for exposing His creatures to the smallest chance, so that frequently the richest buds are thereby crushed and destroyed. Only think that the noblest part of me, my sense of hearing, has become very weak. Already when you were with me I noted traces of it, and I said nothing. Now it has become worse, and it remains to be seen whether it can ever be healed. The primal cause of it is the state of my bowels. So far as the latter are concerned, I am almost well, but I much fear that my hearing will not improve; maladies of that kind are the most difficult of all to cure. What a sad life I am now compelled to lead; I must avoid all that is near and dear to me, and then to be among such wretched egotistical beings such as * * *, etc. I can say that among all, Lichnowski has best stood the test. Since last year he has settled on me 600 florins, which, together with the good sale of my works, enables me to live without anxiety. Everything I write, I can sell immediately five times over, and also be well paid. I have composed a fair quantity, and as I hear that you have ordered pianofortes from * * *, I will send you many things in one of the packing-cases, so that it will not cost you so very much. Now to my consolation, a man has come here with whom intercourse is a pleasure, and whose friendship is free from all selfishness. He is one of the friends of my youth. I have often spoken to him about you, and told him that since I left my native country, you are the one whom my heart has chosen. Even he does not like * * *, the latter is and remains too weak for friendship. I consider him and * * * mere instruments on which, when it pleases me, I play; but they can never become noble witnesses of my inner and outer activity, nor be in true sympathy with me; I value them according as they are useful to me. Oh! How happy should I now be if I had my perfect hearing, for I should then hasten to you. As it is, I must in all things be behindhand; my best years will slip away without bringing forth what, with my talent and my strength, I ought to have accomplished. I must now have recourse to sad resignation. I have, it is true, resolved not to worry about all this, but how is it possible? Yes, Amenda, if, six months hence, my malady is beyond cure, then I lay claim to your help. You must leave everything and come to me. I will travel (my malady interferes least with my playing and composition, most only in conversation), and you must be my companion. I am convinced good fortune will not fail me. With whom need I be afraid of measuring my strength? Since you went away I have written music of all kinds except operas and sacred works.

Yes, do not refuse; help your friend to bear with his troubles, his infirmity. I have also greatly improved my pianoforte playing. I hope this journey may also turn to your advantage; afterwards you will always remain with me. I have duly received all your letters, and although I have only answered a few, you have been always in my mind, and my heart, as always, beats tenderly for you. Please keep as a great secret what I have told you about my hearing; trust no one, whoever it may be, with it. Do write frequently; your letters, however short they may be, console me, do me good. I expect soon to get another one from you, my dear friend. Don't lend out my Quartet any more, because I have made many changes in it. I have only just learnt how to write quartets properly, as you will see when you receive them.

Now, my dear good friend, farewell! If perchance you believe that I can show you any kindness here, I need not, of course, remind you to address yourself first to

Your faithful, truly loving,

L. V. BEETHOVEN (June 1800)

IN LOVE

To Countess Giulietta Guicciardi

MY ANGEL, my all, my very self,

Just a few words today, and only in pencil (with thine) only till tomorrow is my room definitely engaged, what an unworthy waste of time in such matters—why this deep sorrow where necessity speaks? Can our love endure otherwise than through sacrifices, through restraint in longing? Canst thou help not being wholly mine, can I, not being wholly thine? Oh! gaze at nature in all its beauty, and calmly accept the inevitable —love demands everything, and rightly so. Thus is it for me with thee, for thee with me, only thou so easily forgettest that I must live for myself and for thee—were we wholly united thou wouldst feel this painful fact as little as I should—my journey was terrible. I arrived here only yesterday morning at four o'clock, and as they were short of horses, the mail-coach selected another route, but what an awful road! At the last stage but one I was warned against travelling by night; they frightened me with the wood, but that only spurred me on— and I was wrong, the coach must needs break down, the road being dreadful, a swamp, a mere country road; without the postilions I had with me, I should have stuck on the way. Esterhazi, by the ordinary road, met the same fate with eight horses as I with four—yet it gave me some pleasure, as successfully overcoming any difficulty always does. Now for a quick change from without to within: we shall probably soon see each other, besides, today I cannot tell thee what has been passing through my mind during the past few days concerning my life—were our hearts closely united, I should not do things of this kind. My heart is full of the many things I have to say to thee—ah!—there are moments in which I feel that speech is powerless—cheer up—remain my true, my only treasure, my all! as I to thee. The gods must send the rest, what for us must be and ought to be.   Thy faithful,

LUDWIG (July 1801)

Thou sufferest, thou my dearest love. I have just found out that the letters must be posted very early Mondays, Thursdays —the only days when the post goes from here to K. Thou sufferest—Ah! where I am, art thou also with me; I will arrange for myself and thee. I will manage so that I can live with thee; and what a life! But as it is! without thee. Persecuted here and there by the kindness of men, which I little deserve, and as little care to deserve. Humility of man towards man—it pains me—and when I think of myself in connection with the universe, what am I and what is He who is named the Greatest; and still this again shows the divine in man. I weep when I think that probably thou wilt only get the first news from me on Saturday evening. However much thou lovest me, my love for thee is stronger, but never conceal thy thoughts from me. Good-night. As I am taking the baths I must go to bed (*two words scratched through*). O God—so near! so far! Our love, is it not a true heavenly edifice, firm as heaven's vault?

While still in bed, my thoughts press to thee, my Beloved One, at moments with joy, and then again with sorrow, waiting to see whether fate will take pity on us. Either I must live wholly with thee or not at all. Yes, I have resolved to wander in distant lands, until I can fly to thy arms, and feel that with thee I have a real home; with thee encircling me about, I can send my soul into the kingdom of spirits. Yes, unfortunately, it must be so. Calm thyself, and all the more since thou knowest my faithfulness towards thee, never can another possess my heart, never—never—O God, why must one part from what one so loves, and yet my life in V. at present is a wretched life. Thy love has made me one of the happiest and, at the same time, one of the unhappiest of men—at my age I need a quiet, steady life—is that possible in our situation? My Angel, I have just heard that the post goes every day, and I must therefore stop, so that you may receive the letter without delay. Be calm, only by calm consideration of our existence can we attain our aim to live together—be calm—love me—today—yesterday—what tearful longing after thee—thee—thee—my life— my all—farewell—Oh, continue to love me—never misjudge the faithful heart   Of Thy Beloved
                               L.

Ever thine   (1801)
Ever mine
Ever each other's.

THE HEILIGENSTADT TESTAMENT

For My Brothers Carl and ———— Beethoven

O YE MEN WHO regard or declare me to be malignant, stubborn or cynical, how unjust are ye towards me. You do not know the secret cause of my seeming so. From childhood onward, my heart and mind prompted me to be kind and tender, and I was ever inclined to accomplish great deeds. But only think that during the last six years, I have been in a wretched condition, rendered worse by unintelligent physicians. Deceived from year to year with hopes of improvement, and then finally forced to the prospect of lasting infirmity (which may last for years, or even be totally incurable). Born with a fiery, active temperament, even susceptive of the diversions of society, I had soon to retire from the world, to live a solitary life. At times, even, I endeavoured to forget all this, but how harshly was I driven back by the redoubled experience of my bad hearing. Yet it was not possible for me to say to men: Speak louder, shout, for I am deaf. Alas! how could I declare the weakness of a sense which in me ought to be more acute than in others—a sense which formerly I possessed in highest perfection, a perfection such as few in my profession enjoy, or ever have enjoyed; no I cannot do it. Forgive, therefore, if you see me withdraw, when I would willingly mix with you. My misfortune pains me doubly, in that I am certain to be misunderstood. For me there can be no recreation in the society of my fellow creatures, no refined conversations, no interchange of thought. Almost alone, and only mixing in society when absolutely necessary, I am compelled to live as an exile. If I approach near to people, a feeling of hot anxiety comes over me lest my condition should be noticed—for so it was during these past six months which I spent in the country. Ordered by my intelligent physician to spare my hearing as much as possible, he almost fell in with my present frame of mind, although many a time I was carried away by my sociable inclinations. But how humiliating was it, when some one standing close to me heard a distant flute, and I heard nothing, or a shepherd singing, and again I heard nothing. Such incidents almost drove me to despair; at times I was almost on the point of putting an end to my life—art alone restrained my hand. Oh! it seemed as if I could not quit this earth until I had produced all I felt within me, and so I continued this wretched life—wretched, indeed, with so sensitive a body that a somewhat sudden change can throw me from the best into the worst state. Patience, I am told, I must choose as my guide. I have done so—lasting, I hope, will be my resolution to bear up until it pleases the inexorable Parcae to break the thread. Forced already in my twenty-eighth year to become a philosopher, it is not easy; for an artist more difficult than for anyone else. O Divine Being, Thou who lookest down into my inmost soul, Thou understandest; Thou knowest that love for mankind and a desire to do good dwell therein. Oh, my fellow men, when one day you read this, remember that you were unjust to me, and let the unfortunate one console himself if he can find one like himself, who in spite of all obstacles which nature has thrown in his way has still done everything in his power to be received into the ranks of worthy artists and men. You, my brothers Carl and ——, as soon as I am dead, beg Professor Schmidt, if he be still living, to describe my malady; and annex this written account to that of my illness, so that at least the world, so far as is possible, may become reconciled to me after my death. And now I declare you both heirs to my small fortune (if such it may be called). Divide it honourably and dwell in peace, and help each other. What you have done against me has, as you know, long been forgiven. And you, brother Carl, I especially thank you for the attachment you have shown towards me of late. My prayer is that your life may be better, less troubled by cares, than mine. Recommend to your children virtue; it alone can bring happiness, not money. I speak from experience. It was virtue which bore me up in time of trouble; to her, next to my art, I owe thanks for my not having laid violent hands on myself. Farewell, and love one another. My thanks to all friends, especially Prince Lichnowski and Professor Schmidt. I should much like one of you to keep as an heirloom the instruments given to me by Prince L. But let no strife arise between you concerning them; if money should be of more service to you, just sell them. How happy I feel that even when lying in my grave I may be useful to you.

So let it be. I joyfully hasten to meet death. If it come before I have had opportunity to develop all my artistic faculties, it will come, my hard fate notwithstanding, too soon, and I should probably wish it later—yet even then I shall be happy, for will it not deliver me from a state of endless suffering? Come when thou wilt, I shall face thee courageously—farewell, and when I am dead do not entirely forget me. This I deserve from you, for during my lifetime I often thought of you, and how to make you happy. Be ye so.

Heiligenstadt, 6th October, 1802

(*On the fourth side of the great Will sheet*)
Heiligenstadt, October, 1802, thus I take my farewell of thee —and indeed sadly—yes, that fond hope which I entertained when I came here, of being at any rate healed up to a certain point, must be entirely abandoned. As the leaves of autumn fall and fade, so it has withered away for me; almost the same as when I came here do I go away—even the high courage which often in the beautiful summer days quickened me, that has vanished. O Providence, let me have just one pure day of joy; so long is it since true joy filled my heart. Oh when, oh when, oh Divine Being, shall I be able once again to feel it in the temple of nature and of men? Never—no—that would be too hard.

For my brothers Carl and —— to execute after my death.

ON ARRANGEMENTS

To the Publishing House of Breitkopf and Haertel, Leipzig (*Fragment*)
. . . WITH REGARD TO arrangements, I am heartily glad that you decline them. The unnatural mania, at the present day, to wish to transfer pieces for the pianoforte to string instruments, which in every way are so different, ought to be stopped. I firmly assert that only Mozart himself could transfer his piano-forte music to other instruments, and the same of Haydn; and without placing myself on a level with these two great men, I make the same assertion with respect to my pianoforte sonatas; not only would whole passages have to be omitted or

entirely rewritten, but further additions made—and herein lies the whole stumbling-block—to overcome which there must be either the master himself, or at least one possessing the same skill and inventive power. I changed just one sonata of my own into a quartet for strings, which I was pressed to do, and I am sure that no other man could have accomplished the task as I have done.

July 1803

CABALS AND INTRIGUES

To Breitkopf and Haertel, Leipzig

YOU WILL SAY it is this and that, and that and this—it is true there cannot be a stranger letter-writer—but you have received the terzets. One was already finished, when you went away, but I wished only to send it with the second; this latter has also been ready for the last few months without my even thinking of sending it to you—finally the C(opyist) bothered me about it. You will show me a very great kindness, and I earnestly beg you to do so, if you do not publish before Easter all the things you have of mine, for I certainly shall be with you during Lent. Also, until then, let none of the new symphonies be heard, for I am coming to Leipzig, so it will be a real festival to perform these with the, to me, well-known honesty and good-will of the musicians at Leipzig—and when there I will at once see to the correcting.

Finally, I am compelled through intrigues, cabals and low tricks of all kinds to leave the only German Vaterland. I am going at the invitation of his Majesty the King of Westphalia as his Kapellmeister with a yearly pay of 600 ducats in gold. I have sent off by post my acceptance, and I am now waiting my decree so as to make preparations for the journey, when I shall pass through Leipzig. In order that the journey may be the more brilliant for me, I beg you, if not too disadvantageous to you, not to make known any of my compositions before Easter. With regard to the Sonata dedicated to Baron Gleichenstein, please leave out the Imperial Royal draughtsman, for he does not like anything of that sort. There will probably be some abusive articles in the *Musikalische Zeitung* with regard to my last concert. I certainly do not wish everything that is against me to be suppressed, but people should know that no one has more personal enemies here than myself; and this is all the easier to understand, seeing that the state of music is ever becoming worse. We have conductors who understand as little about conducting as about conducting themselves—at the Wieden it is really at its worst—I had to give my concert there, and on all sides difficulties were placed in my way. There was a horrid trick played in connection with the Widows' concert, out of hatred to me, for Herr Salieri threatened to expel any musician belonging to their company who played for me; but in spite of several faults which I could not prevent, the public received everything most enthusiastically. Nevertheless, scribblers will not fail to write wretched stuff against me in the *Musikalische Zeitung*. The musicians were specially in a rage that through carelessness mistakes arose in the simplest, plainest piece. I suddenly bade them stop, and called out in a loud voice, Begin again. Such a thing had never happened there before; the public testified its pleasure. Things became worse every day. The day before my concert, the orchestra in the theatre in the town got into such a muddle in that easy little opera, Milton, that conductor and director and orchestra came to grief—for the conductor, instead of giving the beat beforehand, gave it afterwards, and then only the director appears on the scene. Answer at once, my good friend,

With esteem,
Your most devoted servant,
BEETHOVEN

(On the reverse side of the cover)

I beg you to say nothing definite in public about my appointment at Westphalia until I write to you that I have received my decree. Farewell and write to me soon. At Leipzig we will talk about my works. Some hints might be given in the *Musikalische Zeitung* about my going away from here—also a few stabs, since no one here has been really willing to help me.

(January 1809)

Louis Spohr

A MOZART PERFORMANCE IN PARIS

FOR SOME DAYS I have been less satisfied with the grand opera. I heard *Les Mystères d'Isis*. Too well are justified the complaints of the admirers of Mozart of the mutilation of *Zauberflöte* in the adaptation which the French themselves have rechristened 'Les misères d'ici'. One blushes that it should have been Germans who thus sinned against the immortal master. Everything but the overture has been tampered with, changed and mutilated. The opera begins with the concluding chorus of *Zauberflöte*; then comes the march from *La Clemenza di Tito* and then fragments from other Mozart operas and also a short excerpt from a Haydn symphony. Between these are recitatives manufactured by Mr Lachnitz. Even worse than this is the imposition of serious words on music of a cheerful and even comic character; thus music becomes a parody of the text and of the situation. Papagena is made to sing the air of the Moor 'Alles fühlt der Liebe Freuden'; the trio of the boys 'Seit uns zum zweitenmal willkommen' is sung by the three ladies; the duet 'Bei männern welch Liebe fühlen' has been turned into a trio—and so on. Worst of all are the alterations in the orchestral score. For example in the air 'So wandelt er an Freundes Hand' the imitation in the bass which goes up and down to illustrate the word 'wandelt' is entirely omitted, impoverishing the harmony and robbing the music of its descriptive character. It is not difficult to imagine how insipid and meagre this passage, so much admired in Germany, sounds here. In the trio of women's voices where Mozart strengthens and supports the third voice with the violins only, the adapters have added both violoncello and bass with the result that these delicate phrases for three voices have now a bass with a span of three octaves, unbearable to a cultivated ear.

We must do the French the justice to say that they have always disapproved of the vandalic mutilations of a masterpiece the greatness of which they cannot gauge since they have not heard it. But how is it then that the 'Mystères' have kept their place in the repertory for the last eighteen or twenty years?

To me the performance also was not satisfactory. The overture was not executed as well as it should have been, given the excellence of that company of musicians. It was taken too fast at the beginning so that, with the acceleration of the close, the violins could only play quavers instead of semiquavers. The singers of the grand opera, whose most conspicuous merits lie perhaps in declamatory music, are little qualified to render the soft airs of *Zauberflöte* in a satisfactory manner. They sing them with a blunt roughness that deprives them of all tenderness.

PARIS BALLETS

YESTERDAY FOR THE first time we went to see *Clari*, a grand ballet in three acts with music by Kreutzer. Little as I like ballets and little as, in my opinion, they deserve the aid of art that is lavished on them here, I do not deny that the Parisian ballet may afford agreeable amusement till one begins to weary of monotony of the mimic action and the sameness of the dances. With all the added perfection of the Parisian stage, pantomime, from the poverty of its symbols, is, when compared to recited drama, like a mere outline as against a finished drawing. You may embellish it with golden ornament and decoration (Parisian costumes and décor are magnificent) but it remains an outline—life is wanting. In the same way we may compare drama and opera or a drawing with an oil painting. Only with the powerful aid of harmony can song give expression to the indefinable, imagined emotions of the soul which language can only hint at.

The music of Kreutzer is a great success and in the second and third acts the effects are most captivating. It facilitates the understanding of the action by appropriate expression and abounds in pretty melodies that, to our regret, are not part of an opera score.

ON FRENCH TASTE

BEFORE THE BALLET, the opera *Le Devin du Village* of Rousseau was given. Should we praise or blame the French because in spite of the many excellent things that have enriched their opera repertory during the last twenty years they still produce the oldest things of all? Is it a sign of advanced, cultivated, artistic tastes to give as enthusiastic a welcome to the oldest operas of Grétry, incorrect and poor in harmony, as to the masterpieces of Cherubini and Méhul? It is very singular how all here, young and old, strive only to shine by mechanical execution and men in whom there is perhaps the germ of better things devote whole years to the study and practice of one single piece of music—frequently of the most worthless order —so as to make a sensation in public. In these circumstances it is not to be wondered at if the mind remains inactive and the performer becomes an automaton.

One seldom hears a serious work such as a quartet or a quintet at a musical party; everyone contributes a show-piece; you hear nothing but *airs variés, rondos favoris*, nocturnes and similar trifles with romances and little duets from singers. No matter how incorrect or insipid the composition, the effect is always the same if the execution is sweet and smooth. With a repertory poor in trifles and my serious German education, I feel ill-at-ease in such company—like a man speaking to people who do not understand his words. When these people praise my composition (apart from my playing) I cannot feel gratified since immediately after they will give equal praise to any bagatelle. To be praised by such connoisseurs brings a blush to one's cheek. It is the same in the theatres. The leaders of fashion, like the masses, here positively do not know how to distinguish the best from the worst; they hear *Le Jugement de Midas* (an opera of Grétry) with the same rapture as *Les deux Journées* (Cherubini's) or *Joseph* (Méhul's). It requires no long residence here to conclude that the French are not a musical nation. Their best violinist, in point of execution, is Lafont. His playing combines beauty of tone, purity, power and grace. If he possessed also depth of feeling he would be a perfect violinist. But feeling, without which a man can neither conceive nor execute a good adagio, in him, as in most Frenchmen, appears to be wholly wanting; he trims up his slow movements with elegant and pretty ornamentations, but he remains cold at heart. In this country the adagio is considered by artists and by the public the least important part of the concerto and perhaps is only retained because it divides two quick movements and enhances their effect.

I ascribe to this indifference (the French are generally irresponsive to anything that works upon the emotions) the fact that my adagios and my way of playing them made less impression than brilliant allegro movements. Accustomed to the special applause I had received from Germans, Italians, Dutch and English, I felt hurt to see that the French thought so little of it. But when I noted how rarely their own artists give them a serious adagio and how coldly they respond to it I ceased to worry.

It is sad to see what means artists here have to resort to in order to gain support for their undertakings. While the Parisians rush to any sensual entertainment they have to be dragged to an intellectual one.

The brothers Bohrer wanted me to accompany them on a tour of the southern provinces. I have no desire to do it. The bad orchestra and the bad taste of the provincial towns would make such a journey too disagreeable to me.

WEBER'S 'FREISCHÜTZ' AND SPOHR'S 'JESSONDA'

CARL MARIA VON WEBER'S opera Der Freischütz obtained such success in Vienna and Berlin that the Dresden opera gave the composer permission to produce it on the stage and rehearsals had already started when I arrived in Dresden. As up to that time I had not entertained a very high opinion of Weber's talent for composition it will be easily imagined that I was very curious to hear an opera of his that had won such enthusiastic praise in two German capitals. My interest was all the greater from my having worked a few years before, when at Frankfurt, on the same subject which I found in Appel's book of apparitions and which I abandoned when I accidentally heard that Weber was already working at it.

Closer acquaintance with the opera did not solve for me the riddle of its extraordinary success. I can only account for it by Weber's peculiar gift and capacity for writing for the tastes of the masses. As I well knew that nature had denied the gift to me, I find it difficult to account for the impulse that there and then sent me again to write music for the theatre. But so it happened, and I had scarcely arrived home when I took from my trunk a work I had begun in Paris. On a tedious day there, when rain and mud made it unthinkable to go out, I had asked my landlady to lend me a book. She gave me the old romance 'La veuve de Malabar' and I found the story so adapted for an opera libretto that I purchased the book for a few sous. While in Paris and on the homeward journey I turned over in my mind how the libretto could best be made and immediately on my return to Gandersheim I began to sketch a scene. When I felt disinclined to proceed with the composition of the mass, I turned to the opera and by the time I removed with my family to Dresden I had nearly completed it. I now thought of it again and having drawn up a complete scenario, set about finding a poet who would write the text according to my plan. Such a writer I discovered in Mr Edward Gehe who readily understood my intentions. In this way originated the text of my opera *Jessonda*.

MEETING JOHN FIELD

IN THE EVENING I sometimes accompanied Clementi to his pianoforte warehouse where John Field was obliged often to play for hours to display the instruments to the best advantage for the purchaser. The technical perfection and the dreamy melancholy of that young artist's execution gave me great satisfaction. I still recollect the figure of that pale, overgrown youth whom I have never seen since. Field had overgrown his clothes so that when he placed himself at the piano and stretched his arms over the keyboard his whole figure appeared stiff and awkward; but the moment he touched the keyboard everything else was forgotten. His playing commanded complete attention. Unhappily I could not express my gratitude and my emotion to the young man otherwise than by a silent pressure of the hand; for he spoke no other language but his own. It was generally reported that Field was kept on very short allowance by Clementi and was obliged to pay for the good fortune of having his instruction with many privations.

BEETHOVEN'S QUARTETS NOT APPRECIATED
IN LEIPZIG AND BERLIN

MEETING WITH MANY difficulties in arranging for a concert,
I was desirous to be asked to some musical party in order to
draw attention to my abilities. My wish was gratified. I
received an invitation to an evening party with the request to
play. I selected for the occasion one of the finest of Beethoven's
six new quartets. But after a few bars I remarked that my
colleagues did not know the music and were consequently
unable to enter into the spirit of it. My disappointment was
greater as I noticed that the company soon ceased to pay any
attention to my playing. They began to chat and the conversation became so general and so loud that it almost overpowered
the music. I stopped playing and without a word began to put
my violin back in my case. My action created a sensation and, the
master of the house coming towards me, I went to meet him
saying aloud so that all should hear: 'I have been accustomed
hitherto to find people listening with attention to my playing.
As the contrary happened here I naturally concluded that the
general wish is that I should end the performance.' The host
seemed very much embarrassed, but as I was taking leave of
the company he suggested in a friendly tone: 'If you could
perhaps play something more adapted to the taste of my
friends, I feel sure you would have a very attentive and grateful
audience.' Feeling that I was mostly to blame for having chosen
the wrong music for that audience, I willingly resumed my
violin and played Rode's quartet in E flat which all knew well.
There was now a breathless silence and the interest in my
playing increased with each new section. At the conclusion so
many flattering things were said that I was induced to parade
my hobby-horse, the Variations in G major of Rode. This so
enchanted the company that compliments were showered on
me the rest of the evening.

In Berlin I first played at a party given by Prince Radziwill,
himself a distinguished violoncellist and a talented composer.
I met there Romberg, Moser, Seidler, Semmler and other
distinguished artists. Being solicited to play something myself
I thought nothing could be more worthy of that company than
my favourite quartets of Beethoven. But I was wrong. The

musicians of Berlin knew as little of Beethoven's quartets as the musicians of Leipzig and could neither play nor appreciate them. It is true that as soon as I had finished they hastened to praise my playing but spoke disparagingly of the composition. Romberg said bluntly: 'My dear Spohr, how can you play such stuff?' When I heard one of the most famous artists of the time express such an opinion I began to doubt my own taste and when I was asked to play again later in the evening I chose, as I had done in Leipzig, Rode's quartet in E flat major and the result was the same.

YOUNG MEYERBEER. A CRITIC

I WELL REMEMBER A party where I heard for the first time the now celebrated Giacomo Meyerbeer, then a boy of thirteen, play at his father's house. The talented lad had already excited much attention by his accomplished performances on the piano and his relatives and friends regarded him with the greatest pride. It is said that one friend of the family, returning from a lecture on astronomy, told the boy's parents with the greatest joy: 'Our Giacomo has already been put among the stars.' The lecturer showed us a constellation which is called 'the little bear'—no doubt in his honour.

My playing in Leipzig was received with great applause. There was, however, less favourable criticism which appeared in the Musical Journal published by Reichardt, the conductor of the Royal Orchestra. In his peculiarly offensive manner he took exception to my elastic interpretation of tempo. I felt hurt although I must confess that, giving way to my deep feeling, I had perhaps held back the pace in cantabile and, carried away by my youthful fire, I had hurried the tempo in more impassioned parts. I therefore determined to correct such blemishes in my execution without diminishing its force and by unremitting attention succeeded.

MEETING WITH BOUCHER

IN BRUSSELS WE met another couple who, like ourselves, gave recitals on the harp and violin—Alexander Boucher and his wife. I had heard much about him in Paris and I was therefore anxious to make his acquaintance. He had the reputation of being a distinguished violinist but also a great charlatan. He bore a striking likeness to the exiled Napoleon and had acquired by constant endeavours something of the Emperor's deportment—his way of wearing his hat, of taking a pinch of snuff. When he arrived in a town where he was unknown he showed himself in all public places to attract attention to himself. He even spread the report that he was persecuted by the present Sovereign of France and had been driven from that country because of his resemblance to the idol of the people. On arriving in Lille he announced that, forced to quit his beloved country, he wished to give a farewell concert where he promised to play a Viotti concerto which had won for him in Paris the nickname of the 'Alexander of violinists'.

I was on the point of calling on him when he anticipated me by paying me a visit. He was very amiable and obliging, giving us introductions to musical families at whose parties we later had the opportunity of hearing the Boucher couple play. Both showed great skill but the works they played were poor and dull and I have lost all recollection of Boucher's own compositions. When he played a quartet of Haydn he introduced so many irrelevant and tactless ornaments that I could take no pleasure whatever in the performance.

I was told that once, having failed to play a passage as he meant it should go, he repeated it, murmuring 'Come come; this must go better', but without informing the orchestra of his intention. He concluded his second concert with a long cadenza in which he put all the tricks he knew. At the rehearsal he asked the orchestra to enter after the cadenza with a chord of startling resonance for which he was to give the signal by stamping his foot. At the concert Boucher began the cadenza which seemed to last so long that the players quietly began at first to put away their instruments and, finally, to depart. Boucher, absorbed in his performance, noticed nothing; he played a long final trill, satisfied that with the vigorous entry of the orchestra the enraptured audience would break into enthusiastic applause. He raised his foot at last and let it fall with a loud thump. When nothing happened he stared round and saw nothing but empty desks. The audience, who had anticipated this moment, burst into uproarious laughter in which Boucher had to join with as much grace as he could muster.

FIRST VISIT TO ENGLAND

LONDON IS PROBABLY the only European capital where Spohr's oratorios are still heard occasionally. His visits to England were artistically and financially most happy ventures. His first experience in London, however, was not very promising. The Spohrs had had a rough passage. On arriving at Dover on the ebb of the tide, the ship had to anchor outside the jetty and the passengers were transferred to a little boat. One of the women passengers, frightened by the way the sailors unceremoniously thrust passenger after passenger into the boat as the wave brought her on a level with the ship, threw her arms round Spohr, exciting his wife's 'extreme surprise'. On landing the young girl had scarcely felt firm ground under her feet when she left him without a word, Spohr concluding that she must have been a lady of high rank 'from this truly English behaviour'.

Arrived in London he donned his best waistcoat to meet the directors of the Philharmonic Society, a 'bright red Turkish shawl-pattern waistcoat considered on the Continent a most elegant article of the newest fashion'. But London was in mourning for the death of George III and no one dared appear in public otherwise than in a black suit. The result was that as Spohr walked about without knowing a word of English he attracted the attention of urchins who followed him shouting words which he 'unfortunately' could not understand. Perhaps it was fortunate he did not understand. London urchins and London 'prentices can express themselves very forcibly and gather together, as an Elizabethan observer noted, very quickly. 'You will find yourself in the midst of a host that has sprung up quicker than the men-at-arms, in the fiction of the poets, sprang from the teeth sown by Jason'. (*Happily the house of Ries, already long domesticated in London, was not far and Spohr escaped without molestation. Ed.*)

THE PHILHARMONIC SOCIETY

IN ORDER TO exclude from their programmes the shallow and worthless works of virtuosi the directors of the Philharmonic

Society had made it their rule not to accept concertos except those of Mozart and Beethoven. Ries, however, after long discussion obtained permission for me to play one of my own concertos. I therefore played at my first concert my Gesängscene and met with great and general applause. As a composer it afforded me special gratification that old Viotti, who had always been to me the pattern of what violinists should be, was present at the concert and spoke to me giving me high praise.

THE FIRST TO USE THE CONDUCTOR'S BATON

IT WAS AT that time still the custom that when overtures and symphonies were performed the pianist had the score under his eye, not to conduct from it but to play, when necessary with the orchestra, at pleasure; the outcome was lamentable. The real conductor was the leader (first violin) who gave the tempi, and, when the orchestra began to falter, also the beat with his bow. In the case of a large orchestra like that of the Philharmonic Society, spread over a vast platform, unanimity was out of the question in the circumstances, in spite of the excellence of individual members. I therefore determined when my turn came to remedy this defective system. Fortunately Mr Ries took the piano at the morning rehearsal and readily agreed to give me the score. I then produced from my pocket my baton and taking my stand at a desk in front of the orchestra gave the signal to begin. Alarmed at the unusual procedure some of the directors would have protested but I persuaded them to let me try my way. The symphonies and overtures were all well known to me and I could not only give the tempi but indicate the entries to the horns and wood instruments which much increased the confidence of the performers. I also took the liberty to stop when the execution did not please me and make polite but earnest comments which Mr Ries translated. The novelty roused their attention and, helped by seeing the time beaten out clearly, the players performed with a spirit and correctness unknown before. Immediately after the first movement of the symphony the orchestra loudly expressed their approval of my method, thus over-ruling further opposition on the part of the directors. After explaining the meaning of my gestures, I did the same with the vocal pieces, and the singers repeatedly expressed their satisfaction at the precision with which the orchestra followed them.

In the evening the result was still more brilliant. The audience, at first startled by the novelty, began to whisper, but when the orchestra performed the well-known symphony with unusual power and precision, there was long and loud applause. The baton had triumphed and no one was to be seen again at the piano during the performance of orchestral works.

LONDON AMATEURS

FAVOURABLE NOTICES OF my playing spread my fame through the town and pupils wanting instruction came to consult me, together with ladies who wished to have lessons in accompaniment. They were willing to pay a guinea for an hour's teaching and I accepted them as I felt I owed it to my family to turn to pecuniary advantage the good fortune I had met with in London. Thus, after devoting a few hours in composition, I spent the rest of the day running about the huge town. I was frequently weary of it as the greater part of my pupils had neither talent nor industry, and only came to me because they wanted to be able to say that they were the pupils of Spohr.

I recall with pleasure, however, a few singular individuals who amused me by their oddities and repaid thus somehow the trouble I had with them. One was an old half-pay general who came to my house dressed in full regimentals with medals etc. and played for three quarters of an hour as fifteen minutes were allowed, according to the English custom, for the drive. He came every morning except Sundays in his old state coach; ordered one of his powdered footmen to bring up his violin case and after a dumb greeting sat down at the music desk. He would produce his watch to note the moment when the lesson began and kept it by his side all the time. Although there were many things in his playing that showed inexperience, I soon saw that it would not be wise to point out his errors and contented myself with accommodating my tone as much as possible to that of the old gentleman and so we played duet after duet (mostly Pleyel's) in complete agreement. As soon as we had played three quarters of an hour the general would stop in the middle of the piece, produce a pound note in which a shilling was wrapped, and collecting his watch take his leave in silence—as he had entered.

Another odd character was a lady who passionately admired Beethoven, and would not touch anyone else's music. Her apartment was hung with every portrait of him she had been able to procure. Relics had been given to her from travellers who had visited Vienna, among them a button of his dressing-gown and a piece of music paper with some notes and blots made by his hand. When I told her I had lived some time on terms of close intimacy with him I rose much in her estimation. Some days she had so many questions to ask that we never touched the instruments. Her piano-playing was not bad and I was quite pleased to play with her the sonatas for violin and piano. But when she produced the trios and played them without cello and then the piano concertos where all I could do was to play the part of the orchestral first violin, it became apparent to me that all her enthusiasm for Beethoven was mere affectation and that she had no perception of the greatness of his compositions.

COSTS OF LONDON CONCERTS

MY CONCERT OF June 18th was one of the most brilliant events of the season. Most of the people to whom I had been introduced took boxes—among them the Dukes of Sussex and Clarence—and as many subscribers of the Philharmonic had retained their seats (the lowest charge for which was half-a-guinea) the receipts were considerable. Expenses were reduced because several members of the orchestra refused to accept a gratuity and the use of the rooms cost me nothing. But I had to pay all the singers and I had to give Mme Salmon, then the most popular vocalist in London without whom my concert would not have been sufficiently attractive, thirty pounds for a single song. She also made it a condition that she should appear towards the end of the evening as she had first to sing at a concert six miles off.

I must here mention a singular custom that then prevailed in London and has now been discontinued, according to which the giver of the concert had to provide the audience with refreshments during the interval. It cost me ten pounds. If the company was for the most part people of high rank who ate nothing, the confectioner made a good thing of it. If it was mixed and the evening hot, he was frequently the loser. He never did a better stroke of business than at my concert.

LOGIER'S TEACHING

In LONDON MR LOGIER gives instruction in pianoforte playing and in harmony, but what is most remarkable in his method is that with the very first lessons in pianoforte playing he teaches his pupils harmony at the same time. How he does this I do not know; that is his secret; but the results are wonderful, as children between the ages of seven and ten are able to solve the most difficult problems. When I visited his establishment I wrote on the board a triad and denoted the key to which they were to modulate; one of the youngest girls immediately ran to the board and after a little reflection wrote correctly first the bass and then the upper parts. I repeated this test adding all kinds of difficulties, extending it to remote keys in which enharmonic changes were necessary without ever embarrassing the little students.

HUMMEL AS IMPROVISER

In VIENNA I heard for the first time Hummel play his lovely Septet and other compositions of his. But I was most charmed by his improvisations in which no other piano virtuoso has ever approached him. I specially remember one evening when he improvised in so splendid a manner that I never heard the like of it before or since. The company were about to break up when some ladies who thought the hour too early entreated him to play a few more waltzes for them. Always willing to oblige ladies, Hummel sat at the piano and began to play waltzes for the young people in the adjoining room. Attracted by his playing I stood by his side together with other guests listening attentively. As soon as he noticed us he began to improvise a fantasia, keeping to the rhythm of the waltz so that the dance could continue. He used themes that I and others had used in performing our own compositions earlier, weaving them into waltzes with ever greater ingenuity and variety of expression. At length he made up a fugue in which he poured all his science of counterpoint without ever breaking away from the dance measure. He went back to the romantic style and concluded with bravura passages such as have seldom been heard—even from him. In this finale all the themes he had used were heard again so that the end was artistic in the highest degree. We were enraptured and praised the young ladies' love of dancing which had given us so rich a feast of excellence.

FRIENDSHIP WITH BEETHOVEN

IMMEDIATELY ON MY arrival in Vienna I paid a visit to Beethoven, but not finding him at home I left my card. I hoped to meet him at some musical party but was informed that, when his deafness increased and he could not well hear music, he had become shy of society and had given up attending parties. I tried another visit but was again unsuccessful. Finally, I ran him to earth at the eating-house where I was in the habit of going with my wife. I had already given concerts which had been favourably commented upon by the Vienna Press and as I introduced myself, Beethoven, who must have heard of me, received me in an unusually gracious manner. We sat down at the same table and Beethoven became very talkative, surprising the other guests, for he was usually very taciturn. It was difficult to make him hear me and I was obliged to talk loudly enough to be heard a long distance off. We met again at the restaurant and he ended by visiting me at home. We thus became well acquainted. He was a little blunt, not to say uncouth, in his manner, but there was a truthful eye under his bushy eyebrows. After my return from Gotha I met him at the Theatre An der Wien where Count Palffy had given him a free seat behind the orchestra. After the opera he would accompany me to my house and spend the rest of the evening with us. He

would then be very friendly with my wife and the children.
He very seldom spoke of music. When he did, his opinions
were very decided and he could not bear to be contradicted.
He took no interest whatever in the work of others and I
therefore had not the courage to show him my compositions.
His favourite topic was criticism of the way Prince Lobkowitz
and Count Palffy were running the theatres. He frequently
abused the Count while we were still inside the theatre and in
so loud a voice that the Count himself in his office could hear
him. This embarrassed me greatly.

Beethoven's rough and even repulsive manner at the time
arose partly from his deafness and partly from his poverty. He
was a bad housekeeper and, moreover, was plundered by all
those about him. In the early part of our acquaintance, not
having seen him for several days, I asked him: 'I hope you
were not sick?' He replied: 'I was not; but one of my shoes
was; and as I have only one pair I was under "house arrest".'
Sometime afterwards he was relieved by his friends in the
following circumstances.

Fidelio, performed in unfavourable circumstances during the
French occupation, had met with little success in 1805. Now
the director of the Karthnerthor theatre produced it again for
his benefit. Beethoven had been persuaded to write a new
overture (in E) as well as a song for the jailor and the grand
aria for Fidelio with horns obbligati. In this new form the opera
had been a great success and kept its place for a long succession
of crowded performances. His friends availed themselves of the
favourable moment to give a concert for his benefit in the
great Redouten-Saal where the most recent works of his were
given. All who could fiddle, blow or sing were invited to assist
and all the most celebrated artists in Vienna turned up, including myself and my orchestra. I then for the first time saw
Beethoven conduct. His manner surprised me, although I had
already heard a good deal about his behaviour on the rostrum.
He indicated marks of expression to the orchestra with extraordinary motions of his body. The arms that were crossed on
his breast were suddenly and violently thrust out when a
'sforzando' occurred. When he wanted soft tones he would
crouch down; when a 'crescendo' was needed he raised him-

self by degrees, springing bolt upright when the 'forte' was reached. If he wanted still louder sounds he would shout to the orchestra without being actually aware of it.

On my expressing astonishment at this extraordinary method of conducting, I was told the tragi-comical events that happened at Beethoven's last concert at the Theatre An der Wien.

He was playing his new piano concerto, but at the very first 'Tutti', forgetting that he was the soloist, he began to conduct. When he came to the first sforzando he threw out his arms with such force that he knocked down the lights on the piano. The audience laughed and Beethoven, annoyed, stopped the orchestra and the concerto started again from the beginning. This time the leader took the precaution to order two choir boys to hold the lights for the pianist. When the sforzando was reached a second time, Beethoven acted as before, but instead of hitting the lights he hit one of the boys who, receiving a smart blow, dropped the light in terror. The other lad, guessing what was coming, had saved himself by suddenly bending and dodging the blow. If the public had laughed before, they now became hysterical and Beethoven, enraged, struck the piano with such force that at the very first chord six strings broke.

The concert got up by his friends was a great success. The new compositions were much applauded and the Seventh Symphony in particular made a deep impression, the second movement being encored. In spite of Beethoven's uncertain and, at times, laughable directions the execution was masterly.

It was easy to see that the poor deaf maestro could no longer hear his music. It was particularly noticeable in the second part of the first movement where occur two pauses in succession. The second is marked pianissimo and obviously Beethoven had overlooked it as he beat time before the orchestra had finished the pause. As usual with him he marked crescendo and diminuendo by crouching down and rising, but in this instance when he sprang up for the forte nothing happened. He looked round frightened and only recovered when he realized that the forte was on the way. Fortunately this happened at the rehearsal. The hall being crowded for the concert, Beethoven's friends arranged for a repetition of the event and this realized an equally conspicuous sum so that Beethoven was relieved of

financial worries for some time. But before his death he found
himself once more in poverty and owing to the same cause.

As at the time I made Beethoven's acquaintance he had
already given up playing in public I only had an opportunity to
hear him when I accidentally dropped in during the rehearsal
of a new trio (in D major). It was by no means an enjoyable
experience. The piano was woefully out of tune—a fact which
troubled him little since he could hear nothing—and of his
excellence as a virtuoso there was hardly any evidence because
of his deafness. In the 'fortes' the poor deaf man hammered
upon the keys in such a way that whole groups of notes became
inaudible; the only way of knowing what was happening was
to follow the performance on the score. I was deeply moved
by so hard a fate. It is a sad thing for anyone to be afflicted with
deafness; a musician cannot endure it without being driven to
despair. The cause of Beethoven's continual melancholy was
no longer a mystery to me.

OPINION OF PAGANINI AND OLE BULL

IN JUNE 1830 Paganini came to Cassel to give two concerts
which I heard with great interest. His left hand and the constant
purity of his intonation astounded me. But his compositions,
like his interpretations, were a strange mixture of great
geniality and childishness, so that one felt in turns charmed
and disappointed. The impression he left on the whole was by
no means satisfactory. . . .

Ole Bull gave two concerts that greatly attracted the public.
The variety of his tone and the accuracy of the left hand are
remarkable but, like Paganini, he sacrifices too much for the
sake of effect. His tone on the A and D strings is poor and he
does not exploit these strings in the high positions. This makes
his playing monotonous as we discovered when he played two
quartets of Mozart. He plays with much feeling but not with
cultivated taste.

Felix Mendelssohn

TAGLIONI DANCING IN 'ROBERT LE DIABLE'

THERE IS ONE good thing here. You think I refer to 'La Liberté'? Not at all; I refer to Taglioni. I heard that you were raving about her dancing; I am raving about herself. She is a real artist and dances with an air of lovable innocence. She seems to be the only real musician in Paris. Who knows? I may end by being disappointed in her in spite of my present ideas. In the end she will marry some count or other and leave the theatre to become a great lady or the devil knows what. She is perfect and so is her dancing. I have only seen her so far in *Robert le Diable* where she acts the part of a nun who means to seduce the fat Nourrit. It is a most touching affair because she is so much more pure than either the fat fellow or her audience. After a time he is persuaded to kiss and hug her—much to the delight of the public. There are other nuns who would like to do some seducing; compared with the sweet young child they look like pug-dogs and tomcats. . . .

The opera itself is a great success, although it is just one of thousands that are all alike. The libretto is wretched, muddled, and as cold-blooded, crazy and fantastic as one would expect from young France. The music is not at all bad. Effects are well calculated, there is much suspense, the right touches are provided in the right places. There is melody for those who want to hum; harmony for educated listeners; instrumentation for Germans and contredances for French people—in fact something for everybody, but there is no heart. Such a work is as different from art as decorating is from painting. Decorating may produce at first a greater effect, but if you look at it closely you soon discover that it is just painting done with the feet instead of the hands.

(1831)

THE PARIS ORCHESTRA

. . . WHAT I HAD not heard before and is outstanding here is the 'Orchestre du Conservatoire'. Since it is the orchestra of the Paris Conservatoire it is inevitable that it should be the best in all France; but it is also the best to be heard anywhere. They have brought together the best musicians in Paris with young players from the violin classes of the Conservatoire; they put a capable and enthusiastic musician in charge and rehearsed for two years till they became a single unit and there was no danger of error—then they ventured to give a public performance. If every orchestra did the same, errors in notes and rhythm would not occur. But as this does not happen elsewhere this is the best of all the orchestras I have ever heard. The classes of Baillot, Rode and Kreutzer supply the violinists and it is a joy to see the mass of young people in the orchestra playing with the same bowing, the same style, the same decision and enthusiasm. One can realize how perfectly every player fills his place, how the task has been mastered so that everything could be played by heart. The player's individuality is merged in that of the orchestra. The management is also practical and intelligent. There are not too many concerts; they play once a fortnight on Sunday afternoon making it a feast-day in every respect, as there is no opera that night, and after the concert there is only dinner. The hall is small and the impression made by the music is consequently all the greater as every detail is crystal-clear; the audience is small, very distinguished as on a great social occasion.

(1832)

ON COMPETITIONS

THE INTELLIGENCE FROM Vienna . . . revived my feeling as to the utter impossibility of my ever composing anything with a view to competing for a prize. I should never be able even to make a beginning; and if I were obliged to undergo an examination as a musician, I am convinced that I should be rejected at once as I should not do half as well as I could. The thoughts of a prize or a judge would distract my thoughts. I could never rise above that feeling or forget it.

(1835)

ON BERLIOZ'S SYMPHONY

To I. Moscheles

WHAT YOU SAY about Berlioz's symphony is literally true, and I must add that the whole thing seems to me so dreadfully slow—and what could be worse? Music may be a piece of uncouth, crazy, barefaced impudence and still have some 'go' about it and be amusing; but this is simply insipid and altogether lifeless. . . . If that sort of stuff is noticed and even admired it is really too provoking. But I cannot believe that impartial people will take pleasure in discords or be in any way interested in them. If a few writers puff the thing up it is of no consequence. Their articles will leave no deeper mark than the composition. What annoys me is that there is so little to put on the other side of the account. What our Reissiger & Co. compose is different but equally shallow and what Heller and Berlioz write is not music. Even old Cherubini's *Ali Baba* is dreadfully poor. It is all very sad.

(1835)

ON CHOPIN

. . . YOU ARE NOT just to Chopin. Perhaps when you heard him he was not in the right humour, which often happens. But I must say that his playing has again enchanted me and I am convinced that if you had heard him play some of his better works you would say the same. There is something entirely original in his piano playing. It is so masterly that he may be described as a perfect virtuoso, and as in music I like and rejoice in perfection of every kind, the experience was most enjoyable. It was pleasant to be once more with a thorough musician and not with those semi-virtuosi and semi-classicists who would gladly combine the honour due to virtue with the pleasure of vice; to be with one who has his own perfect and well-defined ways. Although we live in different worlds I can get on famously with such a man while I cannot get on at all with the demi-semi people. Sunday evening was remarkable. Chopin made me play over my oratorio and when between the first and the second part he butted in with his new Études and a new concerto (to the amazement of the Leipzig people) it was just as though a Cherokee and a Kaffir had met to converse. He has also a new nocturne which is just too lovely, a considerable part of which I learnt to play by heart. So we got on famously together and he promised faithfully to return in the course of the winter.

(1835)

ON AUBER

. . . As to AUBER's famous *Leocadie* you cannot imagine anything more pitiable. The subject, taken from a bad novel of Cervantes, has been made into a bad libretto. I could not have believed that such a common, vulgar work could have been kept so long in the repertory, still less that it could have any success with the French public possessing tact and fine feelings. To this novel of Cervantes' crude, wild period, Auber has set music so tame that it is deplorable. I will not even mention that there is no fire, no substance, no life; nor that it is made up of reminiscences of Cherubini and Rossini; nor will I say that there is not the slightest seriousness nor a single spark of passion; nor even that at the most critical moments the singers have to perform gurgles, trills and florid passages. But a grey-haired man, a pupil of Cherubini and the darling of the public, ought at least to know how to orchestrate, especially now that the publication of the scores of Haydn, Mozart and Beethoven has made it so easy. But there is not even that. In the entire opera, full as it is of set pieces, there are perhaps three in which the piccolo does not play the principal part. This little instrument serves to illustrate the fury of the brother, the pain of the lover, the joy of the peasant girl. In fact the whole opera might very well be transcribed for two flutes and Jews' harp ad lib.

(1825)

DESCRIPTION OF ROSSINI

HILLER . . . ALSO LIKES Rossini, Auber, Bellini and . . . yesterday when I went to see him, whom did I find sitting there? Rossini, big, fat, and in the sunniest disposition of spirit. I really know few men who can be so amusing and witty as he when he chooses; he kept us laughing all the time. I promised that the Cecilia Association would sing the B minor Mass for him and several other works of Sebastian Bach. It will be fun to see Rossini obliged to admire Sebastian Bach. He thinks, however, that different countries have different customs and is determined to howl with the wolves. He says he is fascinated by Germany and when he gets the list of wines at the Rhine Hotel in the evening the waiter is obliged to show him the way to his room as he could never manage to find it himself.

He tells the most laughable and amusing tales about Paris and its musicians as well as about himself and his compositions and how he has the deepest respect for all the men of the present time—so that you might really believe him if you had no eyes to see his clever face. Intellect, animation and wit sparkle in all his features and in every word. Whoever does not consider him a genius ought to hear him expatiating in his way in order to change his opinion.

(1836)

ON LISZT

LISZT POSSESSES A certain suppleness and independence in fingering as well as a thoroughly musical feeling that cannot be equalled. I have heard no performer whose musical perception extends to the very tips of his fingers and emanates directly from them as Liszt's does. With his directness, his stupendous technique and experience, he would have far surpassed all the rest if it were not that the main thing is the connection between a man's thoughts and all the rest. And this appears to have been denied him by nature so that in this respect most of the great virtuosi equal and even excel him. But that he, together with Thalberg, represents the highest class of pianists of the present day seems to me beyond doubt. Unhappily Liszt's behaviour here towards the public has not made a favourable impression. . . . His stay caused us almost as much annoyance as pleasure though the pleasure was often beyond words.

(1840)

ON CHERUBINI

WHAT OF OLD Cherubini? There is a man for you! I have got his *Abencerages* and am again and again enjoying his sparkling fire, his clever and unexpected transitions, the neatness and grace with which he writes. I am truly grateful to this fine gentleman. It is all so free, so bold and bright.

(1839)

MUSIC IN BERLIN

I HAVE RARELY ENJOYED anything as much as Gluck's *Armida* at the opera. The mass of well-trained musicians and singers ably conducted by Spontini, the splendid house full to suffocation, made such an impression on me that I said to myself that what is possible here is impossible in smaller towns. Since then I have thought differently. The very next day they gave a so-called Beethoven memorial festival and played his A major Symphony so atrociously that I repented my thoughts about small towns. The coarseness and effrontery of the players were such as I have never heard anywhere and I can only explain it by the nature of the Prussian official which is as suited to music as a straight-jacket is to a man. And it is an unconscious straight-jacket. Since then I have heard much in the way of quartets and symphonies, playing and singing in private circles, and have had to apologize again to the small towns. In most places here music is carried on with the same mediocrity, carelessness and arrogance as ever. . . . It has to do with the sand, the situation, the official life. One may enjoy a good thing here and there but one cannot get to know anything thoroughly. Gluck's operas are among the good things. They always draw a full house and the public is enchanted—which is what happens nowhere else. But the next evening the *Postillion* (an opera of Adam) attracts just as large an audience.

(1838)

QUEEN VICTORIA AND PRINCE ALBERT

GRAHL SAYS THAT the only friendly English house, the house that is really comfortable and where one feels at ease, is Buckingham Palace. I know several others but on the whole I agree with him. Joking apart, Prince Albert asked me to go to him on Saturday at two o'clock so that I may try his organ. I found him all alone but as we were talking away the Queen came in wearing a house-dress. She said she was obliged to leave for Claremont in an hour. Catching sight of the music pages strewn all over the floor by the wind, 'Goodness,' she said, 'how dreadful' and began to pick up the music. Prince Albert helped and I was not idle. Then Prince Albert began to explain the organ stops to me and while he was doing it the Queen remarked that she would put everything straight again.

I begged the Prince to play something so that, I said, 'I might boast about it in Germany'. Thereupon he played me a chorale by heart, with pedals, so charmingly and clearly and correctly that many an organist could have learnt something and the

Queen (who had finished her tidying up) sat beside him and listened very pleased. Then I had to play and I began my chorus from St Paul: 'How lovely are the messengers'. Before I got to the end of the first verse they both began to sing the chorus very well and all the time Prince Albert managed the stops for me so expertly—first a flute, then full at the forte, the whole register at D major and then making such an excellent diminuendo (all by heart) that I was heartily pleased. Then the Crown Prince of Gotha came in and there was more conversation, the Queen asking me whether I had composed any new songs. 'You should sing one to him,' said Prince Albert, and after a little begging she said she would try my 'Frühlingslied' in B flat if 'it is still here as all my music is packed up for Claremont'. Prince Albert went to look for it but came back saying that it had been packed. 'Perhaps it could be unpacked' said I. 'We must send for Lady ——' (I didn't catch the name). The bell was rung and the servants went to look but came back embarrassed. Then the Queen went herself and while she was away Prince Albert said to me: 'She begs you to accept this present as a souvenir', and gave me a case with a beautiful ring on which was engraved 'V.R. 1842'.

When the Queen came back she said: 'Lady —— has left and has taken all my things with her. It is most unseemly.' (I cannot tell you how that amused me.) I then begged that I might not be made to suffer for the accident and expressed the hope that she might sing another song. After consultation with her husband he said: 'She will sing something of Gluck's.' Then we five proceeded through the long corridors to the Queen's sitting-room where, next to the piano, stood an enormous fat rocking horse with two great birdcages and pictures on the walls; beautifully bound books were on the table and music on the piano. The Duchess of Kent came in too, and while they were all talking I rummaged a little amongst the music and found my first set of songs. So naturally I begged the Queen to choose one of those rather than a song of Gluck's to which she consented. What do you think she chose? 'Schöner und schöner' and sang it beautifully in tune, in strict time and with very nice expression. Only where, after 'Der Prosa Last und Mühe' (where it goes down to D and then comes up by semitones) she sang D sharp each time. The first and second time I gave her the D natural, but the last time (when it should be D sharp) she sang D natural. Except for this mistake it was very charming and on the long G at the end I have never heard better or purer tone from any amateur. I felt obliged to confess that the song had really been written by Fanny (I found it difficult; but pride must have a fall) and begged the Queen to sing one of my own. She said she would if I gave her some help and sang 'Lass dich nur nichts dauern' without a mistake and with charming feeling and expression. I thought that one must not pay too many compliments on an occasion of this sort so I merely thanked her very much, but she said: 'If only I hadn't been so nervous; I have really a long breath.' Then I praised her heartily and with a clear conscience as she had sung the last part with the long C so well, taking the C and the next three notes in the same breath as is seldom done. . . .

After this Prince Albert sang 'Er ist ein Schnitter' and then he said I must play (improvise?) something before I went and gave me as themes the chorale which he had played on the organ and the song he had just sung. If everything had happened as usual I should have improvised very badly for that is what happens to me when I am specially anxious to do well. But I have rarely improvised as well. I was in the mood for it and played a long time and enjoyed myself. Of course I also brought in the songs the Queen had sung but it worked in so naturally that I would have been glad to go on for ever. They followed me with so much intelligence and attention that I felt more at ease than I ever did in improvising before an audience. Then the Queen said: 'I hope you will come and visit us soon again in England.' I took my leave and down below I saw the beautiful carriages waiting with their scarlet outriders and in a quarter of an hour the flag was lowered and the papers said 'Her Majesty left the Palace at 30 minutes past three'. It was a delightful day! I must add that I asked permission to dedicate my A minor symphony to the Queen, that having really been the reason of my visit to England and because the English name would be doubly suited to the Scottish piece. Just as the Queen was going to sing she said: 'The parrot must be taken out or he

will scream louder than I can sing', upon which Prince Albert
rang the bell and the Prince of Gotha said: 'I will carry him
out,' but I said 'Allow me' and lifted the cage and carried it
out to the astonished servants.

This long description will make Dirichlet put me down as an
aristocrat but tell him that I swear I am more of a radical
than ever.

(1842)

ADVICE ABOUT PUBLISHING

. . . YOU WRITE TO me about Fanny's new compositions and
say that I ought to persuade her to publish them. Your praise
of those works is quite unnecessary to make me heartily rejoice
in them or think them charming and a miracle, since I know
by whom they are written. No need to say that if she does
decide to publish them I will do everything in my power to
obtain every facility for her and to relieve her as far as I can
from any trouble which she can possibly be spared. But I cannot
persuade her to publish as it would be contrary to my views
and convictions. We have often discussed the subject and my
opinion is unaltered. I consider the publication of a work a
serious matter and I maintain that no one should publish unless
he is resolved to be an author for the rest of his life. For this
purpose a succession of works is indispensable. Nothing but
annoyance can come from publishing only one or two works
which become what I dislike 'MSS for private circulation'.
From my knowledge of Fanny I should say that she has neither
the inclination nor the vocation for authorship. She is too
much of a woman; she manages her home and thinks neither of
the public nor of the musical world till her first duties are
over. Publishing would only disturb her in her first task and
that is what I cannot advise. . . . If she decides to publish
either to please herself or to please Hensel I am ready to assist
her, but I cannot encourage her to do what I do not deem
right myself.

(1837)

Robert Schumann

ON WAGNER'S 'TANNHAÜSER'

WAGNER, THOUGH CERTAINLY a brilliant fellow full of original, audacious ideas, can hardly set down (and think out) a four-measure phrase beautifully or even correctly. He is one of those people who have not learnt their harmony lessons or learnt how to write four-part chorales and this their work makes plain. Now that the whole score is under our eyes, nicely printed—including its parallel fifths and octaves—he would probably like to correct and to erase—too late! But enough! The music is not a bit better than *Rienzi*; if anything, more pallid and forced. But should you say this to people they would suspect you of jealousy, so I say it only to you, aware that you know it all beforehand.

(October 1845)

I was very interested to read what you wrote about Wagner. He is, if I may say it in one word, a poor musician. He lacks all sense of form and of euphony. But you should not judge him from his piano scores. Many passages from his operas once heard from the stage cannot but prove exciting. And if you do not find clear sunlight in them, such as that which radiates from the works of genius, they distil a strange magic which captivates the senses. But, as I said, the music itself (that is disregarding its stage effect) is poor and frequently amateurish, empty and distasteful, and praise of his works at the expense of the many great dramatic works previously written by German composers exhibits an unfortunate decline of taste. But enough of this. Posterity will judge these works as posterity ever judges. . . .

(May 1853)

ON BRAHMS

MANY NEW AND significant talents have arisen; a new power in music seems to announce itself; the intimation has been proved true by many aspiring artists of the last years, even though their work may be known only to comparatively limited circles. To me, who followed the progress of these chosen ones with the greatest sympathy, it seemed that under the circumstances there inevitably must appear a musician called to give expression to his times in ideal fashion; a musician who would reveal his mastery not in a gradual evolution, but like Athene would spring fully armed from Zeus' head. And such a one has appeared, a young man over whose cradle Graces and Heroes have stood watch. His name is Johannes Brahms and he comes from Hamburg, where he has been working in quiet obscurity, though instructed in the most difficult statutes of his art by an excellent and enthusiastically devoted teacher. A well-known and honoured master recently recommended him to me. Even outwardly he bore the marks proclaiming: 'This is a chosen one.' Sitting at the piano he began to disclose wonderful regions to us. We were drawn into even more enchanting spheres. Besides, he is a player of genius who can make of the piano an orchestra of lamenting and loudly jubilant voices. There were sonatas, veiled symphonies rather; songs, the poetry of which would be understood even without words, although a profound vocal melody runs through them all; single piano pieces, some of them turbulent in spirit while graceful in form; again sonatas for violin and piano, string quartets, every work so different from the others that it seemed to stream from its own individual source. And then it was as though rushing like a torrent, they were all united by him into a single waterfall, the cascades of which were overarched by a peaceful rainbow, while butterflies played about its borders and the voices of nightingales obliged. Should he direct his magic wand where the powers of the masses in chorus and orchestra may lend him their forces, we can look forward to even more wondrous glimpses of the secret world of spirits. May the highest genius strengthen him to this end. Since he possesses yet another facet of genius—that of modesty —we may surmise that it will come to pass. His fellow musicians hail him on his first step through a world where wounds perhaps await him but also palms and laurels. We welcome the champion in him.

(1853)

Richard Wagner

ON CONDUCTING[1]

IN THE FOLLOWING essay I propose to speak of my experiences and observations in a field of musical activity
whose practitioners have been hacks and critics. In arriving
at my conclusion I shall rely, not on conductors, but on the
players who alone know whether the conductor is good when,
by way of exception, they meet with a conductor who knows
his job. It is not my intention to put forward a system but to
record observations.

Composers cannot be indifferent to the way in which their
works are presented to the public. It is only through a good
performance that the public can form the right idea of a work;
a bad performance creates wrong impressions although the
public may be unaware of it. If the reader follows my argument
he will learn something of what is already known to the expert
—the weaknesses of our orchestras, both as regards personnel
and standard of playing, the inferiorities of our conductors and
musical directors. The ignorance and carelessness shown by the
highest authorities of our art institutions when appointing conductors grow at the same rate as the demands of composers on
the orchestra become more exacting. In the days when a Mozart
score presented the most difficult task, the conductor was of
the old Kapellmeister type—a musician of great respectability
(at any rate locally), sure, firm, despotic and rough of manner.
When, eight years ago, my *Lohengrin* was produced at Karlsruhe
under old Kapellmeister Strauss, I realized the excellent work
this man and his like were able to achieve in their own particular way—musicians we called 'stick-in-the-mud' on account
of their attitude towards modern music. The dignified old
gentleman looked at my score with astonishment and appre-
hension, yet also with a sense of duty which was shown by
the orchestra. They played with the greatest precision and

---

[1] *Translation by Mosco Carner, from Wagner's 'Gesammelte Schriften', of the essay entitled 'Ueber das Dirigieren'.*

firmness because their conductor was a man not to be
trifled with, who had his players well in hand. This old gentleman, was, oddly enough, the only one I met who had real fire.
His tempi were hurried rather than dragging, but firm and sure.

With the advent of more complicated orchestral music, it
was inevitable that this type of conductor should become unequal to his task. He was accustomed to an orchestra of a
certain size sufficient for the work it had to do. In spite of the
demands of modern orchestral music the disposition of the
orchestra, however, has nowhere been radically altered. Players
of great orchestras are still promoted to the post of principals
by rule of seniority; they reach this position when their best
days are over while younger and better players sit at the second
desk—a fact giving particularly unfavourable results in the
wind department. It is true these disadvantages have in recent
times grown less glaring, thanks to efforts of the musicians
concerned. Yet there is something that still creates an unfavourable effect. This is the way in which the string department
is recruited, affecting the second violins and violas in particular.
Everywhere the viola players are recruited from among former
disabled violinists or old wind players who perhaps at one time
strummed the violin. The first desk boasts at times of a really
good player, chiefly because of occasional solo passages but
I know a great orchestra where out of eight viola players only
one was able to give a correct rendering of difficult passages in
one of my more recent scores. Such methods, pardonable on
grounds of humanity, originated in the old style of orchestration, in which the violas were mostly used to fill in the
accompaniment and in the manner in which Italian opera
composers have orchestrated their works, an essential and the
most popular part of the operatic repertoire in Germany. Since
managers of great theatres, following the notorious taste of
their princes, set store by these favourite operas, it is no
wonder that they then fight shy of works demanding a different
standard. These gentlemen can only be approached and persuaded by a conductor of authority and serious reputation who
clearly understands the needs of the modern orchestra. That
knowledge was lacking in the older conductors who did not
see the necessity of augmenting the strings in proportion to

the increased number of the wind instruments. The little that has been done lately in this respect has not been sufficient to raise the most famous German orchestras to the level of the French. Our violins and particularly our cellos are, without exception, inferior in power and technique.

Now it should have been the foremost task for modern conductors to learn where the kapellmeisters of the old school failed. Yet care was taken lest modern conductors should become dangerous and acquire the authority of the 'stick-in-the-mud' of former days.

It is important and illuminating to see how this new generation, representing as it does the whole of Germany's musical life, rose to office and honour. Since the upkeep of our orchestras is, in the first place, provided for by small and large theatres, we have to acquiesce in the fact that the director appoints the musicians he thinks fit to represent, often for half a century, the spirit and dignity of German music.

Typically German musicians obtained these desirable posts simply by the law of inertia: they were pushed up by a shove. I believe that most of the conductors of the great Berlin Court Orchestra were promoted in this way. This also happened sometimes abruptly when entirely unknown celebrities suddenly rose under the protective wing of the lady-in-waiting of some princess and the like. Being entirely without merits these gentlemen were able to impress their subordinates only by laissez-faire and by submission to a supreme chief who, though an ignoramus, pretended to know everything. These 'masters' abandoned all artistic discipline, which they were in any case incapable of enforcing, and meekly yielded to every stupid demand from above. At rehearsals they overcame difficulties by an unctuous reference to the 'old glory of the orchestra'—a remark met by a smug smirk. Did anybody notice that the standard of this glorious body sank lower from year to year? Where were the judges to be found? Certainly not among newspaper critics who only bark when their mouth is not gagged, which very seldom happens.

The manager sent for a competent hack from somewhere. This is called the inoculation of the lazy kapellmeister with the virus of 'active force'. The newcomer was the sort of man who 'gets up' an opera in a fortnight, expert at making long cuts and inserting in somebody else's scores effective 'cadenzas' to oblige sopranos. It is to such abilities that one of the most 'active' conductors of Dresden owes his post.

But sometimes the need is even felt for a conductor of real fame; 'musical celebrities' are then approached. None are to be found in the theatres, but the *singakademies* and concert societies produce (according to the laudatory articles in the great political newspapers) a few every two or three years. These are our present musical 'bankers' who either graduated from Mendelssohn's school or were recommended to the world through his influence. True, they were quite different from the ineffectual successors of old 'stick-in-the-mud'—they did not rise from the rank and file of the orchestra, but were trained in the new conservatoires; they composed oratorios, psalms, and attended the rehearsals of subscription concerts. They also had lessons in conducting, and received a refined education, such as had never been the good luck of musicians before. There was no longer a trace of rudeness in their manner. The timid, diffident modesty of our poor, native kapellmeisters turned with them to good manners. I believe that these men did exercise some good influence on the orchestras. No doubt, much that was coarse and clumsy in the playing has since disappeared and greater attention is being paid to details and refinement. These conductors were much more familiar with the demands of the modern orchestra which Mendelssohn had treated in an extremely delicate and sensitive manner—a manner which Weber's glorious genius first initiated. Yet these gentlemen lacked the quality necessary to carry further the reorganization of our orchestras—energy such as can only flow from power based on real self-confidence. Unfortunately everything is artificial with them—reputation, talent, education, even faith, hope and charity. These conductors have so much to contend with to maintain their position that it is impossible for them to think of general ideas however logical, coherent and novel. These are not their concern. They do not know what to do with the German art ideal, the focus of everything that is noble in us but alien to their nature. Faced with the difficult problem of modern music, they resort to expedients.

This survey of the qualities characteristic of the older type of conductors (such as still survive) and the modern species, makes it clear that we can expect not much from either. The initiative for further progress has so far come from the players themselves, a fact readily accounted for by the higher standard of their technical proficiency.

It must be stressed first of all that the posts of the conductor and, for that matter, the very existence of the orchestra were bound up with the *theatre*, and that their main activity and achievement lay in the field of *opera*. Conductors had to understand the nature of the theatre, the opera, and learn something else: to apply music to dramatic art just as mathematics is applied to astronomy. Had they properly understood their job, notably dramatic singing and expression, it would have enlightened them about the interpretation of symphonic music, especially of the modern German music. My best guidance as to the tempo and interpretation of Beethoven's music was at one time the inspired, well accentuated singing of the great Schröder-Devrient. I have since found it impossible to let the oboe play the moving cadenza in the first movement of the C minor Symphony in so timid and insipid a way as I have always heard it. Indeed, after the true rendering of this cadenza had become clear to me, I went further back in the movement to the corresponding pause of the first violins and then knew its true significance and expression. Impressed and moved by the pathos of these two insignificant-looking passages, I began to see the whole movement in a new and illuminating light. By this digression I only want to show the possibilities which the theatre offers to the conductor in perfecting his higher musical education in respect of interpretation. Alas, opera to him is tiresome. His ambition is the concert room where he started and where he was discovered. For, as we suggested, as soon as the intendant of a theatre feels the urge to appoint a musician of name, it must be a man who made a reputation not in the theatre.

I remember that during my early youth I received highly unsatisfactory impressions from the performance of classical orchestral music, impressions which other concerts later confirmed. Music which, on the piano or in the score, seemed full of soul and life, I no longer recognized. I was particularly astounded how dull Mozart's cantilena could sound, cantilena which, from a previous study had made a deep impression and seemed so lively and expressive. It was only later that the reasons for this disappointment became clear.

We need but do not possess a German conservatoire, an institute which would preserve the tradition of our classical music as the great masters themselves performed it. In order to get the spirit of a classical work we now rely on the whims of individual conductors and on their views as to tempo and interpretation.

Classical works were not conducted at all in my youth. At Leipzig the orchestra reeled them off like any overture or the entr'acte of a play. One remained completely unmoved by a conductor's readings. The chief classical works, which present no great technical difficulties, were played regularly every winter and the playing was, therefore, smooth and precise. One felt that the orchestra, knowing it all inside out, was enjoying the annual performance of favourites. With Beethoven's Ninth Symphony the system would not work at all although it was a point of honour to perform it every year. I made a copy of the score and a piano arrangement for two hands. How startled I was when I got only confused impressions from the Gewandhaus performance. It made me feel discouraged, it made me doubt Beethoven and, for a time, I gave up studying his music. It was later significant to find true enjoyment in Mozart which came when I had the opportunity of conducting myself and put my ideas about the lively interpretation of the Mozartian cantilena into practice. I learned most from a performance of the, to me, then questionable Ninth Symphony by the so-called *Orchestre du Conservatoire* of Paris, in 1839. The scales fell from my eyes when I realized how much depended on the playing and I learnt where the solution of the problem was to be found. The orchestra had been trained to feel the Beethoven melody in every bar—which the worthy Leipzig musicians of those days never had. The French orchestra *sang* the melody.

That was the secret. The conductor was by no means a musician of particular genius. Habeneck, who with this performance earned great credit, had rehearsed the symphony the whole winter, but the impression he had gained from the work was unintelligent and ineffective. It is difficult to say whether German conductors arrived at a similar conclusion—that is if they ever took pains to form an idea of the work. But Habeneck decided to go on rehearsing for a second and third year, and not to give in until the moment had come when every player began to understand the Beethoven melos. Being musicians with the right feeling for melodic line, they rendered it correctly. But it must be added that Habeneck was a conductor of the old school; *he* was the master, and everybody obeyed him.

I cannot describe the beauty of this performance. To give some idea of it, I might select a passage out of many equally suitable ones, to illustrate the difficulty in playing Beethoven. I have later never been able, not even with the best orchestras, to get the players to play with the perfect smoothness I heard thirty years ago from the Paris Conservatoire Orchestra a passage requiring experience of *movement, sustained line* and *dynamic problems*. The supreme excellence of the Paris musicians was shown by the fact that they were able to play the passage *exactly* as it is meant to be played. Neither at Dresden nor in London, where I later conducted the symphony, did I succeed in getting the musicians to change the bow and negotiate the crossing of the strings with perfect smoothness—still less to suppress casual accents. The average musician always tends to become louder in a rising phrase, and softer in a descending one. On a bar of this passage, there was always a crescendo, leading unwittingly, nay, inevitably, to an exaggerated accent which ill suited the particular harmonic function of the note. It is difficult to make the insensitive realize the bad effect of the playing we commonly hear and to criticize it, not to mention the fact that it is clearly against the intention of the master.

What enabled those Parisian musicians to solve with such infallibility so difficult a problem? They evidently succeeded by taking great pains over it, for that is how musicians work who are not content with paying each other compliments, and do not imagine they know everything as a matter of course. Timid and apprehensive of things they do not understand, they try to tackle them from that angle which is wholly familiar to them: *technique*. The French musician, belonging as he fundamentally does, to the Italian school, has been favourably influenced by the fact that he perceives music only in terms of song. To play an instrument well means to him to sing. And (as stressed already) that glorious Paris orchestra *sang* the symphony. But in order to be able to 'sing', it was necessary to find the right speed, and that was the second feature which impressed itself on my mind. Old Habeneck had certainly no abstract aesthetic notions; he was a man without the affectations of so-called genius, but by *constant, painstaking study he led the orchestra to see the 'melos' of the symphony.*

Only in a true perception of the melos is the right tempo to be found. The two are inseparable and the one presupposes the other. If in considering the majority of performances of classical music in Germany I do not hesitate to declare them grossly inadequate, I will substantiate this statement by the fact that *our conductors know nothing about the right tempo because they know nothing about singing.* I have yet to meet a German conductor or musical director who is able, whether with a good or bad voice, really to *sing* a melody. For these people music is a strangely abstract thing, something between grammar, mathematics and gymnastics; one may well understand how one trained in these faculties should make a good teacher in a conservatoire, but one cannot see how such a man should be able to infuse life and soul into a musical performance. About this I am now going to say a few things which experience has taught me.

In summing up the criteria on which, so far as the conductor is concerned, the correct performance of a given work depends, one would have to mention one thing in particular. This is the right tempo. For the conductor's choice of tempo will at once show whether he has or has not understood the music. To a good musician the *right tempo* will be a help in finding the *right interpretation*. The former argues a recognition of the latter. How difficult it is to decide upon the right tempo is seen from the fact that it can only be found when the conductor is clear in his own mind about interpretation.

The older composers, like Haydn and Mozart, possessed such right instincts that as a rule they gave but very general tempo

indications. Adagio, andante, allegro and slight modifications
of these were all they thought necessary for their purpose.
J. S. Bach normally did not indicate the tempo at all, which
in the true musical sense, is the proper thing to do. He may
well have said to himself: 'Those who do not understand my
themes, my figurations, have no ear for the character and
expression of my music. What then is the use of giving them
tempo markings in Italian?' To speak from my own experience
I may mention that in those of my early operas which have
been performed I gave most explicit indications as to the
tempo, fixing it also by metronome markings to make doubly
sure. But whenever I heard a wrong tempo in one of my works,
for instance in *Tannhäuser*, and objected, my recriminations
were met by the conductor's plea that he had observed my
metronome markings conscientiously. That made me realize
how unreliable mathematics in music are. From that moment
I not only omitted metronome markings but confined myself
solely to very general indications of the main tempo. I was
careful however to mark *modifications* of main tempi as our
conductors know nothing about that. These gentlemen were
only annoyed and confused by my general indications. Accustomed to the old Italian clichés they did not know what to
make of my German directions. I have recently received a
complaint from a quarter associated with a conductor whom
I have to thank for taking three hours over my *Rheingold*
(according to a report in the Augsberg *Allgemeine Zeitung*)
while the opera under another conductor whom I had instructed takes only two-and-a-half hours. Similarly, I was told
that in an Augsberg performance of my *Tannhäuser,* the overture,
for which at Dresden I had taken twelve minutes myself, lasted
twenty minutes. True, these are real bunglers who have a holy
fear of the alla breve beat, and cling to the correct four-beats-
in-the-bar which makes them feel that they are really conducting and doing something useful. God only knows how these
quadrupeds landed in our theatres.

But the fault of 'dragging' is not to be found in the modern,
elegant conductor who, on the contrary, likes to rattle off a
piece at great speed. Thereby hangs a very special tale which
shows the conditions obtaining in our musical world.

Robert Schumann once complained to me that at Leipzig Mendelssohn spoilt his enjoyment because he took too fast a tempo, especially in the first movement of the Ninth Symphony. I heard Mendelssohn conduct a Beethoven symphony once—it was in Berlin, at a rehearsal of No. 8 in F. I noticed that he picked out a detail here and there—almost according to a whim—and worked at it with a certain obstinacy until he got it clear. This was excellent as far as it went, but I could not see why he did not pay the same attention to other details. We talked about conducting, and Mendelssohn told me several times that in his view to adopt too slow a tempo was the worst thing one could do, and that he would always recommend rather taking a piece too fast. To achieve a truly good performance was rare, he said, but it was possible to create the impression of a good performance if the audience was not given time to notice that anything had gone wrong; Mendelssohn must have told his own pupils about that; it could not have been just a casual remark and I had further opportunities of seeing the results and to ascertain why he believed in fast tempi.

Of the results I had experience when conducting the orchestra of the London Philharmonic Society. Mendelssohn had been conducting it for some time, and his interpretation had become a firmly established tradition strictly observed by the orchestra. As a considerable amount of classical music was performed at these concerts (with only one rehearsal) I was often forced to let the orchestra follow the Mendelssohn tradition. Thus I became acquainted with a style of playing that vividly recalled the opinions he expressed. The music rushed along like water from a fountain: to think of stopping it was impossible: each allegro ended as an unmistakable presto. To interfere was painful enough: only after I had taken a well-modified tempo did I discover other deficiencies submerged in this general flood. The orchestra never played otherwise but mezzoforte, there was never a real piano or forte. As far as it was possible, I firmly insisted on what I considered the right style and the right tempo. Good musicians in the orchestra did not take it amiss, on the contrary, they welcomed it. The public also seemed to like it. Only the critics were up in arms

and succeeded in persuading the Society's directors to brow-
beat the committee and ask me to take the second movement of
Mozart's E flat Symphony at the breezy, nonchalant tempo
they had heard from Mendelssohn. Mendelssohn's unfortunate
principle was illustrated by another incident. I was to conduct
a symphony by a Mr Potter (if I remember his name correctly)
who was a very easy-going, elderly double-bass player. At the
rehearsal he came and begged me to take the andante pretty
fast, being afraid that otherwise it might sound dull. I proved
to him that no matter how fast I took it, it would still sound
dull if reeled off in an insipid fashion, but that it would arrest
attention if its pretty and simple theme were played as I sang
it, for that was how he probably meant it to be played. Mr
Potter was visibly moved, agreed with me, and excused his
request on the ground that he was no longer in the habit of
allowing for this style of orchestral playing. In the evening,
after the andante, he came and shook my hand with great joy.
I am really surprised how little understanding our modern
musicians show for correct tempo and correct playing. I have
had such experiences with the most eminent musicians of our
time! It proved impossible, for instance, to convince Mendelssohn that the tempo of the third movement of Beethoven's F
major Symphony was handled in an atrociously careless manner.

We know that Haydn in his symphonies, especially in the
late ones, used the minuet as a refreshing change from the
adagio to the final allegro and, contrary to the character of
the minuet proper, accelerated its tempo noticeably. He also
introduced, especially in the trio, what evidently was the
ländler of his day so that the name 'minuet' was no longer
appropriate. The tempo was only retained for tradition's sake.
None the less, I think that, as a rule, Haydn's minuets are
taken too fast, and so are Mozart's. Take the minuet from the
G minor Symphony, and particularly that from the C major
Symphony. If the latter, which is normally rattled off almost
presto, is taken at a more deliberate speed, it assumes quite a
different character: graceful, festive and firm, whereas the trio
taken fast becomes an insignificant trifle.

Now in the F major Symphony, Beethoven wrote a real
minuet. Intending it as a contrast to the preceding 'allegretto

scherzando', the composer placed it between two allegro movements, and in order to remove any uncertainty as to its tempo, he called it, not simply 'menuetto', but 'tempo di menuetto'. The novel and unusual character of the two inner movements of the symphony passed almost wholly unnoticed: the 'allegretto scherzando' was mistaken for the usual andante and the 'tempo di menuetto' for the scherzo. As it proved impossible to achieve in these two movements the expected effects of andante and scherzo respectively, our musicians began to regard this wonderful symphony as a work of less moment, as if, after the efforts of the A major Symphony, Beethoven's Muse had insisted on having an easy time. Consequently the 'allegretto scherzando' is taken at a dragging pace, while in the 'tempo di menuetto' we are being cheerfully offered an invigorating *ländler*. One usually feels much relieved when the ordeal is over. For, due to the fast tempo at which it is commonly taken, this most charming of all musical idylls becomes a veritable monstrosity because of the triplets of the cellos. Played at high speed the accompaniment becomes most difficult, the players sawing away backwards and forwards in a hurried staccato without producing anything but scratching noises. But the difficulty resolves itself quite naturally if the tempo allows a certain latitude to the delicate cantilena of the horns and clarinet. Thus these instruments can in their turn overcome *their* difficulties which in the clarinet are considerable and make even the best player afraid of a 'crack'. I remember the deep sigh of relief that went through the whole orchestra when I made them play the movement at the correct moderate tempo. The short crescendi of basses and bassoon stood out, the conclusion on the soft *pp* made its effect, and the minuet proper assumed the right expression of comfortable solidity.

I once attended a performance of this symphony at Dresden, conducted by the late Reissiger. Mendelssohn was with me, and, talking about the problem I just mentioned, I told Mendelssohn that I *thought* I had converted Reissiger, who had promised me to take it slower than usual. Mendelssohn fully agreed with me, and we listened. The third movement began and I was startled when I heard the old *ländler* tempo. Before

I was able to express my annoyance, Mendelssohn, well pleased, nodded and said to me with a smile, 'It's all right like that! Bravo!' From shock I fell into surprise. While Reissiger could not be seriously blamed for his relapse, owing to reasons I shall discuss presently, Mendelssohn's insensitiveness aroused in me the very natural doubt whether he was capable of noticing any difference at all.

Shortly afterwards the same thing happened elsewhere. This time it was with one of Mendelssohn's successors at the Leipzig concerts. This well-known conductor, agreeing with me on the tempo, had also promised to take it at the correct pace. Strange was his excuse when he failed: he confessed that, distracted by cares about administrative matters, he remembered the promise *after* he had started the movement; naturally he could not suddenly change the tempo and things had to be left as before. Annoyed as I was by this excuse, I was glad to have found at least one person who accepted and confirmed my views. I do not think that even in this last instance the conductor could have been blamed for real carelessness or 'forgetfulness'. I believe that the real reason for avoiding the slower tempo was that the orchestra, used to a faster tempo, would have been thrown out of gear completely if the conductor had suddenly forced it to adopt a pace which would have entailed *an entirely different style of playing*.

Now this brings us to a point of great importance about which we ought to be very clear if we are to improve the standard of our performances of classical music. Musicians have an apparent right to insist on *their* choice of tempo corresponding to their 'interpretation'. But this very relation between what they feel and what they do is responsible for the fact that if the tempo is changed while the interpretation remains as before, the result is obvious and intolerable discrepancy. A case in point occurs in the opening bars of the C minor Symphony. Our conductors are in the habit of making a very short stop on the pause in the second bar, using it for almost the sole purpose of preparing the players for the clear attack of the figure in the third bar. The E flat is held out as long as a forte can last with careless bowing. Now, suppose that from his grave Beethoven called to a conductor: 'Make my pauses long and terrible! I did not write them to amuse or to give you time to prepare what's coming. The pause of my allegro is still the same sonorous, sustained pause of my adagio, where it serves to express a soaring feeling. When necessary I throw it into the fierce, fast torrent of my allegro to produce a sudden standstill, rapturous or terrifying. Then the life of the note must be squeezed out to the last drop. There I stop the waves of the ocean and allow you a glimpse into the abyss; I stop the course of the clouds, tear the tangled mists apart, and allow you a glimpse of the pure blue sky and the radiant sun. That is the purpose of pauses in my allegros, i.e. *long-sustained* notes. Now you know what I mean by the sustained E flat after the stormy quavers and by the other pauses in the rest of the movement.'

Now suppose the conductor were to follow this advice and ask the orchestra to hold the pause as long as Beethoven intended it. What would be the immediate result? After the first attack of the strings the note being sustained further would grow weaker in tone and peter out in a timid *piano*. Why? Because—and here I am coming to one of the bad habits in our orchestral playing—our orchestras are no longer accustomed to *sustain a note evenly*. I ask conductors to demand an evenly sustained forte from all instruments. They will see astonished faces in response to the unusual demand, and will then realize how persevering their work will have to be to produce the right result. The evenly sustained note is the basis of all dynamics, vocal as well as instrumental; it is the starting point of all those modifications which, in their variety, determine the character of a performance. Without it an orchestra can make a deal of noise, but has no power. It is there that the first weakness of most of our orchestras lies. But conductors who know next to nothing about the sustained forte attach very great importance to an exaggerated piano. This is quite easy to obtain from the strings but extremely difficult to get from wind instruments and from flutes in particular. It is hardly possible to secure a delicate piano from the flute because flautists nowadays are using the instrument, once so soft of tone, as though it were a veritable bellow. An exception is perhaps the clarinettist who can still produce an echo effect, and the French oboeists whose tone never loses its pastoral character. This objectionable fact makes one ask: if it is impossible to tone down the wind, why not demand, for the sake of balance, a fuller tone from the strings? Their exaggerated piano produces an almost ridiculous contrast with the wind and a lack of balance which seems to have escaped our conductors entirely. String players produce no *real forte* and no *real piano*, as in both a full, round tone is lacking. It is quite easy to obtain a mere whisper of sound through light bowing, whereas the wind players require great breath control to produce a clear, clean note, with only the smallest amount of air passing through the instrument. It is from good wind players that violinists could learn how to produce a piano that yet has body, while woodwind players, in their turn, could learn something from good singers.

Sustained softness and loudness are the two poles between which orchestral playing has to range. What variety can there be in playing if these two extremes are never reached? Obviously the variety can only be so limited that Mendelssohn's notion of getting quickly and lightly over difficulties becomes a useful expedient; no wonder our conductors have made it a real dogma, a dogma accepted by the whole crowd of conductors who decry as heresy every attempt to play our classical music correctly.

Before dealing with these conductors, I have to revert again to the question of *tempo* because it is here, as I said before, that a conductor shows his mettle. Now the correct tempo of a piece is obviously determined by its character. We have to agree about the latter before determining the former. The question whether a work tends more to the sustained (singing) style, or the rhythmic (figurative) style, decides the conductor in his choice. The opposites are represented by adagio and allegro movements corresponding to the antithesis of sustained cantilena and fluid movement. The *sustained note* is the law of the adagio, where rhythm dissolves into music pure, absolute, and self-sufficient. In a strict sense one may say that an adagio cannot be taken slowly enough, as the language of pure music must be trusted to convince and make its effect as relaxed tension turns to rapture. The life of music expresses itself in the allegro through quick-moving figures; in the adagio through the infinite variety of inflections of which sustained notes are capable.

Not one of our conductors has the vision to see the adagio quite in this light. The first thing they do is to look out for some figure of short note-values and set the tempo by its presumed speed. I am perhaps the only conductor to have had the courage to interpret the adagio of the third movement from the Ninth Symphony in the above sense, and to set its tempo accordingly. The adagio alternates with an andante in 3/4 time, as if the composer meant to throw its most singular character into particular relief. This fact does not prevent conductors from neutralizing the character of both sections till all that remains is the difference between 4/4 and 3/4 time. The movement, one of the most illuminating examples in this respect, illustrates also very clearly another phenomenon. In the florid writing of the 12/8 section the pure adagio character is modified through the introduction of a more pronounced rhythm in the accompaniment. The accompaniment is independent without, however, affecting the broad character of the cantilena of the melody. It is as if the urge of the adagio to expand had stopped. In the opening section there reigns unlimited freedom to relish the sensuous quality of the sustained note, and the tempo should be flexible and change according to profound laws. By contrast, in the 12/8 section, it is the steady rhythm of the florid accompaniment that fixes the tempo—a tempo firm and without fluctuation.

In the true allegro type (such as we find in the finales of Mozart's E flat and Beethoven's A major symphonies) rhythmic movement has the upper hand. In those movements there is an orgy of rhythm and that is the reason why these movements cannot be taken fast and energetically enough. Yet music that lies between these extremes must in its tempo partake of both. The tempo must be modified, must obey the *law of inter-relation,* a law that should be understood in all its subtle and varied applications, because it is at bottom the same that governs all the possible dynamic modifications of the sustained note. Not only do our conductors know nothing about *modification of tempo* but, in their ignorance, they stupidly cry it down.

We have distinguished two kinds of allegros: one, of recent

date and truly Beethovenish, described as 'sentimental', and the other, older and particularly characteristic of Mozart, which I call 'naïve', adopting the distinction made in Schiller's essay on 'sentimental' and 'naïve' poetry.

I do not think it necessary for our immediate purpose to enlarge further upon the aesthetic problem. I only wish to add that the 'naïve' allegro is seen at best in Mozart's fast, alla-breve movements. The most perfect examples are the allegros of his operatic overtures, above all, those to *Figaro* and *Don Giovanni*. We know that for Mozart they could not be played fast enough; when at last he had forced his musicians to play the *Figaro* overture presto he encouragingly called out '*That* was beautiful! but on the evening I want it a little faster still!' As I said of the pure adagio that in an ideal sense it cannot be taken slowly enough, so the pure allegro cannot be played fast enough. The limits—in the first case indulgence in broad cantilena, in the second, quick figuration—are wholly relative, and the rate of the tempo depends solely on the laws of beauty which mark the frontier line between opposites. On reaching that line the desire for contrast becomes inevitable. There is hence profound significance in the fact that in classical symphonies allegro should lead to adagio, and adagio, after an intermediate, stricter dance-form (minuet or scherzo), to the final allegro which is the fastest movement of all.

That Mozart's *absolute* allegro closely belongs to the 'naïve' kind is seen first, dynamically, in the simple change of forte and piano; and secondly, as regards formal structure, in the indiscriminate juxtaposition, corresponding to the simple order of forte and piano, of completely static rhythmic-melodic sections (containing stereotyped recurrence of loud half-closes). In this treatment Mozart shows surprising unconcern. Yet the character of this type of allegro explains everything, even the indiscrimination in the use of utterly banal movements; Mozart does not wish to attract us by cantilena, rather is it his aim to create a state of excitement by restless movement. It is significant that in the allegro of the *Don Giovanni* overture the speed of the music ends with an unmistakable turn to the 'sentimental'. When the dividing line is reached, a modification of speed is indicated; the pace slows down imperceptibly; it must be slow enough to allow for a gradual transition to the slightly more moderate speed of the first number which follows. The opening number, it is true, is an alla-breve but less fast than the main tempo of the overture.

Now I want to establish, first, that the character of the Mozartian classical, or as I call it, 'naïve' allegro, is worlds apart from that of the modern 'sentimental', Beethovenish, allegro. It was not until he heard the Mannheim orchestra that Mozart learnt the use of crescendos and diminuendos; till then the scoring of the older masters shows that no passages in the forte and piano sections of an allegro were meant to be played 'expressivo'.

Now how does the Beethoven allegro compare with that? To refer to the boldest example of Beethoven's novelties, how will the first movement of his 'Eroica' sound if it is rattled off in the strict allegro tempo of a Mozart overture? I ask: does it ever occur to any one of our conductors to take the tempo of this movement differently from that of a Mozart overture? No, it remains the same throughout from the first bar to the very last! If there were a conductor with the gift for 'interpreting' tempo, one may be sure that he would belong to the smart type who follows above all Mendelssohn's 'chi va presto va sano'.

We have now reached the decisive point in the criticism of our musical life, a point which, as the reader may have noticed, I approached with some caution. I was above all concerned with showing where the problem lay, making it clear to everybody that with Beethoven a very essential change from former times took place in the approach to, and performance of, music. While the principle of strong contrast between the individual sections is still valid, thematic ideas which before lived an independent, self-sufficient life in separate, self-contained sections are now closely brought together; they evolve from each other through the agency of a basic motive. This, of course, must also be realized in the performance and, to achieve that, it is above all necessary that the tempo should be as supple and flexible as the thematic material. The forward tendency of such a thematic texture should make itself felt in the adoption of a free tempo. The difficulties in achieving such constant and effective modification of tempo in a classical piece of more recent date are not less great than those with which the true German genius has to struggle to find the right understanding for its manifestation.

As I wished to avoid details by enumerating my experiences of minor cases, I have devoted my attention mainly to what I experienced with the leaders of modern music. On summing up, I do not hesitate to state that, judging from the way in which Beethoven is performed, the true style of the interpretation still belongs to the realm of pure chimera. This is anything but a restrained statement, yet I would like to substantiate it, and add to this negative dictum some positive evidence. I propose to do that by considering what I believe to be the correct style in Beethoven and music of a similar nature.

Since this subject seems inexhaustible, I shall try to deal again with only a few salient points. One of the main forms of musical composition is that of 'theme and variations'. Already Haydn and, after him, Beethoven, have imparted to this loose form, with its mere stringing together of different elements, a deeper artistic significance. This they did not only through their great inventive power, but also by establishing a relation between the variations. This is best achieved if the development is continuous, that is to say, if one variation leads to another, combining it with a certain element of pleasant surprise—the second variation either develops further what was only hinted in the first, or supplements what was missing in the latter. The real weakness of the variation form lies in that strongly contrasted sections are juxtaposed without relation or link between them. True, Beethoven knows how to turn this very weakness to good account, and in a manner which is neither casual nor clumsy. When he has reached the aesthetic dividing line (to which I referred before) between the extremely sustained tempo of the adagio and unimpeded movement of the allegro, he gratifies our desire for contrast by introducing with apparent suddenness a fast tempo. We find this in the Master's great works, of which the finale of the 'Eroica' is a most instructive example, that is if one accepts it as an extended variation movement and when the performance shows

flexibility and varied expression. In order to become a master
of this style (in this movement as well as in other similar ones)
one has to see all the clearer where the weakness of the
variation form lies and reduce its adverse effect. We often find
that variations have been written independently of each other
and merely strung together according to certain wholly superficial conventions. A most disagreeable effect is caused by such
indiscriminate juxtaposition as when, without apparent reason,
a slow, solemn theme is abruptly followed by a lively and
merry variation. In the second movement of Beethoven's great
A major Sonata for piano and violin, the first variation follows
a supremely beautiful theme; it is played by every virtuoso as
though it were intended to accompany a gymnastic exercise.
This has always angered me and made me wish to hear no more
music. Yet, strangely enough, whenever I complained about it
people said about the music what they said about the 'tempo di
menuetto' from the Eighth Symphony. Everybody agreed 'on
the whole'; but could not understand what I meant. The only
thing which is certain is that the first variation after the
wonderful slow theme has a markedly lively character; in
writing it, the composer did not at first perceive it in its
relation to the theme of which it is the immediate continuation. He was subconsciously influenced by the self-contained
character of the variation form. Yet in performance the variations are played in close succession. Other movements based
on the variation form, yet conceived as an organic whole,
(second movement of the C minor Symphony, the Adagio from
the great E flat major Quartet, and above all the wonderful
second movement of the great C minor Sonata, Op. 111) show
with what subtlety and sensitivity the master made the transition between the individual variations. It follows that in the
so-called Kreutzer Sonata the performer who claims the honour
of doing full justice to Beethoven should try to create the
feeling of correspondence between the mode of the theme and
that of the first variation, whose character, which is always
regarded by pianists and violinists as different from that of the
theme, should, at the beginning, only be hinted at by a slight
acceleration. If that were done with true artistic feeling, the
first part of the variation would thus form a gradual transition

to the more lively second part, and would suggest an agreeable, yet not unimportant, transformation of the basic character of the theme.

A more interesting example of similar nature is found in Beethoven's C sharp minor Quartet, at the entry of the first 6/8 Allegro, after the extended Adagio introduction. The Allegro is marked 'molto vivace'—a very clear indication of the character of the whole movement. Entirely against the rule, Beethoven allows the movements of this quartet to run into each other without the customary break, and, if we look closely at them, we shall see that he develops one from the other in a subtle fashion. Allegro follows an Adagio of dream-like, wistful character such as we hardly find elsewhere in Beethoven; it is a mood picture suggesting some lovely vision rising out of the stream of memory, assuming a more recognizable shape, and rousing in the composer a feeling of lively, intense emotion. Now the question here evidently is: how should the allegro grow out of the melancholy static mood of the preceding adagio, so as to attract us rather than disconcert us by an abrupt and sudden start? The new theme, quite appropriately, starts on a long *pp*, like a delicate dream vision, and dies away again in a ritardando; it then begins to gain momentum and, after a crescendo, enters its proper sphere of lively activity. It is evidently part of the performer's task to allow for the particular character of this passage and modify the tempo accordingly at its entry. It goes against all artistic propriety if, as one can hear without exception in every performance of this quartet, the tempo is not modified and the players start straightaway with a brisk vivace, as if the whole thing were purely a joke. Yet that is what some gentlemen consider 'classical'.

As I have proved in these few examples, modification of the tempo is necessary and of immense importance for the performance of classical music. It is for that reason that I am going to discuss in detail the criteria of a correct performance of classical music, even at the risk of having to tell our musicians and conductors hard truths. I hope to have made clear the problem of tempo modifications as regards classical works of the more modern, German style; and I trust to have explained

the difficulties involved—difficulties which can only be recognized and solved by intelligent minds blessed with artistic
insight.

What I called the 'sentimental' style—a style which Beethoven developed and endowed with eternal values—contains
also the elements of the previous, 'naïve' style. It thus presents
the composer with an ever-ready language to be used as he
pleases. Sustained and short notes, broad lyrical phrases and
quick figurations, are no longer formally separated and opposed;
in variations, individual variations are no longer loosely strung
together but form a close context and run imperceptibly into
each other. Yet there is no doubt that such a piece of symphonic
writing, containing as it does so many different sections, must
be played at a pace that allows its true nature to manifest
itself; otherwise the whole thing will be complete nonsense.
I still remember the critical remarks which in my youth were
made about the 'Eroica' by older musicians. Dyonis Weber of
Prague simply treated it as a monstrosity. And justifiably so,
since he only knew the Mozartian allegro. He made his students
play the first movement of the 'Eroica' in the strict tempo of a
Mozart allegro. Though the symphony is everywhere treated in
the same manner, the public nowadays receives it with acclama-
tion. Unless one wishes to treat the whole phenomenon merely
with mockery, this success is above all due to the fact that for
several decades people have been hearing the music at home
on the piano. For the time being it thus exercises by all kinds
of devious ways irresistible power in an irresistible manner.

How many times have we not heard the overture to *Der
Freischütz*? I know only very few people who are shocked today
when they remember the trivial way in which they often heard
this wonderful tone poem played without realizing how bad the
conducting was. These few were those who in 1864 attended a
concert in Vienna which I had been invited to conduct, the
programme including among other items the *Freischütz* overture. During the rehearsal the orchestra of the Vienna Hofoper,
unquestionably one of the best orchestras in the world, was
completely put out of countenance by my interpretation. The
very beginning showed that the orchestra had been used to
playing the introductory adagio at the pace of a comfortable

andante, in the style of a 'Ranz des vaches' or other pieces of a similarly cheerful nature. This was not only a Viennese tradition; it had become the general practice, as I had known in Dresden where once Weber used to conduct himself. I myself conducted *Freischütz* for the first time at Dresden, eighteen years after the master's death. Unconcerned about the bad habits into which the orchestra had fallen under my older colleague, I took the introduction of the overture in my own tempo, when a veteran cellist who had played under Weber, turned to me and said with a serious face: 'Yes, that's how Weber used to take it; this is the first time I have heard it played correctly since.' My right feeling for Weber who had long been dead caused the composer's widow (she was then still living at Dresden) to express her heartfelt wishes that I should continue as conductor of the Dresden orchestra. She could now, she said, cherish a hope that his music would again be performed correctly. I mention this beautiful and gratifying testimony because it has been a comfort to me in the face of criticism concerning my artistic activities, including conducting. Now on the occasion of that Vienna performance of the *Freischütz* overture her noble encouragement emboldened me to insist on a complete alteration from the first bar to the last. The orchestra, which had played the piece ad nauseam, studied it completely anew. The horn quartet had up till then played the tender forest fantasy of the introduction as though it were a bombastic, pompous virtuoso piece. Now the four players readily changed their embouchure completely, so as to impart to the cantilena with its pianissimo string accompaniment an enchanting fragrance such as the composer had intended. Similarly at the place where Weber indicated it, they increased the volume of tone to mezzoforte, softly dying away again without stressing the sforzando (usually played with a fierce accent) thereby giving the fortissimo after the crescendo its full, terrifying and desperate expression. Having thus restored to the introductory adagio its eerie, mysterious character, I gave full rein to the wild and passionate allegro. I was in no wise hampered by the consideration that the gentle second subject demanded more delicate playing, because I believed myself well capable of *so reducing the pace again at the right time* that on reaching the theme I would have imperceptibly arrived at its proper tempo.

Most or practically all complex allegros of the more modern type consist of two fundamentally very different parts; unlike the early more 'naïve' allegros, they are enriched by the very combination of a pure allegro movement with the characteristic element of a singing adagio with all its graduations. The second subject from the allegro of the *Oberon* overture, which no longer has the character of a proper allegro theme, shows this at its clearest. The composer of course introduces this contrasting theme into the technical form with an eye to fusing it into the main character of the piece. This is to say: on the surface the lyrical theme fits perfectly into the formal scheme of the allegro; yet if its character is to come out in a lively, eloquent fashion *this scheme must be capable of such modifications as to enable the composer to use it equally for both chief characters.*

In Vienna, after obtaining the utmost speed, I arrived at the sustained lyrical theme of the clarinet, which is wholly in adagio character and in which all quick figuration changes to sustained (or tremolando) notes. Despite the more lively bridge figure which follows it, I retarded the tempo by only a fraction so that it was only very slightly slower than the main tempo. Thus I reached the cantilena in E flat, the entry of which was in this way perfectly prepared.

In the reprise the conflict (between two motives) is concentrated into ever shorter periods. It was in this very section that a constant modification of the tempo proved most successful. Being used to a different reading, the musicians were most surprised when, after the glorious, sustained C major chords and the general pauses by which they are separated and thrown into significant relief, I adopted for the apotheosis of the second theme, not the fierce, exciting pace of the first allegro subject, but a slower tempo.

It is most common in our orchestral performances to hurry the main theme toward the end of the overture—and all that we need to recall the circus is the crack of a horse-whip. Increased speed at the conclusion of overtures is frequently intended by the composer, and is quite natural if the lively theme of the Allegro proper is allowed to reassert itself and celebrate its apotheosis. A famous example of this is Beethoven's great *Leonora* overture. But here again the effect of the presto is completely spoilt if the conductor does not know how to modify (i.e. *to retard in good time*) the main tempo according to the changing character of the symphonic texture. The result is that he arrives at a speed which excludes the possibility of further increase. Year in, year out, in every public performance of the *Freischütz* overture we hear the indescribably repulsive effect of this—to put it only mildly—utterly trivial treatment of a theme which expresses the ardent thanks of a loving maiden. Those who find this excellent, who speak of the 'sap and power' of the orchestral playing, and add speculations about music, are indeed well-qualified to warn others 'against the absurdities of misapprehended idealism by pointing to what is genuine, true and for ever valid in art'! Yet a number of Viennese music lovers were once given the opportunity of hearing this ill-used overture played in a different way. Even today this performance is remembered. People said they hadn't really known the overture before and asked me what I had done. Some wanted to know in particular by what mysterious means I had achieved the stirring and novel effect in the conclusion. They would hardly believe me when I pointed to the adoption of a moderate tempo as the reason.

Of my performance and its success, our Herren Kapell-meisters do not like to hear. Herr Dessof, however, thought that the orchestra should play the overture in my way, and he announced this by saying: 'Well now, gentlemen, we will take the overture *à la Wagner*.' Yes, yes—*à la Wagner*! I think, gentlemen, also some other things could be taken *à la Wagner* without detriment to their effect!

This seemed a great concession on the part of the Vienna conductor, while my former colleague Reissiger had made me only *half* a concession. Once when I was conducting Beethoven's A major Symphony at Dresden, where Reissiger had been conducting it frequently, I found that on the orchestral parts of the last movement he had arbitrarily entered a piano. After the repeated strokes on the dominant seventh on A the music continues forte, to become still more violent at the subsequent 'sempre piu forte'. Reissiger did not like this and made the

orchestra suddenly play piano, gradually introducing a noticeable crescendo in the subsequent bars. Of course I took out
the 'piano' mark, restored the 'forte' which I wanted played
most energetically, and thus offended against the 'eternal laws'
of what is 'genuine and true in art'—laws that probably
Reissiger had been observing in his time! When, after I left
Dresden, Reissiger once again conducted the A major Symphony, he hesitatingly stopped at that passage and asked the
orchestra to play it mezzoforte.

On another occasion at Munich I heard not long ago a public
performance of the Egmont Overture which illustrated the
same point. The terrifying, grave sostenuto of the introduction
is taken up again in the allegro of the overture, where in
rhythmic diminution it forms the first part of the second
subject, to be answered by a contrasting motive of pleasing
tenderness. Now at Munich, as anywhere else for that matter,
where the 'classical' style is law, this theme, which tersely
expresses terror and tenderness, was like a faded leaf washed
away by the unimpeded torrent of the allegro, so that it
sounded like a figure from dance music, dancing couples
making ready on the first two bars and, as in a *ländler*, turning
round once in the subsequent two bars. When once, in the
absence of a celebrated older conductor, Bülow conducted
this piece, I induced him to perform it in the correct manner
and then this passage at once became as terse as the composer
had intended. To achieve this it is only necessary to retard
slightly the impassionate, exciting pace of the tempo so that
the orchestra has sufficient time to articulate the change in the
contrasting motives of this theme. Since towards the end of
the 3/4 section this contrast is given more breadth and
emphasis, it follows that only through the necessary tempo
modification will the overture appear in a new light and reveal
its character.

No such suspicion entered the mind of the audience at the
famous Munich Odeon Concerts where I once heard a performance of Mozart's G minor Symphony conducted by a
well-known classical conductor. The playing of the andante
of the Symphony and the success it had showed me something
I would never have thought possible. Mozart's markings are

not numerous, so that it would appear that the composer has allowed us complete freedom, for he only ties us down by the fewest of markings. We are free to lose ourselves in the mysterious awe, the gently surging quaver-movement, and to soar with the ascending violin figure, as ethereal as moonlight.

Such fancies had to vanish before the true and classically strict performance under the famous veteran of the Munich Odeon. It was so grave and sombre that it made one's flesh creep almost as if one had been condemned to eternal damnation. The light-floating andante in particular became a clod-hopping largo, not even a hundredth of a quaver was taken for granted; stiff and ugly like a rod of iron, the baton was waved over the music, and even the feathers of those angel wings grew into well-waxed firelocks from the Seven Years War. Just when I felt as if I were a recruit for the Prussian Guards of 1740, and anxiously demanding to be bought off, who could have described my shock when I saw the conductor turn back the page and repeat the first part of his larghetto-cum-andante? He did it solely because he thought that the usual two dots at the double-bar were not etched into the score without reason. I looked round when I witnessed a second miracle: the whole audience, which had listened patiently, found everything in order and was convinced it had had a true Mozartian treat.

On a later occasion my patience gave out a little. This was at a rehearsal of my *Tannhäuser*; I had quietly put up with various things such as the pedestrian pace for the Knight's March in the second act. Now it became obvious that the conductor didn't even know how to change from the 4/4 to the corresponding 6/4. He had difficulty in negotiating this change. For my poor narration of Tannhäuser in Rome he resorted to a hesitant alla-breve, leaving it to the players to make what they could of the crotchets with the result that the tempo was twice as fast. Musically it was most interesting: but it forced poor Tannhäuser to sing his painful memories of Rome in a highly frivolous, nay, merry and hopping, waltz-rhythm. This reminded me again of Lohengrin's narration of the Grail which I heard in Wiesbaden in scherzando tempo as if addressed to Queen Mab!

The fraternity of modern conductors has always reacted

unfavourably to attempts at modifying the tempo which would improve the performance of classical music, notably Beethoven's. I pointed out in detail that a modification of tempo without a corresponding change in tone-production provides an apparently legitimate reason for objection: yet I showed that the fundamental fault lay in the ineptitude and unsuitability of conductors in general. There is, however, a really valid reason for objection, as arbitrary changes would at once open the door to the whims of every conceited, vain hack who is out for effects, and might distort classical music beyond recognition. Against this there is no other argument but that music must be in a sad state if such fears can arise. It implies that we no longer believe in artistic integrity. Hence the argument boils down to a confession that our conductors are inept; for if the bunglers are not free to treat our music arbitrarily, why don't our most eminent and most respected musicians see that music is performed correctly? They are the very people who steer music into triviality and distortion so that every musician who is alive to the artistic cause turns from them dissatisfied and in disgust.

The reason behind it is ineptitude and mental inertia. Resistance turns to fierce aggression since the inept and lazy are always in an immense majority.

The fact that the majority of our classical works have always been introduced to us in a most imperfect manner (think of the reports about the conditions in which Beethoven's most difficult symphony was first performed) makes us realize how ineptitude and inertia have created a tradition to which one clings studiously. And how even such a master as Mendelssohn treated those works! Of course musicians of far inferior quality cannot be expected to acquire by themselves a knowledge which was lacking in their own master. There is only *one* signpost to the right path—*example*. Their path could never lead to it. They were without guidance and the worst thing about it was that they were so many that there was no room left for those who could lead. That is why I wish here to examine this hypocritical resistance to what I call the right spirit in the performance of great music.

It seems important to examine this attitude closely and to

say bluntly where it originates. Certainly not in the spirit of German music. To assess the positive value of modern music, that is, Beethoven's music, is not easy because it is a very high value, and to attempt to do that we should have to wait for better days. But it may serve if we prove its worth negatively, i.e. by showing the unworthiness of the music-making which at present passes as 'classical'. The opposition of which I have spoken is vocal; to be read in the newspapers where completely uneducated scribblers make a big noise; the real opponents are rather sullen and shy of words. It is the condition of musical life and the complete indifference on the part of the German cultural institutions that enable these musicians to become leaders in high quarters; they are safe in office and honour. As I have made clear from the beginning, this Areopagus of conductors consists of members belonging to two fundamentally different types—the musicians of the older generation who are dying out and who enjoyed a long reputation with the more naïve audiences of South Germany, and the modern, elegant conductors of Mendelssohn's North German school. Owing to recent interference with their prosperous business, these two groups, which before did not think much of each other, have joined forces. In South Germany, Mendelssohn's school, and all that belongs to it, is now appreciated and liked, while the prototype of South German sterility is suddenly welcomed and respected in North Germany. In forming this alliance the first groups had to overcome a certain reluctance; but what helped them out of this predicament is a German national trait which is not particularly praiseworthy—clumsy envy. This has already corrupted the character of one of our most eminent musicians to the point of complete submission to the rule of the second, 'smart' group. As for the opposition of mediocrities, it did not have much to say beyond: 'we can't get on, nor do we want others to get on, but it rankles when they do get on.' This is plain stupidity and dishonest envy.

It is different with the other camp where the strangest ramifications of interests, personal, social, and even national, have established complex rules of behaviour. Without going into details I want only to draw attention to their most important rule of behaviour: *'keep things dark and don't let anyone see them'*. They are anxious to make the 'musician' not too conspicuous, as in former days it was difficult for German musicians to be accepted into society. As in France and England, his social status was held in contempt. It was the Italian musician alone whom courts and the aristocracy regarded as a human being. How humiliating this preference could be was seen in the treatment Mozart received at the hands of the Imperial Court in Vienna.

A musician was an odd being, half savage, half child, and that is how his employers looked upon him. The education of our greatest musical geniuses shows how exclusion from the more refined and sophisticated society worked. One need only think of Beethoven's behaviour with Goethe at Teplitz. The musician was thought incapable of a higher education. When in 1848 I made the greatest efforts to raise the level of the Dresden orchestra, H. Marscher seriously advised me against it, and tried to make me realize that the musicians were incapable of understanding my intentions. There is no doubt about the fact that the higher posts were filled mostly by musicians promoted from the lower ranks, which was not altogether a disadvantage. There was a family feeling between conductor and orchestra. The atmosphere did not lack intimacy but it needed a breath of fresh air coming from an inspired leader who could kindle the spark into a warming, if not a burning flame.

Just as the Jews kept away from manual crafts, similarly our modern conductor did not mix with the musical rank and file. He despised the really hard labour associated with it. He placed himself at the head of a guild of musical craftsmen just as the banker does in commerce. To succeed he had to have something which the rank and file did not possess, or which he could only acquire with the greatest difficulty, and rarely in sufficient quantity. Like the banker with his capital, so the conductor brought along his pseudo-culture. I say 'pseudo-culture' and not 'culture' as those who possess real culture must not be held up to ridicule. 'Pseudo-culture' is prepared to compromise. I know of no case where pseudo-culture succeeded in producing the results of true culture, a true intellectual freedom. Even Mendelssohn, gifted in so many ways and educated with such serious care, clearly showed that he never attained that freedom; he could never overcome that strange self-consciousness which in the eye of responsible observers kept him, despite all his successes, outside German music. This may have been the nagging pain which destroyed his life so prematurely. People brought up in this way are without spontaneity and ease; they are impelled to hide something in their nature rather than to develop it freely. The result can only be false culture. True enough, the intelligence can be keenly developed in particular directions, but at the focal point, where all these directions converge, there can be no true intelligence. Regrettable in a highly gifted and sensitive musician, the result of pseudo-culture in people of inferior and trivial character causes real anger, as this empty pseudo-culture wants to arrogate to itself the right to judge both the spirit and the significance of our glorious music.

It is, generally speaking, a chief characteristic of the representatives of pseudo-culture not to penetrate deeply into things, or, as they put it, not to make much fuss about anything. An idea that is lofty and profound is declared to be something quite obvious, 'a matter of course', within the easy reach of everybody and anybody. To penetrate the extraordinary, the divine and the daemonic, is consequently 'not done'. Hence pseudo-culture speaks glibly of excrescence, exaggeration etc. and it has led to a system of aesthetics that pretends to find support in Goethe above all because he is said to have been against vagueness and obscurity; to have been the inventor of clarity and beautiful poise. 'Innocent' art is praised, Schiller who now and then kicked over the traces is treated with contempt, and, in agreement with the Philistines of our day, a quite new concept of classicism has been developed into which the Greeks have been drawn because theirs was serenity and transparent clarity. This superficial view of everything that is serious and awe-inspiring in existence has been raised into a new system of philosophy where our educated modern heroes of music have been given comfortable and honourable places.

I have already shown how these gentlemen treat German music. It now remains for me to describe the 'Greek serenity'

that was behind Mendelssohn's urgent advice to 'pass over
matters quickly'. It can best be seen in his followers and
successors. With Mendelssohn the matter was 'cover up the
inevitable weaknesses of a performance, and in certain cases,
perhaps also those of the work itself'; with the others the
leitmotif of pseudo-culture is 'cover up everything, do not
make a stir about anything'.

Meyerbeer has been a warning. His association with the
Paris Opéra had already led him to introduce Semitic accents
in his music to such a serious extent that the 'cultured' ones
became frightened. These gentlemen are to a large extent
marked by careful restraint which reminds one of people
afflicted with a stutter, who avoid all passion and excitement
lest they should fall into excessive stuttering and spluttering.
This constant watching of one's own behaviour has certainly
had a beneficial result. Much that was repulsive is now no
longer exposed to glaring light, and social intercourse in
general has become much smoother; this exercised a good
influence on our native character, which is rather rigid and
little developed. As I have mentioned already, musicians became
less rude and began to pay minute attention to detail. But it is
quite another thing if from this need for restraint and perfect
control over certain reprehensible traits of one's nature a
principle is deduced for the treatment of native art. The
German is angular and gauche when he wants to be civilized,
but he has grandeur and is superior to every other nation when the
'*furor*' *comes over him.* Are we to suppress that to please those
people?

When in former days I used to meet young musicians who
had been pupils of Mendelssohn they always told me of the
master's advice that in composing one should never think of
effects and avoid anything that might give rise to them. That
was all well and good, and, indeed, not one of his faithful
pupils has produced anything effective. I believe that all the
teaching at the Leipzig Conservatoire is based on this negative
maxim. Even the greatest talent was of no avail to the student
who had to renounce his taste for anything that did not smack
of psalms.

Most important is the fact that the negative result of this

maxim showed itself in the playing of our classical music
dominated by a fear of falling into extravagance. I am so far
not aware that the adherents of Mendelssohn really study and
play Beethoven's piano works in which the master's particular
style is shown at its clearest. For a long time it had been my
most ardent desire to meet someone who could play the great
B flat major Sonata. It was finally gratified, but by one who
came from quite a different camp from Mendelssohn's. It was
not until the great Franz Liszt came that my wish of hearing
Bach was fulfilled. Bach was also a great favourite with the
other school; for where there were no modern effects
or Beethovenish extravagance, it was possible to apply, with
much assiduity, that smooth, utterly insipid style of playing
considered to be the sole salvation. I once asked one of the
most eminent musicians of the older generation—and a friend
of Mendelssohn's—to play the eighth Prelude and Fugue in E
flat minor from the second volume of the *Well Tempered Clavier,*
which always exercised a magical spell upon me. My request
was readily granted. But I must confess I have rarely had such a
shock. There was no longer any trace of sombre German
Gothic in the music. Under the hands of my friend the piece
flowed over the keyboard so innocuously and with so much
'Greek serenity' that I did not know where to turn, and
imagined myself transported into a neo-Hellenic synagogue
where every vestige of the biblical accentuation was erased
from the religious music. This strange performance was still
in my ears when I finally asked Liszt to cleanse this painful
impression from my spirit. He chose the fourth Prelude and
Fugue in C sharp minor. I had known what to expect from
Liszt, but what I then heard I would not have expected even
from Bach himself. Now I realized what a world there is
between studying a piece and giving an inspired reading of it.
By playing this one fugue alone Liszt revealed what Bach now
means to me. I can now fathom and reach its depth; my faith
enables me to overcome doubts and questioning. I also know
that those who look upon Bach as their property know *nothing*
about him.

I invite anyone from that pietistic musical temperance
society to prove that he had known and understood Beethoven's

great B flat major Sonata before he heard it played by Liszt. Who else can by his playing of Bach and Beethoven move every audience? Is he a pupil of the temperance school? No! He is Hans von Bülow, Liszt's true heir.

Now it is interesting to see how the gentlemen with whom we are dealing have reacted to these wonderful and revealing experiences. We are not concerned here with political successes, i.e. the extent to which they who are so averse from *effect* have *effectively* asserted themselves in the field of German musical life. We are interested in the religious development of their community. Their motto 'avoid effect by all and every means' had originally been due to timidity, caution, and self-conscious restraint. Now this very subtle rule of wisdom has been turned into a hostile dogma. Whenever they happen to meet a real musician the adherents of this dogma turn their faces away in hypocritical disgust as if their eyes had fallen upon something indecent. If this disgust was once only a shield for their own impotence, it has now become an accusation that feeds on calumny and suspicion. The soil on which it grows and prospers is the mentality of the German Philistine, the pettiness and intellectual poverty under which our musical life suffers.

But the main feature of this attitude is a certain reserve against the things one cannot achieve oneself, combined with the slandering of the things one would like to achieve. It is extremely sad that such an excellent composer as Robert Schumann should have been drawn into these intrigues, and that his memory should have served the new congregation as a banner. It was Schumann's misfortune that he undertook more than he was capable of achieving and that the very works whose weakness is due to this failing should have been used by this new music guild as their ensign. The works in which Schumann is lovable, utterly charming, and a real genius, Liszt and his followers (among whom I proudly include myself) played more often and more beautifully than those of Schumann's friends who ignore them and who studiously cultivate those works which show the composer's limitations, viz: works in which he aimed at but did not reach something larger and bolder. If the public is displeased, his 'friends' contend that it is right that music should make no 'effect'. They make great play with the parallel between the works of Beethoven's last period, which in their reading remain unintelligible, and the turgid and uninteresting compositions of Schumann's late years. They mention both composers in the same breath to show that their ideal (Schumann) was on the same lofty plane as Beethoven—the profoundest manifestation of the Germanic genius. They see no difference between Schumann's shallow bombast and the ineffable depths of Beethoven and maintain that the latter's eccentric extravagance is really not permissible while Schumann's insipid and insignificant music is the only right and correct one. On this basis there is of course not much difference between a correct performance of Schumann and a bad one of Beethoven.

Thus these strange guardians of chastity are like the eunuchs in the sultan's harem. They are safe, and our Philistines entrust them with the guardianship of music, music that has great influence on family life. *But where is our glorious German music?* For what really matters is its future. After a glorious century of wonderful works we can proudly ignore the fact that nothing of great importance has been written in the subsequent period. But what makes the people with whom we are dealing so dangerous is that they claim to be the protectors of a wonderful heritage, of the true 'German' genius.

Taking them individually, there is not much to criticize in them, for most of them compose well. Herr Johannes Brahms was once good enough to play to me some variations which I thought excellent, and which showed that he is a serious composer. At a concert I also heard him in other works which pleased me less. Moreover, I thought it impertinent of his followers to credit Liszt and his school with nothing more than 'an extraordinary technique'. I was very painfully struck by Brahms's own technique, which was so wooden and inflexible that I wished it had been lubricated with the oil of Liszt's school. This oil does not flow from the keyboard, but comes from a more ethereal region than that of mere 'technique'. Taking him by and large Brahms is quite a respectable figure. The only thing for which I was unable to find a natural explanation was how his followers could see in him, if not the Saviour himself, one of his most beloved disciples. It may only be that an affected enthusiasm for mediaeval carvings has led them to picture the ideal of holiness in a stiff wooden figure. However, we must protest when our great Beethoven is got up in this holy disguise. This is probably done so that Beethoven's misunderstood genius may be placed side by side with Schumann's. But the latter remains obscure for quite different and most obvious reasons. The Mendelssohnians treat these two composers as if there were no difference between them because they do not know how to make the difference felt.

I have already hinted at the purpose of this unctuous and hypocritical behaviour. On enquiring into it we discover something else.

Some time ago the editor of a South-German newspaper reproached me for the 'hypocritical' tendencies of my theories; the man evidently did not know what he was saying, he was merely anxious to use an invective. But the real nature of hypocrisy was shown by the strange tendency of this disgusting sect (of critics) which vigorously persecutes everything that is exciting and attractive so as to exercise its powers of resistance against excitement and temptation. The real scandal originated in the discovery of the secret of the high-priests who, contrary to the tendency mentioned above, derived pleasure from fighting against excitements. To come back to music, it would not be wrong to accuse of hypocrisy the disciples of Mendelssohn's peculiar school of universal temperance and abstinence. While the lower forms of this school roam about in the sphere of excitement and abstinence—the one lying in the very nature of music, the other imposed on them by dogmatic rules—it can be shown without much trouble that the upper forms only desire the pleasure forbidden to the lower. The 'Liebeslieder Waltzes' by St John—idiotic as the title is—may still be put into the category of studies designed for the lower forms. But the higher forms ardently yearn for 'opera' which absorbs the religious fervour of these disciples of temperance. For if one of them embraced 'opera' with a real success, the whole school would probably break up completely. Only the fact that this never happens keeps the school together. Every failure can be made to appear voluntary restraint such as is taught in the ritualistic studies of the lower forms; and after every unhappy courting, 'opera' can always be made to figure as nothing but a symbol for that excitement which must be fought against, and thus the authors of operatic failure may pass for saints all the better.

Some time ago, in his *Memoirs* (dedicated to Mendelssohn) Herr Eduard Devrient has driven home to us the 'Opernnot' i.e. the need for an opera by his friend Mendelssohn. From it we learn of the strong desire on the part of the master that the opera should be very 'German'. He was to have been provided with a libretto, which, unfortunately, did not materialize. I presume there were natural reasons for it. Much can be done in collaboration, but an opera, 'German, noble and serene', such as Mendelssohn's subtly cunning ambition aimed at, cannot be written because neither the Old nor the New Testament provide a recipe for it. What remained beyond the reach of the master was coveted by his disciple and apprentices. Herr Hiller thought to secure it by simply 'going for' it, merrily and cheerfully, because it all seemed to depend on a 'lucky stroke'. It had happened to others, and he did not see why one day it should not happen to *him*, providing one had the necessary perseverance as in a game of chance. But the wheel of fortune refused to favour them. The lucky number never turned up, not even for Schumann. No matter how many from the higher and lower forms in this temperance school stretched their 'chaste, innocent' hands for the desired operatic success, after a short but painful illusion the lucky draw miscarried.

Such experiences must embitter the simplest souls, and are all the more annoying because, due to the musico-political set-up in Germany, Kapellmeisters and musical directors work primarily in the theatre, a field of musical activity in which these gentlemen are completely unable to produce anything good. But being a bad operatic composer should not prevent a musician from becoming the head of an opera house, i.e. being a good opera conductor. Yet the peculiar fortunes of our artistic life have enabled these gentlemen—who are not even able to conduct our German symphonic music—to be entrusted with the direction of so complicated an affair as opera. Now any intelligent person can imagine what a strange state of affairs has been brought about.

While I took pains to expose their weaknesses in a field where these gentlemen ought to be at home, I have to be brief in discussing their achievements in the *field of opera*, for here we can say: 'Lord have mercy on them, for they know not what they do!' In order to describe their ignominious activities, I would have to produce positive evidence of what could be achieved here in the way of important and beneficial results, but this would lead me too far away from my present purpose. Let me now briefly characterize their achievements as opera conductors. While in concert music they deem it fitting to go about their work in a serious manner, in opera they think it more suitable to show a light-hearted, sceptical, witty, frivolous attitude. They admit that they are not particularly at home here; that they know very little about a style which they think negligible. Hence the chivalrous, obliging manner in dealing with singers whom they are delighted to please. They change the tempo, introduce pauses, ritardandi, accelerandi, transpositions, and above all, 'cuts', wherever and whenever the singers demand. How are they to see the absurdity of such insolent demands? If for once it occurs to a pedantic conductor to insist on this or that point, he is usually wrong. For it fits into the conception of frivolity that it is only the singer who is the real expert and knows what to do and how to do it. If anything of merit is achieved in opera, it is only thanks to singers and their instinct, just as a good orchestral performance is to be credited almost exclusively to the good sense of the players. It is only necessary to look at an orchestral part, for instance, of *Norma* in order to see how a simple musical part may be turned into an odd changeling. Alone the sequence of the transpositions (the adagio of an aria in F sharp, the allegro in F and, between, a transition in E flat because of the military band) presents a truly shocking picture of music to which a highly respected conductor cheerfully beats time. It was not until I went to a little theatre in a Turin suburb that I had the pleasure of hearing a really correct and complete performance of *The Barber of Seville*. Our conductors shirk the trouble necessary to do justice even to this simple score, because they are completely ignorant of the fact that a correct performance of the most insignificant opera can have a relatively very agreeable effect on an educated ear. In the smallest Paris theatre the most shallow theatrical concoctions sound pleasant and even aesthetically satisfying because they are produced in a thoroughly correct and expert manner. So great is the power of artistic principles that even if one of them is applied and adhered to, we at once receive an aesthetically satisfying impression. What we find in the Paris theatre is true art, albeit on a very low level. Of such effects we know nothing in Germany, except in the *ballets* of Vienna and Berlin. There everything is held in one hand, the hand of the man who really knows his job—the ballet master. It is he, fortunately, who lays down how the orchestra is to play and the tempo, and, unlike the individual singer in opera who is only interested in himself, he has regard for the ensemble, the general concord: and the orchestra plays correctly—an extremely pleasant surprise for anybody who, after the tortures of an operatic performance, goes to see a ballet. In opera it is the producer who should create successful team work. Yet, strangely enough, the fiction still remains that opera is absolute music, needing no producer, and this, despite the conductor's proven ignorance which is known to every singer. It so happens that when for once a performance is successful—thanks to the right instinct of talented singers and the enthusiasm of actors and musicians—the conductor, as the supposed representative of the whole team, is rewarded by applause and other signs of approval. This success must surprise him.

But since I only want to talk about conducting, and do not wish to lose myself in further discussion of operatic conditions, I come to an end of the chapter. It is not for me to contest the technique of our opera conductors. This may be left to the singers who complain that one conductor doesn't follow them sufficiently, and another doesn't give them proper cues. One may debate points of technique and experience, which is all that matters here, but as for a really artistic performance, this kind of conducting must be left out of account completely. As I have a better right than any German to speak about opera conducting, I take leave to discuss the reasons for my criticism a little more closely.

I have never been sure (even in my own operas) about which

type of conductor I had to deal with. Was he the conductor of symphonic music or of opera? I believe my trouble is that in my operas these two join hands and supplement each other. When a conductor of the first type, who has gained his experience in classical symphonic music, has been given free scope, as in the introductory instrumental sections of my operas, the results have been disastrous. The tempo was either absurdly hurried (as for instance, the *Tannhäuser* Overture under Mendelssohn at Leipzig) or it got out of control (as in the Prelude to my *Lohengrin* in Berlin and most other places) or it was both dragged and uncontrolled (as in the Prelude to my *Meistersinger* in Dresden and elsewhere). Nowhere was my music treated with the judicious tempo modifications so necessary to an intelligent performance and on which I rely as much as on the playing of correct notes.

To give an illustration of the latter variety of bad performances, I need only point to the way in which my Prelude to the *Meistersinger* is usually played. I have marked the main tempo of this piece 'Sehr mässig bewegt' which, in the older nomenclature, would perhaps be 'allegro maestoso'. In a piece of long duration, and where moreover the formal treatment is markedly rhapsodic (episodic), it needs more modifications than any other tempo. It is very suitable for compositions of a markedly contrapuntal character because of its slow, regular pulse of four beats whose pace can readily be modified, allowing the texture of the music to make its point. In addition the 4/4 time of moderate pace can be used in the most varied ways. Beaten in energetic crotchets, it can express a real allegro and this is how I intended the main tempo to be.

The Prelude was first performed under my direction in a private concert at Leipzig. The orchestra, observing with great accuracy all my directions, played it so well that a very small audience, consisting almost exclusively of lovers of my music from places other than Leipzig, at once demanded an encore, and the musicians, in full agreement with the audience, readily obliged. The impression of the performance seems to have been so favourable that it was decided to introduce the overture to the Leipzig public at one of the Gewandhaus Concerts. Herr Kapellmeister Reinecke, who had attended my own performance of this piece, conducted on the second occasion. The same musicians played it—yet the Prelude was hissed. Whether this 'success' was solely due to the honesty of those who participated in the performance, and their intentional distortions, I do not wish to discuss now, since the patent ineptitude of our conductors is too well known. But well-informed witnesses told me about the tempi adopted by Herr Kapellmeister in the Prelude—it was all I wanted to know.

If a conductor wishes to prove the inferiority of my *Meistersinger*, all he need do is to beat time in the manner in which he is accustomed to treat Beethoven, Mozart, Bach—the manner suitable for R. Schumann. It will thus be easy for anybody to declare that this is indeed most disagreeable music. Imagine that a lively, yet extremely fine-limbed and highly sensitive creature, such as I have shown the tempo of my Prelude to be, is stretched by a classical stick-wagger on the bed of Procrustes, and you will have an idea what happens: 'In with you! what's too long I'll chop off, what's too short, I'll stretch!' And this is accompanied by music to drown the agonized cries of the tortured victim!

Thus firmly 'embedded', not only the Prelude to the *Meistersinger* but the whole opera was first introduced to the Dresden public, a public which once upon a time had heard my best music. To talk again in precise technical terms, the conductor's 'merit' consisted in beating, without the slightest modification, a rigid, stiff 4/4 time which he assumed to be the main tempo for the whole piece. This had further consequences. The final section of the Prelude, where the two main themes combine in an ideal tempo 'andante alla breve', serves me, like the refrain of an old folksong, for a serene conclusion of the whole opera. Against a more elaborate and richer combination of the two themes—the whole passage being treated in the manner of an accompaniment—Hans Sachs sings the praise of the Mastersingers, concluding with his own consoling verses on German Art.

Despite the seriousness of its content, this final apostrophe should create the effect of calm serenity and only towards the end, at the entry of the chorus, does the rhythmic movement assume a broader, more festive character. For a very particular reason I refrain from going further into the significance of my dramatic work, and for the sake of pure, naïve 'opera' I shall only deal with conducting and time-beating. In the Prelude the conductor completely ignored the need for modifying to an 'andante alla breve' the opening tempo, meant only for that part of the music where it has the character of a broad, festive processional march. Similarly, in the final chorus of the opera which is by no means closely related to that march, he omitted the modification of the tempo. The wrong tempo of the Prelude became here the guiding principle: the conductor harnessed the singer of Hans Sachs, an artist of lively imagination, to a most rigid 4/4 beat, and inexorably forced him to sing the concluding apostrophe in as stiff and wooden a manner as possible. From a friendly quarter I was asked to sacrifice this ending and 'cut' it on account of its too depressing effect. I refused, yet complaints stopped. Eventually I learned the reason for it: the Herr Kapellmeister, taking up the cudgels for the obstinate composer (wishing to help his work, of course), had followed his own artistic judgment and cut the concluding apostrophe. Cut! Cut!—that is the *ultima ratio* of our Herren Kapellmeisters. Thus their ineptitude comes to terms with their inability to achieve a correct solution of the problem. 'What the eye doesn't see, the mind doesn't grieve about' is their motto, and the public must put up with it. On the surface, everything seems to run smoothly: the public cheers, at the end acclamations for the conductor bring the Sovereign, applauding, back to his box. But afterwards come mortifying reports about old and new cuts and alterations. For all the insensible treatment, the vital power of the work cannot be broken—that is a comforting thought. To the author it seems a miracle, especially when he can no longer bring himself to attend performances of his work. Yet, curiously enough, from the proven effect of his works he draws an oddly consoling conclusion about the relation between these conductors and great classical music. This music continues to live despite the indifferent treatment it receives. This very fact makes the author realize the power of survival. Such music cannot be killed, and it is this conviction that is becoming a kind of dogma for German genius. Faith gives peace and comfort, and enables one to continue his creative work in his own fashion.

One more question: what is one to think of these strangely famous conductors as musicians? The fact that there is complete unanimity among them about everything leads one almost to suppose that after all they know their job and that despite one's own feelings to the contrary their style is, perhaps, classical. Their excellence is taken for granted to such an extent that the whole of Germany has not a doubt as to who should beat time when the nation is in need of music. The Beethoven Centenary Festival simply could not be celebrated if these gentlemen sprained their hands. But unfortunately I do not know of a single conductor to whom, I felt, I could entrust a single tempo of my operas, at least not one from the general staff of the time-beaters' army. Now and then I came across some poor devil in whom I noticed real ability and talent. These people ruin their chances because they see through the ineptitude of the great Kapellmeisters and carelessly talk about it. It is of course no recommendation for them if they point out bad mistakes in the orchestral parts which had been played, God knows how often, without such a 'general' noticing anything. These talented wretches perish just as did the heretics of old.

What the Kapellmeisters fail to grasp in great music is precisely that which makes it great and can never be explained in words. Could it be that Mozart's tremendous gift for mathematics serves here as an explanation? It seems that in him—whose nerves were so hypersensitive to any discord and whose heart overflowed with goodness—the two ideal extremes of music closely touched one another, and were fused into a wonderful organism. Mathematical problems had certainly nothing to do with Beethoven's creative designs. Compared with Mozart, he appears, in the degree of his sensitivity, as a *monstrum per excessum*. Though lacking the intellectual counter-weight of mathematics, his sensitivity was saved from ruin by an abnormally vigorous constitution—robust to the point of coarseness. This music can no longer be measured in numbers, while in Mozart's there is sometimes an almost trivial regularity that can be explained by the naïve mixture of the two extremes of musical perception.

It is to be hoped that a new school is going to be formed. As I understand, a 'Hochschule der Musik' (Music Academy) has been founded under the auspices of the Royal Academy of Art and Science in Berlin, and Herr Joachim, the famous violinist, has already been appointed as its director. To found such a school without Joachim would have seemed a grave error. I consider it a good omen that, from what I have heard about his playing, this virtuoso knows the kind of interpretation I demand for our great music. Next to Liszt and his school, Joachim is the only musician known to me to whom I can refer as evidence and example of the truth of my preceding statements. It is no matter that Herr Joachim, as I hear, is annoyed at being mentioned in this company. For if we really know a thing, it is quite irrelevant what we pretend to stand for. If Herr Joachim deems it necessary to pretend that he has developed his style through the influence of Hiller and R. Schumann, we may leave it at that, as long as his playing shows the good results of an intimate association with Liszt which lasted for several years. I also regard it as hopeful that in founding a Music Academy they should have thought at once of an artist distinguished for his *interpretative* powers. Had I to explain to a theatre conductor how to conduct certain works, I should refer him to Signora Lucca rather than to the late Leipzig Cantor Hauptmann, even if the latter were still alive. On this point I agree with both the simple-minded members of the public and the connoisseurs of opera in that it is the executive artist who matters because he reaches our heart and ear by direct means. All the same, it would seem dangerous if Herr Joachim were to sit in the Chair of the Academy with only a fiddle in his hand. The baton does not quite obey Joachim, and his compositions seem to have embittered him rather than given pleasure to others. How a 'High School' is to be conducted solely from the 'High Chair' of the leader, I cannot quite conceive. Socrates, at any rate, did not think that because Themistocles and Pericles were distinguished generals and orators, they were capable also of leading the state to happiness and prosperity. As he was unfortunately able to show, their career as statesmen did them no good at all. It may be different in music. But there is one thing that arouses new doubts. I understand that Herr Joachim is hoping for a *New Messiah* in music. He should leave this hope to those who

have made him Professor of Music. I say to him: 'On with the
job.' Should he turn out to be a Messiah he will not need to
fear that the Jews will crucify him.

PERFORMANCE OF THE NINTH SYMPHONY

MY CHIEF UNDERTAKING for the winter was the careful
preparation of Beethoven's Ninth Symphony which was to be
performed in the spring, on Palm Sunday. The performance
involved many a tussle, besides experience that was to have a
strong influence on my own development. . . . I had a great
desire to do this symphony and I chose it because it was almost
unknown in Dresden. Imagine my emotion when I saw for the
first time since early boyhood the mysterious pages of the
score. Then the sight of those pages had cast me in a deep
mystical mood, a reverie, and I spent many nights copying it
out. At the time of my Paris embarrassments the rehearsal of
the first three movements at the Conservatoire had carried me
back from a past of errors and doubts to my earliest days,
stimulating thoughts in new directions. Similarly now that well-
remembered music awakened the mystery and visions of those
days. I had by this time experienced much which, in the depth
of my soul, drove me almost unconsciously to a process of
summing-up, to an almost despairing inquiry about my destiny.
The old despair was now converted into a new enthusiasm.
The heart of a disciple has never been filled before with such
rapture by the work of his master as was mine by the first
movement of the Ninth. . . .

I began by drawing up a programme for which the words of
the chorus provided the pretext. I did it in order to furnish a
simple guide to the understanding of the work, hoping to appeal
not to the critical judgment but to the emotions of the
audience. This programme, in the framing of which passages
in Goethe's *Faust* were very helpful, was well received not
only on this occasion but later elsewhere. I also used the
Dresden paper, writing short and enthusiastic paragraphs in
order to whet the public taste for a symphony that had not
enjoyed a good reputation in Dresden.

As regards the artistic side of the performance, I aimed at
obtaining from the orchestra as expressive a reading as possible,

making to this end all kinds of annotations in the parts to make quite sure that the interpretation would be as clear and colourful as I wanted. It was then the custom to double the wind instruments, a custom that led me to a very careful study of the advantages of the system, the prevailing rule being that all passages marked piano should be executed by single instruments while those marked forte were to be played by the double set. As an instance of the way in which I ensured a more intelligent rendering, I may point to a passage in the second movement, where all the strings play the characteristic rhythm in C major for the first time. The pattern, in three octaves, is played in unison and serves as an accompaniment to the second theme, assigned to the weak woodwind. As the directions for the whole orchestra say fortissimo, the result can only be that the melody of the woodwind disappears, as it cannot be heard above the strings which are only accompanying. I have never carried reverence to the point of interpreting directions literally and, rather than sacrifice the effect really intended by the master, I made the strings play a moderate forte instead of the real fortissimo till they alternate with the wind in continuation of the new subject. Thus the theme, rendered with all possible force by the double set of wind instruments, was heard distinctly for the first time since the symphony was written. I proceeded in this manner throughout, ensuring the greatest exactitude of dynamic effects. No passage—no matter how difficult—was allowed to be played in a way that did not arouse the interest of the audience. For example many have been puzzled by the fugato in 6/8 time after the chorus 'Froh wie seine Sonnen fliegen' in the 'Alla Marcia' of the last movement. In view of the inspiring verses that precede it, which seem to prepare for combat and victory, I conceived this fugato as a happy but earnest war-song and I took it at a continuously fiery tempo and with the greatest vigour. The day after the performance I had the satisfaction of having a call from music-director Anacker of Freiburg, who came to tell me penitently that, although he had been one of my opponents, after hearing the symphony he had become one of my supporters. What had absolutely overwhelmed him was my interpretation of the fugato.

I also devoted special care to that extraordinary passage of the cellos and double basses resembling a recitative in the last movement, which once caused my old friend Pohlenz to come to grief in Leipzig. Thanks to the exceptional excellence of the players, I felt sure I could obtain a perfect reading and, after twelve special rehearsals for the instruments concerned alone, I succeeded in getting them to play it in a way that sounded perfectly free but also expressed exquisite tenderness and utmost energy in a thoroughly impressive way.

I realized from the beginning that the only way to succeed in impressing the public with this symphony was to overcome the extraordinary difficulties of the choral section. I realized that its demands could only be met by a large and enthusiastic body of singers. It then became necessary to secure a very good and large choir. So, besides adding the somewhat feeble Dreissig Academy of Singing to our theatre choir, I enlisted the help of the choir from the Kreutzschule, with its fine boys' voices, and of the choir of the Dresden seminary. In my own way I now tried to get these three hundred singers assembled for rehearsal in a state of real enthusiasm. I succeeded, for instance, in persuading the basses that the passage 'Seid umschlungen Millionen' and especially 'Bruder, uber'n Sternenzelt muss ein guter Vater wohnen', could not be sung in an ordinary manner but must convey the impression of great majesty and rapture.

It gave me particular pleasure to give, with the co-operation of the singer, an overwhelmingly expressive rendering of the baritone recitative 'Freunde, nicht diese Töne'. In view of its exceptional difficulty this passage might almost be considered impossible of execution, yet it was sung in a way that showed the result of mutual interchange of our ideas. I also took care to obtain favourable acoustic conditions by arranging the orchestra according to a new system of my own. I was thus able to place the orchestra in the centre and surround it, in amphitheatre fashion, by the throng of singers on raised seats. This was not only a great advantage to the powerful effect of the choir but gave precision and energy to the finely organized orchestra in the purely instrumental movements.

(Dresden 1846)

QUEEN VICTORIA

To Minna

I AM QUITE HOARSE with too much talking to—The Queen!
. . . Don't think this is a joke. It is all true: The Queen of
England has had a long conversation with me. Further I can
assure you that she is *not* fat but very short and not at all pretty,
with, I am sorry to say, a red nose. Still there is something
uncommonly friendly and easy about her and, although she is
decidedly not a person of great weight, she is pleasing and
amiable. She does not care for instrumental music and when
she attends a concert she does it for the sake of her husband
who goes in for music and is fond of German instrumental
music. But this time she seems to have been impressed. Sainton
(the leader of the orchestra) who kept his eye on her all the
time declared that she followed my conducting and the pieces
we played with quite unusual and increasing interest; she and
Prince Albert were quite stirred by *Tannhäuser* in particular.
So much is certain: that when I turned round at the close of
the overture both applauded most heartily, smiling at me in a
most friendly manner. Naturally the audience backed them up
and this time honoured me with very marked, unanimous and
prolonged applause. That was at the end of the first part of the
concert, whereupon the Court withdrew to the refreshment
room, whither I was immediately summoned, being first
handed over to the Lord Chamberlain, to be presented. I
treated that lord very much *en bagatelle*, but I confess I was
really touched when this kind and gracious Queen assured me
quite simply that she was pleased to make my acquaintance,
because I could not help remembering what my ostensible
standing with her was—one that could not well be more
difficult and embarrassing. Here was I, pursued by the police
in Germany like a highway robber, difficulties made about my
passport in France, yet received by the Queen of England
before the most aristocratic Court in the world with un-
embarrassed friendliness. That is really quite charming.

(1855)

'PARSIFAL' FOR BAYREUTH

To A. Neumann

'PARSIFAL' IS TO be performed nowhere but in Bayreuth and this for reasons of idealism which my illustrious benefactor, the King of Bavaria, saw so clearly that he has quite given up the idea of repeating the Bayreuth performances in Munich. I ought not, and cannot, allow it to be performed at other theatres unless a true 'Wagner Theatre' were to arise, a sacred theatre which, moving from place to place, should propagate throughout the world the thing that I have founded and brought to perfection at Bayreuth.

(1881)

To A. Neumann

I do not know how to reply to the request you have made again about *Parsifal*. *Parsifal* must belong exclusively to my own Bayreuth creation and my Dramatic Festival Theatre there will be used exclusively for producing this one work for a given season year after year. This exclusiveness is founded on the whole conception of the subject. My Bayreuth creation stands and falls with *Parsifal*. . . . If my strength should fail much before my death so that I am unable to take part in the performances, I shall have to consider other ways of keeping my work pure as far as possible for the world. If by then you have attained the right standing for your Wagner theatre by the exclusive and constantly improving production of all my earlier works, Sacred Dramatic Festivals might be entrusted to it and to it alone at special seasons. On this understanding alone could I surrender my *Parsifal*.

(1882)

Hans von Bülow

CONDUCTING OPERA IN ZÜRICH
WITH WAGNER

THE SINGERS WHO, for a wonder, are extremely good, at first intrigued with the orchestra against me because I am young and inexperienced. Wagner, however, who is perfectly satisfied with my work, defeated their plot by threatening to resign if they did not behave properly. People here have a tremendous respect for him. I have now made a few friends among the artists and soon hope to have them all under my thumb. With a monthly salary of fifty gulden, Ritter and I must get along till the new year. The morning coffee is suspended and we enjoy a water-soup which we make ourselves and to which I have grown quite accustomed. We dine with Wagner, where the cooking is excellent. His wife understands it thoroughly and is most kind and obliging. For instance the other day she mended my umbrella (which badly needed it) without saying a word.

WAGNER CONDUCTING MOZART

YESTERDAY 'DON GIOVANNI' was produced under Wagner's conductorship with an overflowing and yet dull, stupid, ungrateful audience. Wagner had taken exceptional trouble and we had all three been busy several days and nights correcting errors in the orchestral parts, replacing instruments which were wanting. Wagner had had the Italian recitatives translated into good German dialogue; he had also simplified the scenery and reduced the everlasting scene-shifting to a single change in the middle of the first act. He had further arranged that the last aria of Donna Anna, which is usually sung in a room, should be sung in the churchyard where she goes with Ottavio, for whom a little recitative composed by Wagner preceded the aria by way of introduction. Thus he has given to the dramatic action a consistency which, alas! is always wanting. It has driven me nearly wild to think how Wagner used to be accused in Dresden of conducting Mozart's operas badly on purpose, being too conceited to appreciate them. The warm and living artistic feeling shown by the Zürich performance will remain unknown to the would-be-adorers of Mozart. It is clear that *Don Giovanni* as given everywhere up to the present does not give the pleasure nor produce the effect it can and ought to do.   There is need for ample reform in this matter.

LISZT'S PIANO PLAYING

THE GREAT MASTERY of Liszt rests mainly on his marvellously expansive and manifold power of expressing outwardly what he feels inwardly; not merely in the perception and grasp of a musical work, but in the way he can make the reading an extraordinarily faithful reproduction of his spiritual conception. Nothing is further from him than the thought of 'effect' arrived at by cold reasoning. His genius gives him complete confidence in the effects of his own brilliant imagination.

BRAHMS

MOZART—BRAHMS OR Schumann—Brahms does not give me sleepless nights. It is about fifteen years since Schumann was speaking in the same eulogistic way of the 'genius' of W. Sterndale Bennett. (1853)

I have got to know Robert Schumann's young prophet, Brahms, pretty well. He has been here a couple of days and was constantly with us. A very lovable, candid nature and something really of God's grace (in the best sense) in his talent.

(1854)

CHERUBINI'S 'REQUIEM'

I HEARD CHERUBINI'S 'REQUIEM' lately in the church. It is a magnificent, grand, yet clear, sacred work and wonderfully beautiful. And, what I did not venture at first to assert out of diffidence, as a whole I think it much grander than Mozart's. I do not hesitate to say so now seeing that Franz and Hauptmann —two very different temperaments—are of the same opinion.

RONDO FORM

I HAVE PRAISED VERY highly Litolff's trio but that dry old stick, F. Geyer, did not agree with what I said. He considers that Litolff had violated the inflexible, sacred, unimpeachable trio form. Litolff has kept as strictly as possible—but not pedantically—to the old forms. Only in the last movement he has gone a step further. It is a very bad habit of composers, which betrays an imperfect sense of form, to lay out their finale on as large a scale as the first movement and, if possible, spin it out even longer. The hearer cannot stand it; repetition grows wearisome and there is no justification, if the form is not new, for a fourth movement at all. The rondo form is old-fashioned and insupportable. Litolff has taken the right road. He has hit the nail on the head whether by instinct or in conscious imitation of the finales in many a Beethoven symphony. In the first movement and in the Andante the composer must give himself over to the purest subjectivity. The last movement—and, perhaps, the Scherzo—must be treated objectively so that the hearer must be satisfied and see the necessity for a concluding section. To avoid insipid objectivity the composer has carte blanche and is free to introduce a piquant 'capriccioso' element. This is what Litolff has done. And now a Flodoard Geyer puffs himself up crying: 'The critic must be the guardian of the sacredness of form.'

BERLIOZ

BERLIOZ'S OPERA *Benvenuto Cellini* which made a semi-fiasco in Paris will be given here (in Weimar) next February; the composer will probably be present. I am delighted to think I shall make his acquaintance. Although I do not like the course Berlioz is pursuing—anti-Wagnerian, pseudo-imitation of Beethoven—yet his genius, felt in so many departments of musical art, interests me. Music has much cause to be grateful for his rich technical acquirements especially as regards orchestration. Berlioz has taken the initiative in many innovations and has shown us the right way to apply them. He is certainly a Frenchman through and through and his brilliance rests on externals.

   That Liszt produces his opera is due in the first place to his personal friendship for Berlioz; then there is his desire to do justice to a man who is almost more misjudged in Germany than in his own country. Yet another inducement is the desire to raise the standard of singers and orchestra to a higher level

by making them face difficult and unaccustomed tasks. The
French and Italian rubbish that has come to Germany since the
July revolution has done incalculable harm. These composers
are the obedient slaves of the singers and the singers are so
spoiled that they no longer submit to the discipline of correct
declamation and dramatic expression laid upon them by Wagner
and Gluck and hardly trouble to comply with the very
moderate demands of Cherubini, Spontini, Weber, Spohr or
Marschner. Liszt alone cannot put an end to the scandal but
the presence of a living conductor—indeed the only really
alive conductor—carrying through the radical regeneration of
opera may perhaps wake up the rising generation.

                                                          (1852)

To Liszt

  I am happy to be able to give you news of an event which
cannot be nearer your heart than it is to mine for I have felt
my enthusiasm for Berlioz increase with each concert. Last
night's concert was one of the most brilliant triumphs that
Berlioz ever scored in Germany. A house full to overflowing
with all that is most notable and elegant in Dresden society
received the composer with utmost warmth on his entrance.
. . . They encored the third number and clapped hands in
frenzy when a laurel wreath thrown from one of the boxes fell
at the composer's feet. In spite of fatigue the orchestra surpassed themselves in their playing of the last piece, the *Cellini*
overture. An ovation started by the younger members of the
orchestra terminated this memorable evening in the midst of
the wildest applause of the audience. Reissiger has behaved well
in regard to Berlioz but his enthusiasm freezes when it reaches
envy-point. . . . We have had four concerts instead of two,
and the almost certain prospect of a performance of *Cellini* to
which the playing of the two overtures will have contributed
not a little. Perfidious criticism of Mr Banck has jeopardized
the chances of a revival of *Faust*. The more numerous audience
of the later concerts promised well for a revival of *Faust*—but
for those villainous insects, the critics.

  Orchestra and singers are most enthusiastic and happy to be
able, thanks to the incomparable conductor, to make the most
of their own talent and ability. They feel the disgrace and

sterility of the last five or six years and would like to keep
Berlioz in Dresden as their conductor. After the first rehearsal
M. Berlioz had stifled every germ of opposition. But a week
ago Krebs bitterly reproached the orchestra for having played
so magnificently under a 'foreigner'! What a humiliation for
the local conductors under whose direction the orchestra could
never show such zeal and ardour. Perhaps it would not be amiss
to remind M. Berlioz that his best and warmest friends in
Dresden in the orchestra and in the audience belong to the
Wagner party and have long belonged to it. I am writing this
because of some words in Mme Berlioz's chatter which
irritated me much. She is, on the whole, an excellent woman,
but rather a chatter-box, telling a lot of stories to which it is
perhaps wrong to pay any attention.

(1854)

Johannes Brahms

VISIT TO ROBERT SCHUMANN IN THE ENDENICH ASYLUM

To Clara Schumann

MY MOST BELOVED FRIEND!

I feel that I have so many beautiful things to tell you this evening that I really don't know where to begin. From two o'clock till six I was with your beloved husband, and if you could see my blissful expression you would know more than any letter could tell you. He received me as warmly and cheerfully as he did the first time, but did not show the same subsequent excitement. Then he handed me your last letter and told me what a delightful surprise it had been to him. We spoke about your travels. I told him that I had seen you in Hamburg, Hanover, Lübeck, and even in Rotterdam. He then asked particularly whether you had occupied the same room in Holland as you had the previous winter. I told him your chief reason for avoiding it, which he quite understood. He was very much pleased with the Bach, Beethoven, Schumann programme.

Then I showed him your portrait. Oh, if only you could have seen how deeply moved he was, how the tears almost stood in his eyes as he looked ever more closely at it. 'Oh, how long have I wished for this!' he said at last, and as he laid it down his hands trembled. He continued to look at it and often stood up to get a closer view of it. He was delighted with the inkstand and also with the cigars. He said he had not had any since Joachim's. This is probably true and he may have left some of those lying about. But he told me that he does not like to ask the doctors for anything (he also said to me most emphatically, 'Clara must certainly have sent me some often, but I do not get them').

He then invited me to go into the garden with him, but as to what we talked about, I cannot possibly remember it all, but I don't think you could mention anything we did not discuss. I asked him quite calmly whether he was composing anything. He then told me that he had written some fugues, but that I was not to hear them because they were not properly arranged yet. He spoke much and often about you—how wonderfully, how magnificently you play, for instance the canons, particularly those in A flat and B, the Sketches, 'It would be impossible to hear "Abend" and "Traümeswirren" played more beautifully than by her!' He inquired after all the children and laughed heartily over Felix's first tooth. He also asked after Frl. Bertha, Frl. Leser, Frl. Junge, and Frl. Schönerstedt, Joachim (and how earnestly!), Hasenclever,[1] etc. etc. Later on he asked after Bürgermeister Hammers, Nielo,[2] Massenbach,[3] etc. inquiring whether they were still in Düsseldorf. He told me a lot about your travels, the Siebengebirge, Switzerland and Heidelberg, and also spoke of Gräfin Abegg.[4] He looked through my C major Sonata[5] with me and pointed out many things. I begged him to send you a greeting (in writing) and asked him whether he did not wish to write to you more often. 'I should love to,' he replied, 'always and always, if only I had paper.' And he really hadn't any. For he does not like to ask the doctors for anything and they think of nothing unless he asks for it.

Whereupon I had paper brought. He disliked its large size very much, nor was he at all pleased with my way of reducing its dimensions. Again and again he sat down and with a most friendly expression on his face seemed as if he wished to write. But he declared that he was much too excited and would write the next day. I can only hope that the next day will not keep us waiting as long as usual. He wrote in my notebook with a pencil the things I was to get for him—a scarf; his everyday one is worn out and the one he was wearing was too 'grand' for his taste! As for the copies of the *Signal*, I will look through this

---

[1] *Dr H., Schumann's doctor and a member of the Committee of the 'Gesängverein'.*

[2] *Member of the Committee of the 'Gesängverein'.*

[3] *'Regierungs Präsident' (Governor of the District).*

[4] *Meta Abegg, to whom, as Countess Pauline d'Abegg, the Variations Op. 1 were dedicated.*

[5] *Op. 1.*

year's numbers and send them to him (when I have made my selection), then I will write to Senff to tell him that Herr Sch. wishes to read this paper. We also spoke about the new *Zeitschrift für Musik* and what a lot of nonsense and gossip it contained. . . . He spoke very enthusiastically of Joachim, as enthusiastically as he usually speaks only of you. He talked a good deal about the musical festival,[1] and of how beautifully J. had already played at the rehearsal. Surely such sounds had never been heard on the violin before! We then played a duet. He asked me to play the *Caesar* Overture[2] with him, but he would not take the lead. 'I am the bass,' he said. We did not keep strictly together but how long it must be since he played a duet! He said that with you he used to play it much faster or else that you used to play it so. He thought highly of the arrangement. . . . The piano was badly out of tune; I have arranged for it to be tuned.

When I wished him goodbye he insisted on accompanying me to the station. On the plea of going to fetch my coat I went downstairs and asked the doctor whether this could be allowed, and to my great joy he said it could. (I did not say any more to the doctor and had not even seen him before this.) An attendant followed us or walked beside us all the time (a few steps away).

It was very fine to see the heavy doors, which are usually bolted, opened for us to go out. . . . He was very pleased with my Hungarian hat just as he used to be in the old days with the cap etc. You can imagine my joy when I found myself walking cheerfully along with my friend for quite a long time. I never once looked at my watch and in reply to his questions always said that there was no hurry. So we went to the cathedral, and to the Beethoven monument, after which I brought him back to the road.

He often made use of my glasses because he had forgotten his own and incidentally found no difficulty in keeping up with the well-known Brahms pace which is often too much for you. On the way he asked me whether his Clara also took a walk

[1] *Of 1853.*
[2] *Op. 128.*

every day. I told him (though not quite truthfully) that whenever you were in Düsseldorf or any other place with me I took you for a walk every day, as you did not like going out alone. 'That I readily believe,' said your Robert, very sadly, 'in the old days we always went out for walks together.' We talked a good deal about his books and his music and he was as happy as a king when he saw how well I knew them all and their proper places. We chaffed each other a good deal over this, for in the case of some of the books he had to stop to think and I had to do the same in the case of others.

I left him on the Endenich Road. He hugged and kissed me tenderly, and on parting sent greeting to you alone. . . . On the way there were moments when I felt intoxicated with happiness, and you can well imagine how much I longed for you to be in Düsseldorf. Your letter was a real joy. It made me feel as if I were holding your hand.

I cannot write you anything sad about him except that occasionally he expressed an emphatic wish to be out of the place. At such moments he always spoke in low and indistinct tones, because he is frightened of the doctors; but he said nothing that was not lucid or showed any signs of confusion. He mentioned the fact that in March he would have been in Endenich a year, and it seemed to him as if he had first known the place when everything was beautifully green, the weather perfect and the skies blue overhead. But alas! I can only tell you in simple and dry language all that we had to say to each other. The beautiful side of it all I cannot describe—his fine, calm demeanour, his warmth in speaking of you and his joy over the portrait. Just picture all this as perfectly as you can.

Surely you will have no questions to ask after such an exhaustive letter? But how I wish I could write more briefly and more beautifully. . . . And so with heartiest greetings from your Robert and myself; and be content at least with my good intentions, for you know how gladly I would give you more joy if I could, with heart-felt love and respect,

Your Johannes

Heartiest greetings to dear Joachim

(1855)

Gustav Mahler

ON THE RIGHT TEMPO

THE TEMPO IS right if one can hear every note; the tempo is *too fast* if the clear perception of the musical figure is no longer possible. The speed of a Presto is that which allows all the notes to be heard *distinctly*; beyond that the effect is lost.

ON WAGNER

ONE ALMOST HAS to forget Wagner's writings in order to give his genius due admiration.

ON BRAHMS

I HAVE NOW gone through almost the whole of Brahms. He is a mannikin with a somewhat narrow chest. Lord, how small it all is compared with Wagner! How Brahms must economize to make both ends meet! The trouble is in his so-called 'developments'. Beautiful as the themes often are, he rarely knows what to do with them; that is what only Beethoven and Wagner knew.

ON HIS THIRD SYMPHONY

IN CONCEIVING THE work (Symphony No. 2) I was most concerned with expressing *an emotion*—not with telling a story. The intellectual basis of the work is clearly defined in the words of the final chorus; and the alto solo throws, on its sudden entry, a revealing light upon the preceding movements. That I should afterwards see in some parts a real, dramatic action can easily be explained by the very nature of Music. The parallel between Life and Music goes perhaps deeper and further than one is able to grasp. But I don't expect that everybody should follow me; I rather leave it to the imagination of the individual listener to make what he pleases of the detail.

(1895)

ON HIS SECOND SYMPHONY

HAVEN'T I TOLD you that I am working at a big symphony
(No. 3)? Don't you understand how this absorbs my whole
being? I am so deep in it that one becomes dead to the world
around. Now think of a work so big that the whole world is
reflected in it—one is a mere instrument on which the
universe plays. . . . The whole of Nature begins to speak in
it, telling us of mysteries that are perhaps sensed in dream.
Some passages make me feel strange as if it was not I who wrote
the work.

(1896)

EMOTION IN WORDS AND MUSIC

. . . WE TOUCH NOW upon the important question *how* and
perhaps *why* music should be explained in terms of words. . . .
In my own case I know that as long as I can express an
experience in words, I would certainly not express it in music.
The need to express myself in music, that is symphonic music,
only comes when *indefinable* emotions make themselves felt—
when I reach the threshold that leads to the 'other world'—the
world in which things are no longer subject to time and
space.

Just as I consider it trivial to invent music to a programme,
so I think it unsatisfactory and futile to add to a programme.
That does not alter the fact that the *incentive* for a composition
may have been an experience in the life of the author, something real and tangible enough to be clothed in words. We
have now arrived—and I am sure of it—at the crossroads where
everybody who understands the nature of music will see that
the two divergent paths of symphonic and dramatic music are
going to separate for ever.

If you compare a Beethoven symphony with a music-drama
by Wagner, you will already see the essential difference between
the two. True, Wagner assimilated the *devices* of symphonic
music just as the symphonic writer of today will be fully
entitled to borrow, consciously, some of his means from a
style of expression that was developed by Wagner. In that

sense all arts are linked with one another, and even art with nature. But as yet we have not thought enough about this problem because we still lack the *perspective* for it. I have not constructed this 'system' and composed accordingly. It was rather that, after writing a few symphonies and constantly coming up against the same questions, I began to see the whole matter. It is, therefore, just as well if the listener to whom my style is unfamiliar is given, to begin with, signposts and milestones on his journey, or, if you like, a chart of the stars so that he may find his bearing in the night sky. That is all a programme can be. The human mind must start with familiar things, otherwise it goes astray.

(1896)

ON PROGRAMME MUSIC

AFTER BEETHOVEN THERE is no modern music that does not have an inner programme. But no music is worth anything in which the listener has first to be told what the composer meant and felt, and what he, the listener, is expected to feel and see in it. So once more! repeat every programme! One must have heart and ears and, last but not least, the will to surrender oneself to the Rhapsodist (bard). A mystery always remains— even for the creator himself!

(1901)

THEATRE ACOUSTICS

I MUST APPLY MY musical faculty to practical work so as to provide a counterweight for the great things that go on in my mind while I compose. And to conduct a symphony orchestra has been my desire all my life. I am glad for once to indulge it, not to mention the fact that I am again *learning a few things*. For the technique of conducting is different in the theatre, and I am convinced that many failings in my orchestration are due to the fact that I have been used to hearing music in the theatre under entirely different acoustical conditions.

(1910)

Richard Strauss

COMPOSITION OF 'DER ROSENKAVALIER'

I BEG YOU WILL not let my criticism discourage you; I can only judge from my own feelings when I say that nothing stimulates my ambition and fertilizes my creative powers so much as the adverse criticism of one whose opinion I value. My criticism is meant to spur you on, not to discourage you—my aim is to get the best possible out of you.

I am sure you will be able to find something better for the scene of the courtship between the Baron and Sophie, more broadly comic in your new version. I know how vexed one gets when something one has done does not meet with another person's approval, but one ceases to worry as soon as one has found something better. All the additions to Act I safely to hand. I always forget to acknowledge receipt right away, so you must never worry.

Don't forget that the public must be made to laugh! Laugh—not smile or grin. So far as we have gone, our work lacks a really comic situation—it is all merely gay, but not *comic*!

The last act of Verdi's *Falstaff* begins with such a capital monologue that I have a similar notion for the Baron's scene after Octavian has left the stage. The Baron on the sofa, the doctor with him, silent servants grouped around the end of the couch—the Baron talking intermittently, now to himself, now to others, half boasting, half sorry for himself—with constant orchestral interruptions. He is alternately groaning with pain, cursing Quinquin and appraising his bride. This is a good scheme, but I shall want additional matter—about 8 lines.

Act I arrived yesterday—I am simply ravished by it; it is really extraordinarily charming, and so subtle—a little too subtle perhaps for the general public, but that doesn't matter. The middle part (the levee scene) is not easy to put into shape, but I shall manage it all right—I have the whole summer before me.

The concluding scene is splendid—I have already had a shot at it—I only wish I had already got so far. But in order to preserve the symphonic unity I shall have to compose it all in the order in which it is written—so I must have patience.

When shall I have the rest of it? The characters are all excellent—so clearly cut; only, as before, I shall need very good actors for them—the usual opera singers wouldn't do at all.

It would be very nice if in Act II you would write something for a contemplative ensemble, just after the moment of the dramatic explosion, when the action comes to a standstill and all are lost in reflection. Such points of repose are always very telling; for example, the great ensemble in *Lohengrin,* Act II, known as 'the heavy brooding' or the quintet in *Die Meistersinger,* or again, in *Il Barbiere,* the A flat ensemble at the end of Act I, 'Freddo ed immobile'. Every musician knows these things and can play them over for you.

(Letter to Hoffmannsthal, 1909)

WAGNER'S AUTOBIOGRAPHY

HAVE YOU READ Wagner's autobiography yet? A really affecting book which one cannot put down without tears of sympathy. What creative power and what a truly wretched existence! The story of his life forms one of the saddest chapters in the history of German culture. . . .

(1911)

THE FIRST WORLD WAR

IT IS SAD indeed that mature artists with serious aims and strictly loyal to their principles should have to be on their guard against men to whom 'this glorious time' is a mere pretext for bringing forward their own mediocre achievements. They see a fine opportunity to cry down real artists as shallow aesthetes and bad patriots; people have forgotten my *Heldenleben,* the *Bardengesang,* the military marches I wrote before the war; I now maintain a reverential silence in the face of the present great upheaval while they take advantage of the favourable moment to launch their amateur rubbish under the flag of patriotism. It is disgusting to read about the regeneration of German art in the very newspapers that only twenty years ago were reproaching Wagner with 'romantic ardour'—to read how 'young Germany' will come back from this glorious war purged and enlightened, whereas one must be thankful if the poor fellows return to us purged of their lice and bugs, cured of infectious disease and weaned from the habit of murder.

When one thinks how seriously one has taken one's art (even when forced to turn to Paris for the first production of a ballet) one is seized with a deep disgust for all this humbug.

(1917)

ITALY

Niccolò Paganini

GOSSIP AND LEGEND

F. J. Fétis

THE FRENCH PUBLIC has given me so many proofs of kindness and appreciation that I must conclude that my performances have not been below my standard. To entertain any doubt on the subject is impossible in view of the pains artists have taken to reproduce my features in the portraits with which the walls of Paris have been plastered. And it is not merely portraits; these gentlemen have gone much further. Yesterday walking along the Boulevard des Italiens, I saw in the window of a print shop a lithograph representing 'Paganini in prison'. 'Good,' I said, 'here are honest men trying to make capital out of the slander that has followed me for fifteen years.' I was examining with amusement the careful drawing of details the artist's fancy had suggested, when I noticed a group of people standing by and, no doubt, comparing the lithograph with the original, noticing how much I had changed since the days of my alleged detention. I realized then how gullible people were taken in, repaying the artist for his labour. It came into my head to suggest that, as the world must live, I should myself provide artists with anecdotes similar to that which is the subject of that jest. I beg you therefore to publish this letter in your *Revue Musicale*.

These gentlemen have shown me as a prisoner. They don't know why I was sent to prison. They know as little about it as I know myself or the men who started the story. Now there are many tales to provide artists with attractive subjects. It has been said, for instance, that finding a rival in my mistress's apartment I jealously stabbed him in the back when he could not defend himself. Others have asserted that jealousy led me to attack my mistress herself. They do not agree as to the manner in which I killed her. Some say I used a dagger; others assert that I poisoned her and laughed at her sufferings. They do as they please and there is no reason why artists should not enjoy the same freedom.

I now speak of what actually happened to me in Padua fifteen years ago. I had given a concert which had been fairly successful, and the day after I went to the ordinary. Arriving late, I was not noticed. One of the guests was discussing my playing; his neighbour, while praising my performance, added that there was really nothing unusual in the playing of Paganini since he had practised assiduously for eight years in a prison cell where his violin comforted his captivity. 'He had been condemned to a long term of imprisonment for the cowardly murder of one of the speaker's friends who had been Paganini's rival in love.' All the guests were horrified at the enormity of my crime. I then joined the conversation asking the speaker to tell me where it had happened. All eyes turned towards me; they were face to face with the principal actor of that tragic tale. The man who had told the story became terribly embarrassed. It was no longer a friend of his who had been murdered . . . he had heard people say . . . he had thought . . . he did not believe they could have lied . . . it was possible that he had made a mistake. That, sir, is the way in which the reputation of an artist is besmirched by lazy people who cannot believe that one can work as hard at liberty as under lock and key.

A still more ridiculous story, current in Vienna, tested the credulity of the enthusiast. I had just played my variations entitled *The Witches*, and had been applauded. A gentleman, described as pale, sad, with glowing eye, asserted that he found nothing remarkable in my playing since he had clearly seen the devil guiding the bow across the strings. A resemblance between myself and the demon proved a common bond; he was dressed in red, had a tail and horns. You will understand that after so detailed a description it was impossible to doubt the truth of the story and many were persuaded that they had learned the secret of my *tours de force*.

These rumours worried me for some time. I tried to show how absurd it all was. I pointed out that since I was fourteen years old I had been giving concerts and constantly before the public; that I had been orchestral leader and court musician for sixteen years, and that if I had been condemned to prison for killing a rival it must have happened when I was seven years old. In Vienna I appealed to the ambassador of my country to bear witness to my respectability, which he did, and for a time the slander was silenced. But something always remains, and I am not surprised to hear the old story again here. What can I do? I am resigned. But before closing this letter, I will add one more anecdote which has been the origin of these tales.

A violinist whose name ended in 'i' plotted with two villains to murder a village priest who was said to be rich. At the last moment one of the assassins lost courage and denounced his accomplices. They were arrested and condemned to twenty years imprisonment. But General Menou, then Governor of Milan, set the violinist at liberty after he had served two years of his sentence. It is on this that my slanderers rely. The violinist's name ended in 'i'—hence it must have been Paganini; the victim, instead of a country priest, was either my mistress or my rival. I was imprisoned but, fortunately, my arms were free and I could use the bow. I thus discovered a new system. They insist in spite of all I can say. What can I do but accept the inevitable?

One hope remains, and it is that when I am dead my libellers will quit the game and those who make me pay so dearly for my success will leave my ashes in peace.

(Paris, 1831)

(*Even this last hope of the violinist was not fulfilled. For many years after his death the ecclesiastical authorities would not allow his body to be buried in consecrated ground, alleging that Paganini was an atheist and, no doubt, suspected of dealing in the Black art. Yet the last will of the alleged atheist ends with the words: 'I commend my soul to a merciful God.'*)

Gioachino Rossini

ON BELLINI

To F. Florimo

THE GENTLE FEATURES of Bellini reflected admirably the character of his music. Bellini had still much to learn; he died too young to learn all the secrets of his art. Had he lived two or three years longer he would have learnt all that he needed. He was gifted by nature, and determined to rise above his rivals. They, on the other hand, could never hope to acquire the qualities that were his. Bellinis are born, not made.

ON MOZART

THE GERMANS HAVE always excelled in harmony as we Italians excel in melody. But after the north gave birth to Mozart we Italians were beaten in our own field. This man rises above all, combining in himself the charm of Italian melody and the depth of German harmony. He roused my admiration when I was young; he caused me to despair when I reached maturity; he is now the comfort of my old age.

ON VERDI

To Duprez

VERDI HAS A melancholy nature; he is a serious character. From that nature springs a rich vein of music which I appreciate and value highly. But it is certain that such a man will never write a light opera, like *Linda* or a comic one, like *L'Elisir d'amore*.

ROSSINI ANECDOTES

ROSSINI WAS A great executant as well as a composer. His memory must have been phenomenal. Many instances are reported of his sitting at the piano to play from memory music from a wide repertoire.

When he first called on Cherubini in Paris he was denied admittance, the older composer sending a message to the effect that, as he was busy, he could see no one, were the caller Mozart himself. On a second attempt he was admitted and while waiting in the drawing room sat at the piano and sang from memory an aria from an already forgotten opera of Cherubini, *Giulio Sabino*. The old master heard and was charmed by the performance, which laid the foundations of a friendship that lasted till Cherubini's death.

Discussing with F. Hiller and others the many excellences of Haydn, while most musicians present were declaring their preference for *The Seasons* or *The Creation*, Rossini claimed that the cantata *Arianna* was at least as admirable and, sitting at the piano, proceeded to play and sing from memory many pages from all three works.

One evening, after playing movements from the works of Mozart and Haydn, Rossini turned to Panseron who was standing by and asked him: 'Why don't you give Haydn's *Arianna* at the Conservatoire? It is beautiful.' To prove it he began to play, then to sing, getting more and more interested, ending only after he had played by heart the whole work from the first to the last page.

MEETING WITH BEETHOVEN

CLIMBING THE STAIRS that led to the apartment of the great composer, I was deeply moved. When the door was opened I found myself in a room in a state of indescribable disorder. I remember that the roof above the bed was all cracks which let the rain pour in.

The portraits we have of Beethoven reproduce his features accurately enough. But no brush, no etcher's tool, could reproduce the sadness of his countenance or the deep-set eyes hidden under heavy eyebrows which gave the impression that they could wound with a glance. His voice was tender and mellow. When we came in he was correcting proofs. 'Rossini,' he said, 'the author of *The Barber of Seville*? I congratulate you. That is an excellent comic opera which I have read with great pleasure. It will be performed as long as Italian opera exists. Don't write anything else. If you were to try serious opera you would have to do violence to your nature.'

Carpani, who was with me, then interrupted: 'But Maestro,

Rossini has written serious operas as well. I sent you some scores a little while ago. You should read them.'

'I have seen them,' said Beethoven, 'but, believe me, serious opera is not for the Italians. They have not enough science to deal with real drama. Indeed, where could they acquire science in Italy? On the other hand, no one can surpass the Italians in light opera; their speech and their temperament are made for it. Look at Cimarosa. The comic scenes of his operas are infinitely superior to the rest. You may say the same of Pergolesi. You Italians think highly of religious music, and in his *Stabat Mater* the sentiment is very touching, but the form lacks variety and the effect is monotonous, while in *La Serva Padrona*. . . .'

I then expressed the admiration I felt for his genius and my gratitude for allowing me to tell him of it in person. He answered with a deep sigh: 'I am an unhappy man.'

He then asked me news of the Italian theatres and singers. He wanted to know if Mozart was being performed and if I was satisfied with the company singing in Vienna. He wished success to my *Zelmira* and accompanied us as far as the door saying once more: 'Don't forget to write many "Barbers".'

Coming away from that meeting I was moved to tears at the thought of the great man alone and in poverty. 'It's his own wish to live like that,' said Carpani. 'He is an ill-tempered misanthrope who cannot keep a single friend.'

The same evening, while I was remembering with pain my morning's visit, I was dining at Prince Metternich's. Beethoven's 'I am an unhappy man' was still ringing in my ears and I felt ashamed at being treated with such deference in that brilliant company. I had to say what I thought of a Viennese court and aristocracy that ignored the greatest musical genius of the time. The answer I got was a repetition of Carpani's words. I then remarked that Beethoven's deafness should have made him an object of compassion and that it was unfair to make his weaknesses an excuse for withholding the help he needed. I said that if the rich families of Vienna got together and opened a subscription it would be an easy matter to secure the capital necessary to place him above the fear of poverty. But no one listened to my suggestion.

MEETING WITH WAGNER

As SOON AS Wagner showed himself, Rossini welcomed him: 'Herr Wagner, our new Orpheus, do not be afraid to enter. I know that they try to make you hate me, attributing to me jests for which I am in no way responsible. Why should I behave so? I am neither Mozart nor Beethoven. I do not pretend to be a learned man, and I am very careful not to injure in any way the reputation of a musician who is trying to extend further the frontiers of our art. Malicious people who amuse themselves at our expense might at least give me credit for common sense. Moreover, I cannot disparage your work because I don't know it. It is for the stage and I never go to a theatre. I have only heard the march from *Tannhäuser* which I heard at Kissingen and liked very much. And now that there is no further cause of misunderstanding between us, tell me how you are getting on in Paris. I know that you are negotiating a production of *Tannhäuser*.'

Wagner, impressed by this opening of the conversation, began: 'Allow me to thank you for your words which show how noble your character is. In any case, even if I had believed you to be the author of the remarks attributed to you, I could not have resented it since my own writings have often been misunderstood. When one tries to explain a new and complicated system of ideas, even the best judges are apt to mistake their true purport. That is why I am anxious to prove through good performances that my ideas are practical.'

'Facts count more than words.'

'At present I am trying to secure a performance of *Tannhäuser*. Carvalho who has heard it was impressed and is willing to try; so far, however, nothing has been decided. Unfortunately the press has long been hostile and I am afraid Carvalho will be frightened. . . .'

'There has never been a composer who has not been a victim of plotters, beginning with Gluck. I myself. . . .' Here Rossini told of the hostility he met in Rome, in Vienna, in Paris and spoke of his wandering life.

'I am surprised how, travelling about as you did,' said

Wagner, 'you were yet able to write pages in *Otello* and *Mosè* which show not only facility but cerebral work.'

'I had a certain instinct,' said Rossini, 'and the little I knew I had learnt from German scores—*Creation, Figaro, Magic Flute,* which had been lent to me by an amateur of Bologna. At fifteen I hadn't the means to buy them. If I could have studied music in your country I might have written better stuff.'

'The "darkness scene" in *Mosè*, the conspiracy in *Tell* and, in another field, "Quando corpus morietur". . . .'

'You are quoting the high lights of my career. But what does it amount to in comparison with the work of a Mozart or a Haydn? I cannot say how deeply I admire the easy mastery of these composers, the certainty and naturalness of their touch. But all that must be learnt at school and, besides, one has to be a Mozart to use it effectively. As for Bach—another country-man of yours—his genius is astounding. If Beethoven is a prodigy of humanity, Bach is the miracle of Heaven. I have subscribed to the publication of all his works. See on the table yonder the last volume. I wish it were possible before dying to hear a satisfying performance of the *Passion*. But here, in France, it is hopeless to think about it. . . . Why don't you follow the example of Gluck, Spontini and Meyerbeer and write an opera to a French libretto?'

'As far as I am concerned that would be impossible. After *Tannhäuser* I wrote *Lohengrin* and *Tristan*. These three operas represent logical steps in the development of my conception of music drama. My style developed accordingly and I could not resume now the manner of *Tannhäuser*. If I were to give the Parisians something more advanced, something still more different from customary opera, I should meet with failure.'

'But what does your reform consist of?'

'My system has developed gradually. The germ lies in poetic rather than musical considerations. My first object in fact was literary. But when I came to consider musical means to clarify and amplify its purpose, I saw how the customary form of opera stood in the way and set limits to my ideas. Those arias, those duets cut to the same pattern, those ensemble pieces, like septets which interfere with the continuity of the drama, where the various characters casting aside all pretence come to the footlights to sing in harmony (and often—what harmony!) to perform a stereotyped piece. . . .'

'Do you know what we used to call those ensembles in Italy? "Rows of beans". I felt it to be ridiculous, but unless I did it there was the risk of being hissed.'

'As to the orchestra, what can I say of the usual colourless accompaniments which repeat the same formula over and over again without taking into account the characters and the dramatic situation? In short, all that "concert room" music, extraneous to the action, is only a piece of conventionalism, contrary to common sense and incompatible with an art that can be described as noble.'

'Arias! Bravura pieces! They were my curse! To have to please at the same time the prima donna, the tenor, the bass. Some of them sang a few bars of their aria and then refused to go on because somebody else had a longer one or one with more trills and roulades.

'I quite see that your purpose is the rational, regular and rapid development of the action. But how can you secure the independence demanded by the literary conception when it is yoked to a musical form that is conventional? I am quoting your own words. If we are to be strictly logical it follows that there can be no singing where there is dialogue. An angry man, a conspirator, a jealous man does not sing. You may make an exception for lovers who may, presumably, coo. But does one face death singing? Opera, we must conclude, is conventional through and through. Even orchestration is a convention. The orchestra cannot differentiate between storm, conflagration, revolt. . . .'

'A large measure of conventionality is inevitable; otherwise we should have to put aside opera and even comic opera. But it is beyond question that conventionality raised to an art must be understood as avoiding all the excess that turns it into something ridiculous and absurd. It is against excess that I protest. Those who say anything else misrepresent my thought. They say I am arrogant . . . that I disparage Mozart. . . .'

'That would be sacrilege. He is the angel of music.'

'They say I depreciate all the music of the past except Gluck's and Weber's; they deliberately misrepresent all that

I have written. I do not question the beauty of many pages which are justly famous. I protest only against that music which is made to play the part of the slave, and is foreign to the action and whose only purpose is to tickle the ear.

'According to my ideas, opera in its complexity is destined to form an organism which combines harmoniously its component arts—poetry, music, design. You must see that it is a lowering of the composer's art to look upon him as the embroiderer of a libretto suggested by the impresario and cut up in so many arias, duets, concerted pieces . . . "pieces" being the right word, implying breakages, bits. I do not deny that there are passages where a composer, inspired by a moving situation, has put the stamp of immortality, but other pages of the same score will seem even more futile owing to the vicious system I condemn.

'We shall never have true music drama until music and text form a whole, a double conception unified by the same impulse.'

'If I understand you aright, in order to achieve your ideal it will be necessary for the composer to write also his libretto—a difficulty which seems to be almost insurmountable.'

'But why? There is nothing to prevent the composer from studying literature as well as counterpoint, from reading history or searching among legends. If he does so he will grow fonder of the subject, poetic or tragic, that best suits his temperament. If he should lack the skill or the experience to construct a dramatic plot, he will still be able to ask an experienced dramatist to collaborate. Not a few dramatic composers have possessed literary and poetic instincts which enabled them to change and alter the text or the order of the scenes and improve on the work of the librettist.

'To go further, did you follow slavishly the indications of your librettist in the conspiracy scene of *William Tell*? I do not believe it. Anyone who looks closely will find many passages in the declamation and in the disposition of the words which bear the stamp of, if I may say so, "musicality", of a spontaneous inspiration which I can only attribute to your own intervention. A librettist, however clever, cannot, especially in ensemble pieces, grasp the design the composer has before him when setting on paper the picture he has in mind.'

'You are right. That scene was modified and not without some trouble, according to my wishes. I wrote *Tell* in the villa of my friend Aguada where I used to pass the summer months. I had there my two librettists—Marrast and Crémieux who helped me to alter the text so as to conform to my notions of the conspiracy.'

'Your confession confirms all that I have said. You have but to go a step further and conclude that my ideas are neither contradictory nor impracticable. A natural, if, perhaps, slow evolution will lead not to that "music of the future" which my opponents say I mean to create all alone, but to the future music drama which will give composers, singers and public a new starting point.'

'It will be a radical change. Do you think that singers who have been used to parade their talents and their virtuosity will accept the declamatory melody or that a public, accustomed to the ways of the past, will tolerate innovations contrary to their habits? I very much doubt it.'

'Of course, as far as the singers are concerned, it will be necessary to educate them. As for the public—does the public create the master composer, or is it the composer who creates his public? I see in you yet another proof of what I am saying: was it not your own personal way of composing that caused every Italian who preceded you to be forgotten? What won for you unexampled popularity and, when you passed the frontiers of Italy, caused your influence to be felt everywhere?

'As for the singers, they will have to accept a situation that must finally redound to their credit. When they fail to find in the new lyric drama the elements of easy success through lung-power or sheer beauty of voice, they will see that art demands from them a nobler task. Forced to think of their part, they will grasp the aesthetic and philosophical aim of opera; they will live in an atmosphere where, as a part of a whole, nothing is of secondary importance. Freed from the ephemeral lure of virtuosity, freed from the torment of having to adapt their voices to absurd words arranged in banal rhymes, they will add to their fame by representing characters with thorough understanding of the *raison d'être* of the drama; they will study the ideas, the customs, the characters of the times in which the action takes place, combining irreproachable pronunciation to a declamation that will be true and exact.'

'From the artistic point of view, from the point of view of pure art, your views are undoubtedly wide and seductive; from the standpoint of musical art they will lead fatally to the end of melody. How can one reconcile declamation true in every syllable with melodic form whose outline is dictated by the fixed design of rhythm and by the symmetrical concordance of all the parts which go to the making of it?'

'Certainly the system, rigorously applied, would be intolerable. But, if you will allow me to say so, I do not repudiate melody. I want it; but completely free. Is not melody the expression of every musical organism? Without melody there can be nothing. But let us understand one another. I want a different type from melody bound by conventional ideas, tied to monotonous rhythms, harmonic progressions that can be foreseen, to obligatory cadences. I want melody free and independent, melody which in its characteristic lines will describe every character not only in such a way that it will be impossible to mistake the one from the other but will differentiate also every episode of the drama . . . melody clear in form blending with the poetic sense of the text, but able also, when necessary, to grow in accordance with the musical effect the composer has in mind. You yourself have written such a melody in the prayer of William Tell, ''Sois immobile'', where the unfettered voice gives to every word its true accent and, sustained by the anxious notes of the cellos, touches the greatest lyrical heights of expression.'

'I have then written music of the future without knowing it?'

'You have written some of the best music of all times.'

'I must tell you that the greatest love of my life has been for my parents and that in that I found the right note for the scene of the apple. One more question, Herr Wagner. How does your system fit in with the combining of two or more voices of the choir?'

'It would indeed be logical for musical dialogue to be modelled on spoken dialogue, every actor speaking in turn. But it must be admitted that two people may at a given moment feel the same emotion and consequently join their voices to express the same thought. Similarly when two or more people are on the stage at the same time and when there is a conflict of emotions, they will be able to express themselves at the same time though individually the music will give each of them a true determining character.

'You will understand how much the composer will gain by being able to apply to every member of the cast, to every incident of his drama, a melodic formula that, while maintaining its original character, can yet be adapted to fit new developments. In consequence, those ensemble pieces where every actor appears in his own individuality but where all combine polyphonically will no longer be the absurd "pieces" in which everyone—no matter what his feeling or his temperament—has to join in a sort of apotheosis set to patriarchal harmonies which make us think of *on ne saurait être mieux q'au sein de sa famille*. As for the choir, it is a psychological fact that a mass of people will respond with greater energy to such passions as fear, anger, pity, and it is hence quite reasonable to allow the mass to express its emotion in the language of sound without, therefore, being nonsensical. In fact the intervention of the choir when the dramatic situation permits can be a great force and a precious means of theatrical effects. Let me quote the chorus "Let us fly" in *Idomeneo* and your own fine setting for the "Chorus of Darkness" in *Mosè*.'

'My own? Did I not say that I had a marvellous instinct for the music of the future? If I were not so old I would begin again and then . . . *gare à l'ancien régime!*'

'Ah, Maestro. You gave up composing at thirty-seven after *William Tell*—that was a crime! You cannot know what might have come from that mind of yours. You might have made a new start. . . .'

'You see . . . I had no children; if I had had a family, I would certainly have continued to work. But quite frankly, after having laboured for fifteen years, and having written forty operas—they say I was slothful!—I felt the need for rest and I went to live quietly in Bologna.

'Besides, the conditions of the Italian theatres, bad when I began, got worse. The art of singing was ruined; it was bound to happen. . . . These are the reasons why I thought best to say no more. I have said no more and now the comedy is over.

'Dear Meister Wagner, I cannot thank you sufficiently for your visit and, above all, for the very clear and interesting account of your system. I am too old to look to new horizons (at my age one does not think of composing but of de-composing), but it is certain that no matter what your opponents may say your ideas will give much food for thought to our young men. Music, because of its essential idealism, is of all the arts the one which must evolve and there is no end to evolution. Who could have guessed that after Mozart there would be a Beethoven or a Weber after Gluck? Everyone must go ahead and forget that ancient traveller, Hercules, who having reached a headland placed his columns to mark the limit and turned back. Let us hope our art will never find such columns on its path. As for myself I have been of my time. Now it is for others to carry on—you particularly. You are full of vigour; you can do new things and succeed; your ideas are masterly. I do wish you success with all my heart.'

(*All these Rossini passages are taken from the book on Rossini, by Radiciotti.*)

Giuseppe Verdi

HOW 'MACBETH' SHOULD BE PERFORMED

I KNOW THAT YOU are getting together a company for *Macbeth* and as this opera interests me more than any other work of mine you will allow me to say something about it. The part of Lady Macbeth has been given to Mme Tadolini and I am surprised that she should have accepted it. You know how highly I think of her abilities—she knows it herself; my objections concern her interests as well as mine. Mme Tadolini possesses qualities that are too great for that part. This may seem nonsense, but she looks well and gentle and I should like Lady Macbeth to look ugly and wicked. Mme Tadolini is a perfect singer and I should like Lady Macbeth not to sing at all. She has a marvellous voice, pure, clear, powerful, where I want a hard, dark, sombre voice. Her voice is that of an angel; Lady Macbeth's should be diabolic.

Please tell this to the impresario, to Mercadante and to Mme Tadolini herself, and do what you think best. Note that there are two chief situations in the opera—the duet between Lady Macbeth and her husband, and the sleep-walking scene. If these fail to make the right effect the whole opera is doomed. These pieces are *not* to be sung: they must be acted, declaimed in a dull, veiled voice. Unless this is done the right effect can never be achieved. The orchestra must be muted and the stage quite dark. In the third act the kings must appear through a hole in the canvas—not puppets but real men of flesh and bone who walk over ground that rises and falls (I saw it in London) so that the spectator will see them coming up and descending. The stage must be absolutely dark except where the apparitions are seen. For your theatre it may be necessary to reinforce the music under the stage but, mind, neither trumpets nor trombones. The sound must be distant and dumb, hence bass clarinets, bassoons, double bassoons and nothing more.

(1848)

'RIGOLETTO' AND THE AUSTRIAN CENSOR

I HAVE HAD little time to read the new libretto, but I have read enough to convince me that the new version has no character, interest or life. If it was thought necessary to alter the name of the characters they should have altered also the place or transferred the action to another period—say the times of Louis XI when France was not a united nation and we could have had a Duke of Burgundy or Normandy, but in any case, a tyrant. The curse of the old nobleman, so terrible in the original, becomes ridiculous in the new version, since there is no longer a purpose. Without the curse, what can be the dramatic interest? The duke is a nobody; he must be shown as a licentious youth, since otherwise Triboletto's[1] fear is unjustified and the whole drama becomes futile. I do not know why they will not allow the body of Gilda to be given to Triboletto in a sack. How can the sack interest the police? Will they allow me to ask whether they know more about my opera than I know myself? Finally they will not allow Triboletto to be an ugly hunchback—why not? I do not know whether the character will be effective, but do *they* pretend to know it? I find this misshapen and ridiculous being, yet full of passionate affection, extremely attractive. These are the very things which guided me in the choice of subject. If these original traits of the character have to go I can no longer write the music. If I am told that my music will fit the new libretto I answer that my notes, pleasing or displeasing, are always meant to fit character. Out of an original and powerful drama they have made a cold, commonplace affair. I can only repeat that as a conscientious artist I cannot write music for such a libretto.

(1850)

THE PARIS OPERA

IT IS NOT the labours of writing, nor the taste of the Parisian public, that prevent me from writing (for Paris) but the certainty that an opera can never be produced there as I want it. It seems very singular to me that the author should be always opposed in his ideas and his directions ignored. In your

---

[1] *Rigoletto was so named originally.*

theatres there are too many servants; everyone looks upon a work of art from his own point of view or, what is worse, from the point of view of his system, without considering the talent and character of the author. Everybody wants to give his opinion, to express his doubts, and the poor composer living in that atmosphere begins to question his own judgement, to make alterations, to correct or, rather, to spoil his work. That is the way to make up a mosaic, very beautiful if you like, but still mosaic. It will be said that the Paris Opéra presents many masterpieces in this fashion. It may be; but it would be better still if no one were allowed to add his bit and make adjustments as he thinks fit. No one will deny Rossini's genius. But in spite of his genius one perceives in *William Tell* the fatal influence of the atmosphere of Paris. Perhaps less frequently than with other composers, *William Tell* has the little more and the little less which betray a touch less sure in the composer of the *Barber*. With this I do not intend to condemn all you do; I mean to say only this—that for me it is an impossibility to pass the Caudine Forks represented by your theatres. I can only write when I am not thwarted by foreign influence and think no more of Paris than of the moon. Not in any other circumstances can I hope to succeed. The singers must sing, not as they want to do, but as I want them to sing; the masses, which are very capable, must be also willing. In other words, everything must be as I want it; one will alone must dictate to all—my will. All this may sound rather tyrannical to you and perhaps it is; but if the opera is one whole, the dominating idea is also one and everything must point in that direction. You will say perhaps that it can't be done. In Italy it can be done and I invariably do it. In France, I cannot. If I go with a new opera to an Italian theatre, no one ventures to give an opinion or ask a question before understanding my intentions. They respect the work and its author and it is left for the public to approve or disapprove. At the Opéra instead, after four chords one hears: 'That's no good; that's commonplace . . . in bad taste . . . it will never do for Paris.' What on earth does it mean? For Paris? Why, a work of art is for the whole universe.

The end of it is that I am no composer for Paris. I do not

know whether I have talent but I do know that my ideas as regards art are very different from yours. I believe in inspiration; you believe in workmanship. Your ways lead to discussion; I want enthusiasm, failing which one can neither feel nor judge. I want art in all her manifestations and not the amusement, the artifice, the system which you prefer. Am I right? Am I wrong?

I am within my rights in telling you that your ideas are not mine and that my backbone is not supple enough for me to act contrary to opinions that are deeply rooted, and of long standing. I should be most unhappy if I were to write for you an opera that would be shelved after a dozen performances. If I were twenty years younger I would say: let us wait and see whether things will change. But time passes very quickly and I see no way out of the difficulty unless something at present unimaginable were to happen.

(1869)

TRAINING YOUNG MUSICIANS

. . . I WILL GIVE you a general idea of what I think about possible reforms in the teaching of music in schools and colleges. I will say nothing of the instrumental side, which has always been satisfactory. Nothing to reform there. I will talk instead of composers and singers. I would suggest long and severe study of every branch of counterpoint for the composer; the study of old music, sacred and secular; complete disregard of modern work. Many will think it odd, but, while I see so many operas today cut to a pattern—much as a bad tailor will cut cloth—my opinion is unalterable. I know that somebody will suggest that there are modern works as good as the old. What does it matter? When the student has gone through a severe course of study, when he has acquired a style of his own, when he can feel his own strength, let him then study modern opera, and there will be no danger of his becoming a mere imitator. They will ask me: Who will teach him orchestration, who will instruct him in ideal composition? I answer: His head and his heart—presuming that he has a heart.

For the singer I would suggest vast knowledge of music; exercises on voice production; long study of solfeggio as in the old days; exercises for the voice and words pronounced perfectly. Then, instead of a teacher of singing to instruct him in affectations, I should like the young student, well grounded in music and voice production, to sing guided entirely by his own instinct. It would no longer be a student who sang, but a man inspired. The artist would have an individuality; he would be himself or, rather, the character he represented on the stage. It is hardly necessary to add that the study of literature must go hand-in-hand with the study of music.

(1871)

THE IDEAL SCHOOL OF MUSIC

IF ANYTHING COULD flatter my self-esteem it would be the invitation you send me to fill the post of Director of your Conservatoire. It grieves me not to be able to give you the answer I should like to give. My duties, my habits, my love of independence prevent me from accepting new and serious duties. You will say: what about art? I have done what I could for music and if I can do more I must be free to do it. But for this I should have been proud to occupy a position that has been filled by Alessandro Scarlatti, by Durante and Leo. It would have been my pride to lead young musicians through the study of those early fathers. I would have planted one foot in the past and one in the future (I am not afraid of the music of the future) and I would have said: practise the art of fugue constantly, tenaciously, till you are full of it, till the hand is strong enough to bend the note and force it to do your will. You will thus learn to write well, to space your parts accurately and to modulate without affectations. Pay attention to Palestrina and to a few of his contemporaries. Then go on to Marcello and pay special attention to his recitatives. Attend a few performances of modern operas without allowing yourself to be overcome by harmonic combinations, orchestral devices or that chord of the diminished seventh which is the refuge and the rock on which we who cannot write a dozen bars without half a dozen such chords come to grief.

After these studies and after sound literary culture has been acquired, I would say to the young people: now put your hand on your heart and you will be composers, or at least you will not be one of a crowd of imitators, of the sick who, today, search and never find. In the study of singing I would also expect the student to learn the old masters together with modern declamation. In order to carry out such a programme, the twelve months of the year could hardly suffice. How can I undertake it, having house and duties elsewhere? I hope you will find somebody who is learned and severe. Licence and errors of counterpoint can be admitted (and are at times even beautiful) in the theatre—never in the schools.   (1871)

HIS MEMOIRS

NEVER AND NEVER will I write my memoirs. It is enough for the world of music to have had to put up with my notes for so long. I will never condemn it to read my prose.   (1895)

ON GLUCK AND HANDEL, ROSSINI AND BELLINI

I HAVE READ your book with great attention. I will only say something about the musical opinions you express. I applaud with you the three giants—Palestrina, Bach, Beethoven, and when I consider the melodic and harmonic meagreness of his times, Palestrina seems miraculous.

Everybody will agree with you about Gluck but, in my opinion, in spite of his dramatic genius, he was not greater than the best men of his day and, as a musician, inferior to Handel. . . . You say much about Rossini and Bellini that may be true enough. I confess that, to my thinking, the *Barber of Seville* for verve, declamation, and abundance of musical ideas is the finest of all comic operas. Like yourself I admire *Tell*, but how many excellent, nay sublime, things are found also in other operas of his! Bellini's harmony and orchestration are poor . . . but he is rich in melody which has a melancholy character all its own. Even in the less known operas, like *Straniera, Pirata*, there are long, long melodies such as no one wrote before him. And what power and truth in his declamation as, for instance, in the duet between Pollione and Norma! There is noble thought in the Introduction of *Norma*, badly scored, but heavenly.

I do not intend to pass sentence. Heaven forbid that I should. I am only giving you my impressions.   (1898)

MODERN TENDENCIES

I CANNOT TELL what the outcome of the present movements
is likely to be. One man wants to be a melodist like Bellini;
another wants to specialize in harmony like Meyerbeer. I want
neither the one nor the other. I should like the young composer
to resist any desire to be melodist, harmonist, realist, idealist or
futurist—may the devil take all these pedantries. Melody and
harmony are the means the artist has at hand to write music.
If a day should come when there will be no more talk of
melody, of harmony, of schools, of past and future, then the
kingdom of art will perhaps begin. Another mischief of the
present time is that these young men are afraid. No one lets
himself go; when they write they are afraid of public opinion;
they want to court the critics. You tell me that my success is
due to the blending of two schools. No such thought has ever
entered my head.

(1875)

ON BERLIOZ

BERLIOZ, POOR FELLOW, was ill, angry with everybody,
bitter and malicious. A great and keen intelligence; he had a
feeling for instrumentation and in many orchestral effects he
comes before Wagner. The Wagnerians will not have it, but
it is so. He lacked balance; he never had that peace of mind,
that equilibrium, which results in a complete work of art. Even
when he wrote something fine there was exaggeration.

His present success in Paris is well deserved and an act of
justice. But reaction plays a great part. He was badly treated
when he was alive; now that he is dead they cry 'Hosanna'.

(1882)

ANSWERING BÜLOW

*(In 1874 Bülow published a bitter attack on Verdi. Eight years
later, profoundly moved by a performance of Otello, he wrote to Verdi
apologizing for his early sin. This is Verdi's answer:)*

THERE IS NOT a shadow of 'sin' and it is out of the question
to speak of repentance and absolution. If your opinion was
different in those days, you were entitled to express it and
I should be the last to complain. Moreover . . . you may have

been quite right then. However this may be, the letter, which was unexpected, written by a musician of your worth and importance in the artistic world, has given me great pleasure. It is not a case of personal vanity but of realizing that true artists are free from the prejudices of schools, nationality and time. It is right that the artists of north and south should differ in their tendencies and be true to the character of their nation, as Wagner well said.

You, children of Bach, are happy men. We, heirs of Palestrina, had once a school that was great and our own. Now it is a hybrid, and threatened with complete collapse. What would happen if we were to start again from the beginning?

(1892)

PRODUCTION OF 'FALSTAFF'

WE ARE WASTING time in writing letters and telegrams. You —all of you—are on the wrong tack. I alone am steering the right course and I cannot allow anyone to interfere with my rights. I am not going to produce *Falstaff* as others wish. There must be:

No exorbitant fees for the artists.

No payment for rehearsals.

No obligation to give *Falstaff* where others wish.

As for the first point, I do not wish the impresario to lose money even if the opera is a success. As for the rehearsals, there must be no new departure. Paid rehearsals for *Falstaff* would establish a disastrous precedent.

Now my last point. Supposing that after the Scala production I should decide to make a change here and there? It would be altogether unthinkable for one of the performers to come to me saying 'I cannot wait for your alterations as I am engaged to sing the opera in Madrid, London etc.' It would be too humiliating! I said you are on the wrong tack and so, too, is Maurel.[1] Does he not see that if the libretto is good and the music tolerable, by performing the title role excellently he

---

[1] *Maurel wanted the sole right to sing Falstaff for some time and Mme Maurel had tried to secure a clause to this effect in her husband's contract.*

will be sure of success without pretending to rights that cannot help him but must hurt others? Mme Maurel, who is very intelligent, may feel disappointed today but in a month's time she will say 'Le maître avait raison'.

Let us put our cards on the table. I demand to be master in my own house without interference from other people. If I have to choose between your acceptance of these conditions and burning *Falstaff*, I shall not hesitate to throw Falstaff and his great belly on the fire myself.

(1892)

To Ricordi

There are a few mistakes in the score and I beg you to mark them so that they can be corrected. The printed libretto looks better than ever, but at page twenty a line is missing. On page twenty-one a word has been cancelled, probably because I omitted to write it. Tell Boito about it. You ask me about entrances and exits. Nothing simpler. The scene painter will have to draw a picture such as I had in mind when I was writing the music. Nothing more than a large garden with avenues, plenty of shrubs and bushes so that the characters can hide, appear and disappear as the action demands. . . .

I am told that Hohenstein means to put the screen close to the wings, saying that it is natural for a screen to be resting against the wall. Nothing of the kind. Here the screen is part of what I might call the action and must be used according to the requirements of the action, especially as Alice says: 'more to this side; nearer to that side'. The scene at the end of Act II should be empty so that all the principal groups—by the screen, by the window and by the basket—can be seen easily.

Let me say again that I do not want to insist on my own notions—on the contrary I am anxious that others should find better things . . . but, on the other hand, I shall not give my approval unless they can convince me that they are right.

(1892)

Arrigo Boito

THE THIRD ACT OF 'FALSTAFF'

To G. Verdi

NO DOUBT ABOUT IT—the third act is rather chilly; a
pity. Unfortunately that is the law of the comic
theatre—in tragedy it is the opposite that happens.
Getting closer to the final catastrophe (either foreseen as in
Othello or unforeseen as in *Hamlet*), the interest grows enormously as the end is terrible. Hence the finest acts of tragedies
are the most beautiful. In comedy all that happens is that the
knot will be untied and the interest wanes as the end is happy.
You have recently read Goldoni and you must remember how
in his last scenes, in spite of the marvels of the dialogue and of
the character-drawing, the action loses impetus and the interest
grows cold. In spite of his immense powers, Shakespeare in
The Merry Wives of Windsor has not been able to escape the
common law. It is so with Molière, with Beaumarchais and
Rossini. The last scene of the *Barber* always seems to me less
admirable than the rest. You will correct me if I am in error.
In comedy, a point is reached when the audience says 'It is
over'; but on the stage all is not over yet.

It is impossible to untie a knot without slowing down the
pace and when that happens the end becomes a foregone
conclusion: the interest is gone before the knot is unravelled.
The knot is untied in comedy; it is broken or cut in tragedy.
Hence the third act of *Falstaff* is rather cold. But as the law is
common to all comedy the mischief is not as serious as it
appears to be. But we must do what we can to warm things
up, to speed action and knit it more closely together. We must
make the most of the last scene which has certain advantages.
The unexpected fantastic atmosphere may help—it is a light
and new touch. We have, moreover, three good comic
moments: (1) Falstaff, disguised as Herne the Hunter and
wearing horns; (2) the questioning of Falstaff by Bardolph and
Pistol who will beat him and force him to confess a sin with
each blow; (3) the marriage ceremony. The little duet of Anne

Page and Fenton will be transferred to the first part of the act as evening begins to fall. This love duet must peep in and out often—in every scene in which they have a part they will kiss cunningly, boldly, without being caught, with short, fresh, quick dialogue from the beginning to the end of the play. It will be a merry love-making, always interrupted and always starting again. This point seems to me good—we must not lose sight of it. Certainly the aria of Fenton has been added to give the tenor his chance, which is not desirable—shall we cut it out?

(1889)

Before answering your questions I have been thinking much and now my mind is quite clear. The fact is that when I speak, write or think of you no notion of your age ever occurs to me. The fault is yours. I know that *Otello* is two years old and is now being performed by Shakespeare's own countrymen. But there is one consideration more important than your age and it is this: after *Otello* it has been said that it would be impossible to end your career better. This is a truth which implies great and rare praise. This is the only serious considera-tion—serious for your contemporaries, but not for history, which judges men according to their essential worth. It is a rare thing to crown the work of a life-time with a great victory such as *Otello*. All the other arguments—strength, age, labour—have no weight whatever, and are mere obstacles to new enterprise. As far as I am concerned, I will assure you that if I were to undertake the libretto of *Falstaff* I should hand it to you on the date agreed upon. Of this I am certain.

Now for your doubts. I do not believe that the writing of a comic opera would prove too heavy a task. Tragedy causes real suffering in its author, as the brain feels the suggestion of pain which irritates the nerves. The jest and the smile of comedy exhilarate mind and body. 'A smile adds one thread to the web of life.' I do not know whether I am quoting Foscolo correctly, but I do know this to be true. You have a great desire to work; this is the real proof of your health and your powers. Ave Marias are not enough—you need much more.

All your life you have wanted a good subject for a comic opera; it shows that the vein of art at once refined and gay is in your temperament; instinct is a good councillor. There is only one better way of concluding a career than with *Otello*—with the victory of *Falstaff*. After having sounded every note of human sorrow to end with a magnificent outburst of merriment —that would indeed be astounding!

I beg you hence, dear Maestro, to think again about the sketch I sent you. If it has the germ of a masterpiece, the miracle is accomplished. Meanwhile we must keep it secret. I have spoken to no one. If we work in secret we work in peace. I await your decision which, as usual, will be free and final. I must not influence you in any way. Your decision will be wise, be it 'yea' or 'nay'.

(1889)

To Bellaigue

While in Genoa I talked with Verdi about your subject (old Italian composers). Verdi adores Palestrina and of all the masterpieces of the 'Principe della Musica', he has a special admiration for the Madrigali, the Improperia, one Stabat (the one beginning with open fifths) and, of course, for the Mass of Pope Marcello. Verdi cherishes Pergolesi's *Stabat Mater, Salve Regina, La Serva Padrona,* and *Olimpiade.* Of Marcello he likes the *Psalms* only—and he is right. It is in the *Psalms* that Marcello reveals his powerful originality; there is nothing as good in the sonatas for viola da gamba or in the cantatas. I have read your 'Psychology of Music'. It is not criticism but art grafted on to art. But I have a bone to pick with you. You don't share my feeling for the god I adore—Bach. You revere him— you do not love him.

(1893)

ON CANTATAS

To G. Negri

CANTATAS ARE THE despair of poets, composers and audience. These hybrid compositions are cold, conventional, rhetorical, and their sole purpose is to fill an hour with boredom.

The first difficulty is in finding a theme and a lyrical form that is not commonplace. This is the task of the poet—infinitely more difficult and unsatisfactory than the composer's. In the poem of a cantata the seed of boredom exists; in the music it is in full flower.

VERDI'S CHRISTMAS EVE

To Bellaigue

THIS IS THE day of the year he loved best. Christmas Eve
recalled for him the enchantments of childhood and a faith
which is heavenly when it believes in the miraculous. Like the
rest of us he had lost that faith in early years, but all his life
he seemed to regret it. He has set an example of Christian
faith in the moving beauty of his religious works as in the
observance of ceremonies (you cannot have forgotten his noble
head bowed in prayer in the Chapel of St Agata), in his homage
to Manzoni, in the directions about the funeral found in his
testament: 'one candle, one priest, one cross'. To those who
were about him, labourers in the field, men stricken by sorrow,
he offered himself humbly, without ostentation, seriously to
aid their conscience. . . . In the ideal sense—moral and social
—he was a great Christian. But let us beware of thinking of
him as a Catholic in the political and theological sense of the
word for nothing could be further from the truth.

(1912)

Giacomo Puccini

A STUDENT IN MILAN

I HAVE NO NEWS of the examination as the Council of the Conservatorio must first have a meeting, but I have good hopes. Tell my dear teacher Angeloni that the papers were quite easy. . . . I often visit Catalani who is most kind. In the evening when I have enough cash I go to the café, but as a glass of punch costs forty centimes I go there very seldom. I keep early hours, as walking up and down the gallery is a wearisome business. I have a nice little room with a magnificent table in polished walnut. I am quite comfortable. The cuisine is not all that could be wished but I do not go hungry. I fill myself with minestrone, thin broth and similar food so that my belly is satisfied. Today the weather has been bad. I have heard *Stella del Nord* and *Fra Diavolo* but am not much out of pocket. A few centimes secured entrance to the dove-cot (upper gallery) and the ticket for *Fra Diavolo* was a present. . . .

Yesterday I had my second lesson from Bazzini—all is well. Next Friday I start musical aesthetic. I have made for myself a timetable. I get up at 8.30 and if I don't have to attend classes I practise piano for a bit. I am not making a serious job of it but I must play a little better. I am going to buy one of those methods to teach oneself. At 10.30 I have breakfast and then I go for a stroll. At one o'clock I start work for Bazzini which keeps me till 3.0; from 3.0 to 5.0 more piano practice and reading of classical music. I should like to join a lending library but I haven't enough money. At 5.0 I have my dinner—a minestrone (three platefuls), something to follow, a piece of cheese and a little wine. After that a cigar and a walk in the gallery and I am home again by 9.30. As there must be no music at night I study counterpoint; then to bed to read seven or eight pages of some novel. This is my life.

I should like to ask for one thing but I am afraid to say it because I know that you have little money to spare. Yet it is a small matter. I should like a little oil, new oil for my beans. They gave me beans here once but their oil was so bad that

I could not eat them. A very little will do. I promised the people here to taste it and it would be most kind of you, if you could, to send me a can costing 4 lire.

The other night I went to hear Gounod's *Redemption,* which bored me. Yesterday I heard an opera of Catalani. People here are not enthusiastic about it, but it is artistically a fine work and if they give another performance I shall not miss it. A seat at La Scala costs fifty lire—the Milanese must be very rich.

A MAN OF THE THEATRE

To his librettist G. Adami

I DO NOT SAY that the second act (of *La Rondine*) is poor, thin and untheatrical, but I do say that it is not striking, polished and as theatrical as it should be. Reading an account of Labiche's *Le chapeau de paile* caused me much worry. Why? Because in our libretto there is nothing like the verve, the variety, the plot that is necessary to interest and amuse the public. The public wants to be amused, my dear Adami. Unless you do this, a fiasco is certain, and we don't want that. The first act is good and the third still better, but the second will not do. Let us scrap everything and find something more alive, more colourful, the best we can discover. I don't know what to suggest on the spur of the moment just now while I feel angry. But the sense that torments me all the time I work tells me that our affair will not do. I am not enjoying work, I do not laugh, I am not interested. In this rotten world something very different is needed. We want a second act—let us set about writing it while we are in time. Let us keep the main lines but let us also find episodes that are new and attractive.

(1914)

Do you have the libretto of *Il Tabarro*? I hope you do. Now on page twenty-three during the duet between Giorgetta and Michele I find that I must keep the baritone languidly at it while Giorgetta says nothing and goes on saying nothing. Thus the duet is no duet at all and followed by the baritone's monologue about the river—much too much stuff for the baritone. *Ergo* I ask you to arrange it so that the duet will be a real duet between Michele and Giorgetta. I realize that it will not be easy to find words for her but it is necessary if we are to avoid monotony which would jeopardize the success of the opera.

(1916)

I should have to write much to give you all the reasons which induced me to give up the thought of setting to music 'Conchita'. I was not afraid to offend the prudishness of the Anglo-Saxons in Europe and America, nor was I afraid of repeating the experience of *Salome* in New York. My only fear was that the musical atmosphere might recall *Carmen*—a point that must cause any composer to think hard. In the many long hours when I thought of it I have criticized the libretto from the point of view of the spectator and from that of the composer. Through the many episodes which have only one purpose—to describe how Conchita is attracted to Matteo, and then repulses him—there is nothing but a succession of scenes *à deux*—five duets or rather six. Then the final scene seems to me unrealizable in the theatre unless we present the sort of action that might have appalled even Pietro Aretino. Yet this finale is indispensable to the action. Nothing less will do. I do not deny that Louys's work is attractive. But in order to make an opera of it, it would have been necessary either to get away from the story altogether or else give it another turn in order to make clear to the public what is happening.

(1907)

Ferruccio Busoni

ON SARASATE

SARASATE IS A creature without brain, and without temperament. But he has seen a great deal of the world and has been on intimate terms with great artists. That gives him a certain historical varnish. He told us that once at Leipzig he was sitting with Rubinstein in the hotel lounge playing whist while at the Gewandhaus a new symphony was being performed—I forget the name of the composer—which Rubinstein did not want to hear. At about 10.0 p.m. people were returning from the concert. 'How was the new symphony?' Rubinstein asked the very first guest. 'O, very musical,' the man replied. 'C'est jugé,' Rubinstein cried out, and thumping the table with his fist said: 'Quand les allemands disent "musical", c'est sûr que c'est embêtant.'

(1906)

PLAYING AND COMPOSING

I HAVE GOT to force myself to practise the piano; one can't do without it. It's like a monster with many heads. They keep growing no matter how many you chop off. Composing is a different thing. It's like taking a path which is now beautiful, now full of difficulties, where distances grow longer and longer and one passes many stops, while the end remains unknown and unattainable.

(1907)

VIENNA TODAY

VIENNA! WHAT A CITY! But for the fact that Beethoven composed good music here, I shouldn't think it were possible to write anything of worth in this city. To judge by the succession: Beethoven, Brahms, Hugo Wolf—Vienna's inspiring atmosphere has gone or vanished to a large extent (history, nature, and statistics prove such phenomena). Wolf, a spiritual cripple (*vulgo*: idiot) was the last to benefit from the vanishing artistic atmosphere of which nothing was left for

241

later years. 'Finished', say the Viennese, his mourning admirers. In Berlin I could enjoy being idle, but in Vienna it
would be completely futile.

(1908)

SERIOUS COMEDY

YOUR REMARK THAT I am of too serious a cast of mind to
write a comic opera made me think. It seemed like criticism,
but knowing that you did not intend it as such I must account
for it by our different views of what constitutes seriousness.

I see much more seriousness in humour than in tragic make-
beliefs. To me *The Mastersingers* is more serious than *Cavalleria*,
and *Figaro* more serious than *The Prophet*. Leporello is the
creation of a more serious mind than that which created Fides
(in *The Prophet*). *Don Quixote* is a profounder work than *The
Battle of Rome*. With a poet, lack of humour is as bad a sign as
is the predominance of pathos, viz. Victor Hugo.

Only tragedy of the *soul* suited Beethoven, he could do little
when it came to tragic *situations*. The latter argue a conflict
between at least two people, while the former lies in the heart
of the individual. Beethoven would have been the right man
to write a comic opera of the higher order.

(1906)

ORCHESTRAL PLAYERS

HAVE YOU EVER thought about the 'Orchestra'? Each of its
members is a poor disappointed devil. Collectively they are
like a suppressed crowd of rebels, and, as an official 'body',
they are bumptious and vain. Routine gives their playing the
varnish of perfection and assurance. For the rest, they loathe
their work, their job and, most of all, music.

(1911)

Ildebrando Pizzetti

MAURICE RAVEL

THERE IS NOT a great deal of music which, like Ravel's, reveals at a glance its characteristics. If you glance at *Miroirs* or *Gaspard de la Nuit*, you are at once struck by two different, yet related, features in the writing: the notes constituting the melody are either supported by an equal number of chords running on parallel lines or the melody is submerged in wide waves of arpeggios. In both cases one musical organism—melody—moves against a background that has no life of its own but lives through the impressions it receives from melody that rises or falls, is slow or rapid—a single line expresses the feeling and emotion in the mind of the composer. This, to my thinking, is one of the most important differences between the music of Ravel and that of Debussy.

Debussy, who has dramatic genius and sensibilities, may use procedures similar to those of Ravel, but must of necessity add to his music accessories (combinations of different rhythms, unexpected variations in rhythm and melody) which are the outward signs of things felt and seen. Ravel, on the other hand, appears impressed not by the changing life, but by the moment; one would say that moments—static, immobile—generate in him a melody, a song which reflects them. While the spirit of Debussy lives dramatically, Ravel's lives lyrically. You never know which of the elements in Debussy is most prevalent (chords, melodies); in Ravel, and especially in compositions for pianoforte and for orchestra, it is the melodist that excels. Not only does a single line prevail, but the elaboration of the theme (in works in classical form like the Sonatine for piano) is, as regards expression, inferior to the exposition.

In the music of Ravel, as also in most of the music of modern France—elegant, *spirituelle*, interesting as it is—one looks in vain for broad, human expressions. Joy sings very rarely or when it does the tone is subdued; it is short-lived; nor do we find an echo of human sorrow. Instead of joy there is a felicitous cheerfulness that does not smile and instead of sorrow we have sadness, grey and weary. Let us glance for instance, at 'Barque sur l'Océan' or at 'Vallée des Cloches'. Apart from the new effects of sound, luminous, mysterious, apart from the ingenious devices of harmony, we have an impression of deadly melancholy. It is the voice of the musician singing about one aspect—an exterior one—of Nature. But the composer sings about Nature arrested in its course by some frightful event; his voice rises to a heaven that has no atmosphere of its own and no warmth.

It will be said that it is just because music of this type is concerned solely with the moment that sentiment and humanity have no share in it. But Beethoven's Nature is calm yet not dead; there is always something that lives in it, vibrating, singing for all men.

Thus while in the music of all the great masters of the past we find side by side with the expression of grief the expression of joy—which, in a sense, is the outcome of pain—in the work of those admirable French musicians of today we have no joy, free and sincere; we have in its place irony, jest, caricature, humour.

In Ravel we have the exquisite lyricist whose song is tinged with melancholy—and the brilliant humorist, without bitterness, full of verve. Do you know the *Histoires Naturelles*? Their author is a Renard less profound, but much less bitter, than the author of *Poil de carotte*. It is music that does not stir great emotion, light, intelligent and a real prodigy of finesse and exquisite taste. This is the music of Ravel I like best—and *L'heure Espagnole,* a comedy in one act, is a perfect mine of happy thoughts, of irony and musical caricature.

Alfredo Casella

CLAUDE DEBUSSY

IN HIS PERSONAL appearance Debussy did not at all resemble the slender, refined, delicate creature fondly
imagined by young ladies who delight in playing—somehow
or other—the first 'Arabesque' and 'Jardins sous la pluie'. He
was of middle height, broad-shouldered and very strong. The
shape of his head was peculiar; a wide forehead bulged forward
while the back seemed to recede; the eyes were small and
deep-set; the Roman nose was short and straight, the hair and
beard thick and black. Even in his fiftieth year there was hardly
a grey thread in it. His hands were the true artist's—perfect in
shape. The voice, rather rough by nature, suffered owing to
his excessive smoking habits. Nervous in speaking, he was most
neat and even elegant in his dress. He walked in a curious way
recalling the steps of a woman wearing high-heeled shoes. He
was something of a gourmet and it was a common occurrence
to meet the author of *Pelléas* in the Avenue Victor Hugo about
midday, carefully appraising the rarest fruit and cheeses that
were to appear later on his luncheon table. He disliked
strangers. He was never seen at a concert or in the theatre; he
had a horror of appearing in public. His friends were few and
he had no pupils. He seldom left the wife and daughter he
loved passionately. But he was a great worker and he needed
light to create. His study was lit by three great windows which
admitted shafts of sunlight to light up every one of the many
nick-nacks (mostly Asiatic) he had collected.

He was not a good conductor and confessed that when he
was obliged to conduct he felt ill before, during, and after the
performance. But he was a most admirable pianist. No word
can describe his playing of some of the *Préludes*. He had not the
virtuosity of the specialist, but his touch was extremely sensitive. One had the impression that he was playing actually on
the strings of the instrument without the mechanical aid of
keys and hammers. He used the pedals as no one else ever did;
the outcome was pure poetry.

He was not only a superb interpreter of his own compositions; he excelled in music of older masters and especially of Mozart. He knew all the Chopin repertory and told how a meeting with a pupil of Chopin in his youth influenced his outlook both as pianist and composer. He demanded much from his interpreters. He hated the famous virtuoso; he was fond of the cultured, intelligent player who, though not enjoying a great reputation, shared his earnest outlook.

He was a very cultured man—especially as regards literature and the plastic arts; he did not like the latest fashions in painting. Nor did he care for the new, anti-impressionistic music. Thus while he admired Stravinsky's *Petruchka*, he disliked *Sacre du Printemps*. After listening to Ravel's *Valses Nobles et Sentimentales,* he said: 'One should do much better with that type of music.'

He remained to the end the true 'grand enfant'. The lucidity that characterizes his art was reflected in his words and in his gestures. At fifty he delighted in playing with the toys his wife had bought for their daughter and he treated domestic animals with the egotism of a little urchin. He much preferred the English music-hall to the theatre. He was passionately fond of the sea; he did not like mountains. To a friend who asked him the reason why he felt an antipathy for mountains he replied shortly: 'Because mountains are too high.'

Pizzetti finds Debussy's art egotistical, rapt in itself, too aristocratic. In considering the work of a great artist, I am only concerned with the emotion and interest his art arouses; I am not concerned with its effect on humanity. Art is neither moral, socialistic, nor propaganda for patriotism or religion. Art is an expression of the artist's fancy, of his sensibility, of his imagination, and lives in its own world. I do not know how the historian of the future will look upon the 'humanity' of Debussy. I only know that at present I owe to it some of the most memorable and deepest experiences of my artistic career.

POLAND

Frédéric François Chopin

ON KALKBRENNER

HERZ, LISZT, HILLER—they are all zero beside Kalkbrenner. If Paganini is perfection, Kalkbrenner is his
equal but in quite another style. It is hard to describe
to you his calm, enchanting touch, his incomparable evenness
and the mastery that is displayed in every note; he is a giant
walking over Herz and Czerny and all—including myself. What
can I do? When we met he asked me to play something. I should
have liked to hear him first; but knowing how Herz plays,
I put my pride in my pocket and sat down. I played my E minor,
which the Rhinelanders and all Bavaria raved about. I astonished
Kalkbrenner, too, who at once asked me whether I was a pupil
of Field, as I have Cramer's method and Field's touch. This
delighted me. I was still more pleased when Kalkbrenner,
sitting down at the piano and wanting to do his best for me,
made a mistake and had to begin all over again. But you should
have heard him when he did start. I had not dreamed of
anything like it. We have been meeting every day since; he
comes to me or I go to him. After a time he made me an offer
to study with him for three years, saying he would make
something of me. I answered that I know how much I need
advice but that I could not abuse his kindness, and three years
is a long time. He has convinced me that I can play admirably
when I am in the mood and badly when I am not—a thing that
never happens to him. He told me that I have no school, that
I am on an excellent road but slip off the track; that after his
death there will be no representative of the great pianoforte
school; that even if I wished it I couldn't build a new school
without knowing the old; that I am not perfect technically and
that this hampers the flow of my thoughts; that having made
my mark in composition it would be a pity not to become
what I promise to be. If you had been there you would have
said: 'Learn, my boy, while there is a chance.' Many have tried
to dissuade me, thinking that I shall do well without it, that
the offer is made out of arrogance so that I may be known

afterwards as his pupil. That is rubbish. You must know that Kalkbrenner is as much hated as his talent is respected. He does not make friends with every fool and, as I love you, he is superior to everybody I have heard. . . .

To my mind, in order to appear before the musical world a man is fortunate if he is both composer and performer. I am known in certain parts of Germany as a pianist; some people have spoken of my concerts raising hopes that I may shortly take my place among the virtuosi. Today I have the opportunity to realize that hope—why not seize it? In Germany I could not have learnt anything from anybody; they felt I lacked something but could not say what. Three years is a long time—even Kalkbrenner admits it. But I would be willing to stick it if it would allow me to take the forward step I mean to take. I know enough not to become a mere imitator of Kalkbrenner and nothing can interfere with my, perhaps, overbold, but not ignoble, desire to create a new world of my own. If I work, it is to achieve a firmer footing. Ries found it easier to win laurels with *The Bride* in Berlin because he was known as a pianist. Spohr was well known as a violinist before he wrote *Jessonda, Faust,* etc.

(1831)

'ROBERT LE DIABLE' AT THE OPERA

I DON'T KNOW whether there has ever been such magnificence in a theatre or whether the pomp of Meyerbeer's new opera *Robert Le Diable* has ever been attained before. It is a masterpiece of the new school. A huge choir of devils singing through speaking trumpets; the dead rise from the grave; there is a diorama of the theatre in which at the end you see the interior of a church—the whole church—at Christmas (or, is it Easter?) lighted up, with monks and congregation—even an organ the sound of which on the stage is enchanting and also amazing as it nearly drowns the orchestra. Nothing of this sort could be put on anywhere else. Meyerbeer has immortalized himself but he has spent three years in getting it done and it is said that he paid 20,000 francs for the cast. Mme Cinti-Damoreau sings superbly; I prefer her to Malibran. Malibran amazed; Cinti delights; and her chromatic scales are better than those of Toulon, the famous flautist. No voice could be more highly trained; it seems to cost her so little effort to sing—as if she blew the notes to the audience. Nourrit, the tenor, has much feeling and Cholet is the lover— seductive, tantalizing, marvellous, a genius with the real voice of romance. He has created his own style.

(1831)

HOW TO BE FAMOUS IN PARIS

I HAVE GONE into the highest society. I sit with princes, ambassadors, ministers. I don't know how it happened; I made no effort yet it is very useful. You are supposed to be more gifted if you have been heard at the English or the Austrian embassy. You play better if Princess Vaudemont was your patron—I don't say 'is' because the lady died a week ago. She was a lady like poor Zielonkowa; she did some good and hid many aristocrats during the first revolution. She lived surrounded by a multitude of little black and white dogs, canaries, and parrots, and she also possessed a most amusing monkey which at evening receptions would bite other countesses.

(1831)

ON LISZT

I WRITE TO you without knowing what my pen is scribbling because at this moment Liszt is playing my *Études* and transporting me outside my thoughts. I should like to steal from him the way to play my own *Études*.

(1832)

JENNY LIND IN LONDON

I AM JUST returned from the Italian theatre. Jenny Lind sang for the first time this year and the Queen showed herself in public for the first time since the Chartist riots. Both produced a great effect on me and so did old Wellington who sat underneath the Queen's box like an old monarchical dog in his kennel under his crowned Lady. I have met Jenny Lind and she very graciously sent me an excellent stall with her card. As I had a good place I heard well. She is a typical Swede; not in the ordinary light but in a sort of Polar dawn. She is enormously effective in *Sonnambula*. She sings with extreme purity and certainty and her soft notes are steady and even.

A stall cost two and a half guineas. . . .

Jenny Lind came to my concert. It means a lot for the fools; wherever she is people turn their opera-glasses on her. I had never dreamed of asking her although she is a kind woman and we are on excellent terms. It is not the same with others. One may call it the Scandinavian streak. It is something totally different from southerners like Pauline Viardot. Lind is not pretty but pleasant, looking 'at home'. On the stage I don't always like her but in *Sonnambula* from the middle of the second act she is perfectly beautiful in every respect as an actress and singer. People say that she will marry Mrs Grote's brother but I know for certain that it is not true.

(1848)

THE TALLEST CHIMNEY IN MANCHESTER

SINCE WRITING TO you I have been to Manchester. They received me very well: I had to sit down at the piano three times. The hall is fine and holds 1,200 people. I stayed in the country as there is too much smoke in town; all the rich people live outside. I stayed with the kind Schwabe's. He is one of the foremost manufacturers, owns the tallest chimney in Manchester (it cost £5,000) and is a friend of Cobden. His wife is particularly kind.

(1848)

IN SCOTLAND

ART HERE MEANS painting, sculpture and architecture. Music is not called an art and if you say artist the Englishman will understand you to say painter, architect or sculptor. Music is not an art: it is a profession. Ask any Englishman and he will tell you that I am right. No doubt it is the fault of the musicians. These queer people play for the sake of beauty but to teach them is a joke. Lady X, one of the first ladies here, is regarded as a great musician. One day after my playing, and after hearing various songs by other Scottish ladies, they brought a kind of accordion and she began with the utmost gravity to play on it the most atrocious tunes. Everybody seems to me to have a screw loose. A lady showing her album told me the Queen had seen it; another told me she was the thirteenth cousin of Mary Stuart. The Princess of Parma told me that one lady whistled a tune for her with guitar accompaniment. They all look at their hands and play the wrong notes with much feeling. Eccentric folk—God help them!

My Scotswomen are kind; I have not seen them for two or three weeks but they are coming today. They want me to stay and go visiting from one Scottish palace to another. They are kind but so boring. Every day I get letters and answer none of them; wherever I go they follow if at all possible. Perhaps that has given someone the notion that I intend to get married but there should be some physical attraction, and the unmarried one is too much like myself.

Even if I could fall in love with someone, as I should be glad to do, I could not marry, as we should have nothing to eat and nowhere to live. A rich woman expects to marry a rich man, or, if a poor one, one at least who is young and handsome—not a sickly one. It is bad enough to go to pieces alone, but two together—that indeed would be the greatest misfortune. I may peg out in a hospital; I will not leave a starving wife behind me.

(1848)

IN LONDON

AFTER MY MATINÉES many papers had good criticisms except *The Times* whose critic is a certain Davison—a creature of poor Mendelssohn. He does not know me and imagines, so I am told, that I am an antagonist of Mendelssohn. It does not matter to me, but you see how everywhere in the world there are people actuated by something that is not truth. My fee for an evening in London was £20. I have only had three such evenings.

(1848)

RUSSIA

Peter Ilitch Tchaikovsky

ON WAGNER'S 'RING'

BAYREUTH HAS LEFT me with disagreeable recollections. My artistic ambition was flattered more than once, as it appears that I am by no means as unknown in Western Europe as I thought. The disagreeable recollections are raised by the uninterrupted bustle in which I was obliged to take part which finally came to an end on Thursday. After the last notes of the *Götterdämmerung* I felt as though I had been let out of prison. The *Nibelungen* may be a magnificent work, but it is certain that there never was anything so endlessly and wearisomely spun out. . . .

I brought away the impression that the trilogy contains many passages of extraordinary beauty, especially symphonic beauty, which is remarkable, as Wagner has certainly no intention of writing an opera in the style of a symphony. I feel a respectful admiration for the immense talent of the composer and his wealth of technique is such as has never been heard before. And yet I have grave doubts as to the soundness of Wagners' principles of opera. I will, however, continue the study of this music—the most complicated which has hitherto been composed.

Yet, if the *Ring* bores one in places, if much of it is, at first, incomprehensible and vague, if Wagner's harmonies are at times open to objection, being complicated and artificial, if his theories are false, even if the results of his immense work should eventually fall into oblivion and the Bayreuth theatre drop into eternal slumber, yet the *Nibelungen Ring* is an event of the greatest importance to the world, an epoch-making work of art.

(1876)

I have seen *Walküre*. The performance was excellent. The orchestra surpassed itself; the best singers did all within their powers—and yet it was wearisome. What a Don Quixote Wagner is! He expends his whole force in pursuing the im-

possible and all the time, if he would but follow the natural
bent of his extraordinary gift, he might evoke a whole world
of musical beauties. He is gifted with a genius which has
wrecked itself on his tendencies. His inspiration is paralysed
by theories which he has invented and which, *volens nolens*, he
wants to put into practice. In his effort to attain reality, truth
and rationalism, he lets music slip quite out of sight, so that
in his four latest operas it is, more often than not, conspicuous
by its absence. I cannot call music that which consists of
kaleidoscopic, shifting phrases which succeed each other without break and never come to a close, that is to say, never give
the ear a chance to rest upon musical form. Not a single broad,
rounded melody, nor yet one moment of repose for the singer!
The latter must always pursue the orchestra and be careful
never to lose his note, which has no more importance in the
score than some note for the fourth horn. But Wagner is a
wonderful symphonist. I can prove to you by a single example
how far the symphonic prevails over the operatic style in his
music. You have probably heard the celebrated *Walkürenritt*?
What a great and marvellous picture! How we actually seem to
see these fierce heroines flying on their magic steeds amid
thunder and lightning. In the concert room this piece makes an
extraordinary impression. On the stage, in view of the card-
board rocks, the canvas clouds and the soldiers who run about
very awkwardly in the background—in a word, seen in this
very inadequate theatrical heaven, which makes a poor pretence
of realizing the illimitable realms above—the music loses its
power of expression. Here the stage does not enhance the
effect, but acts rather like a wet blanket. Finally, I do not
understand, and never shall, why the *Niebelungen* should be
considered a literary masterpiece. A national saga perhaps; but
a libretto—distinctly not.

  Wotan, Brünnhilde, Fricka and the rest are all so impossible,
so little human, that it is very difficult to feel any sympathy
with their destinies. And how little life! For three whole hours
Wotan lectures Brünnhilde on her disobedience. How wearisome! And with it all there are many fine and beautiful episodes
of a purely symphonic description.

(1877)

Yesterday I began to study the score of *Lohengrin*. I am not very sympathetic to Wagnerism in principle. Wagner's personality arouses my antipathy, yet I must do justice to his great musical gift. This reaches its climax in *Lohengrin*, which must always remain the crown of all his works. After *Lohengrin* began the deterioration of a talent ruined by his diabolical vanity. He lost all sense of proportion and began to overstep all limits so that everything he composed after *Lohengrin* became incomprehensible, impossible music which has no future. What chiefly interests me in *Lohengrin* at present is the orchestration. In view of the work which lies before me I want to study this score very closely and decide whether I want to adopt some of his methods of instrumentation. His mastery is extraordinary, but for reasons which would necessitate technical explanation I have not borrowed anything from him. Wagner's orchestration is too symphonic, too overloaded and heavy for vocal music. The older I grow the more convinced I am that symphony and opera are in every respect at the opposite poles of music. Therefore the study of *Lohengrin* will not lead me to change my style; it has been interesting but of negative value.

(1879)

Yesterday I heard *Tristan und Isolde*. The work does not give me any pleasure, although I am glad I have heard it, for it has done much to strengthen my previous views, which, until I had seen all Wagner's works, I felt not to be well grounded. Briefly summed up this is my opinion: in spite of great creative gifts, his talents as a poet, his extensive culture, Wagner's services to art—and to opera in particular—have only been of a negative kind. He has proved that the older forms of opera are lacking in all logical and aesthetic *raison d'être*. But if we may no longer write opera on the old lines, are we obliged to write as Wagner does? I reply, decidedly, 'no'. To compel people to listen for four hours at a stretch to an endless symphony which, however rich in orchestral colour, is wanting in clearness and directness of thought: to keep singers all these hours singing melodies which have no independent existence, but are merely notes that belong to symphonic music (in spite of lying very high these notes are often lost in the thunder of the orchestra)— this is certainly not the ideal for a contemporary musician to aim at. Wagner has transferred the centre of gravity from the stage to the orchestra, but this is an obvious absurdity, therefore his famous operatic reform—viewed apart from its negative results—amounts to nothing. As regards dramatic interest, I find his operas very poor, often childishly naïve. But I have never been quite so bored as with *Tristan und Isolde*. It is an endless void, without movement, without life, which cannot hold the spectator or awaken in him any true sympathy for the characters on the stage. It was evident that the audience—although German—were bored but they applauded loudly after each act. How can this be explained? Perhaps by a patriotic sympathy for a composer who actually devoted his whole life to singing the praise of Germanism.

(1883)

In *Parsifal* we deal with a master, a genius, even if he has gone somewhat astray. His wealth of harmony is so luxuriant, so vast that at length it becomes fatiguing even to the specialist. What then must be the feeling of an ordinary mortal who has wrestled for three hours with this flow of complicated harmonic combinations? To my mind Wagner has killed his colossal creative genius with theories. Every preconceived theory chills his incontestable creative impulse. How could Wagner abandon himself to inspiration while he believed he was grasping some particular theory of music-drama, or musical truth, and, for the sake of this, turned from all which, according to his predecessors, constituted the strength and beauty of music? When the singer may not *sing* but, amid the deafening clamour of the orchestra, is expected to declaim a series of set and colourless phrases to the accompaniment of a gorgeous but disconnected and formless symphony—is that opera?

What really astounds me, however, is the seriousness with which this philosophizing German sets the most inane subjects to music. Who can be touched, for instance, by *Parsifal*, where, instead of having to deal with men and women similar in temperament and feeling to ourselves, we find legendary beings, suitable perhaps for a ballet, but not for a music-drama? I cannot understand how anyone can listen without laughter, or without being bored, to those endless monologues in which Parsifal, or Kundry and the rest, bewail their misfortunes. Can we sympathize with them? Can we love or hate them? Certainly not, we remain aloof from their passions, sentiments, triumphs and misfortunes. What is foreign to the human heart should never be the source of musical inspiration.

(1884)

BRAHMS

YESTERDAY I LOOKED through a new symphony in C minor by Brahms, a composer whom the Germans exalt to the skies. He has no charm for me. I find him cold and obscure, full of pretensions, but without any real depth.

(1877)

In the music of Brahms there is something dry and cold which repels me. He has very little melodic invention. He never speaks of his musical ideas to the end. We seldom hear an enjoyable melody that is not engulfed in a whirlpool of unimportant harmonic progressions and modulations as though the special aim of the composer were to be unintelligible. He excites and irritates our musical senses without wishing to satisfy them and seems ashamed to speak a language which goes straight to the heart. His depth is not real. He has set himself once and for all the aim of trying to be profound, but he has only attained to the appearance of profundity. The gulf is wide. It is impossible to say that the music of Brahms is weak and insignificant. His style is invariably lofty. He does not strive after mere external effects. He is never trivial. All that he does is serious and noble, but he lacks the chief thing—beauty. Brahms commands our respect. We must bow before the original purity of his aspirations. We must admire his firm and proud attitude in the face of triumphant Wagnerism; but to love him is impossible. I, at least, in spite of many efforts have not succeeded. I will own that some early works (such as the sextet in B flat) please me far more than those of a later period and especially the symphonies which seem to me exceptionally long and colourless.

(1888)

Brahms is a caricature of Beethoven.

(1888)

BEETHOVEN

THERE IS NO padding in Beethoven. It is astonishing how equal, how significant and forceful this giant among musicians always remains and how well he understands the art of curbing his vast inspiration, never losing sight of balanced, traditional form. In his last quartets, which were long regarded as the productions of an insane and deaf man, there seems to be some padding until you study them thoroughly. But ask someone who is familiar with these works, say, a member of a quartet who has performed them frequently, if there is anything superfluous in the C sharp minor quartet. Unless he is an old-fashioned musician brought up on Haydn, he will be horrified at the thought of abbreviating or cutting any part of it. In speaking of Beethoven I am not thinking merely of his last period. Could anyone show me a bar in the 'Eroica'—a long symphony—that could be called superfluous, or any portion that could really be omitted as padding? Thus everything that is long is not too long; many words do not necessarily mean empty verbiage and terseness is not an essential condition of beautiful form. Beethoven, who in the first movement of the 'Eroica' has built up a superb edifice out of an endless series of varied and ever new architectural beauties upon so simple, and seemingly poor, a subject, knows on occasion how to surprise us by the terseness and exiguity of his forms. Do you remember the Andante of the pianoforte concerto in B flat? I know nothing more inspired than this movement; I go cold and pale every time I hear it.

Of course, the classical beauty of Beethoven's predecessors and their art of keeping within bounds are of the greatest value. It must be owned, however, that Haydn had no occasion to limit himself, for he had not an inexhaustible wealth of material at command. As to Mozart, had he lived another twenty years and seen the beginning of our century, he would certainly have tried to express his prodigal inspiration in forms less strictly classical than those with which he had to content himself.

(1888)

Although every art is related to the sister arts, they all have their peculiarities. As such we must regard the 'verbal repetitions' which are only possible to a limited extent in literature but are a necessity in music. Beethoven never repeats an entire movement without a special reason, and in so doing rarely fails to introduce something new. But he has recourse to this characteristic method in his instrumental music, knowing that his idea will only be understood after many statements. I cannot understand your objection to the constant repetition of the subject in the Scherzo of the Ninth Symphony. It is so divinely beautiful, strong, original and significant! It is quite another matter with the prolixity and repetitions of Schubert who, with all his genius, constantly harps upon his central idea—as in the Andante of the C major Symphony. Beethoven develops his idea fully before repeating it; Schubert seems too indolent to elaborate his first idea and—perhaps from his unusual wealth of thematic material—he hurries through the beginning to arrive at something else. It seems as though the stress of his inexhaustible inspiration hindered him from carefully elaborating the theme in all its depth and delicacy of workmanship.

(1888)

GLINKA

Glinka's 'memoirs' reveal a nice, amiable, but commonplace man. We can hardly realize that the same man created *Slavia*, which is worthy to rank with the work of the greatest genius. And how many more fine things there are in *Russlan* and in the overtures! How astonishingly original is his *Komarinskaya*, from which all the Russian composers who followed him (including myself) continue to this day to borrow contrapuntal and harmonic combinations whenever they have to develop a Russian dance tune. This is done unconsciously. But the fact is that Glinka managed to concentrate in one short work what a dozen second-rate talents would only have invented with the whole expenditure of their powers. And it was this same Glinka who, at the height of his maturity composed so weak and trivial a thing as the *Polonaise for the Coronation* (written a year before his death) or the *Children's Polka*, of which he speaks in his *Memoirs* at length and with self-satisfaction—as though it were a masterpiece.

Mozart, too, expresses himself with great naïveté in his letters to his father, and, in fact, all through his life. But his was another kind of simplicity. Mozart is a genius whose child-like innocence, gentleness of spirit and virginal modesty are scarcely of this earth. He was devoid of self-satisfaction and boastfulness, and he seems hardly to have been conscious of the greatness of his genius. Glinka, on the other hand, is imbued with the spirit of self-glorification. He is ready to be garrulous over the most trivial events of his life, or the appearance of his least important work, and convinced it is all of historical importance. Glinka is the gifted Russian aristocrat of his time, and has the faults of the type: petty vanity, limited culture, intolerance, ostentatiousness and a morbid sensibility to and impatience of all criticism. These are generally the characteristics of mediocrity; how they come to exist in a man who ought to dwell in calm and modest pride, conscious of his power, is beyond my comprehension. In one page of his *Memoirs* Glinka says he had a bulldog whose conduct was not irreproachable and his servant had to be continually cleaning the room. Kukolnik, to whom Glinka entrusted the revision of the *Memoirs*, remarked in the margin 'Why put in this?' Glinka pencilled underneath 'Why not?' Is not this highly charac-teristic? But, all the same, he did compose *Slavia*.

(1880)

An amateur who played violin and piano a little, who concocted a few insipid quadrilles and fantasias on Italian airs, who tried his hand at more serious musical forms without accomplishing anything rising above the jejune tastes of the thirties, suddenly in his thirty-fourth year creates an opera which for inspiration, originality and irreproachable technique is worthy to stand beside all that is loftiest and most profound in musical art! We are still more astonished when we reflect that the composer of this work is the author of the *Memoirs* published some twenty years later. Like a nightmare the question haunts me: how could such colossal artistic force be united to such emptiness? How came this average amateur to

catch up in a single stride such men as Mozart and Beethoven?
For he did overtake them. One may say this without exaggeration of the composer of *Slavia*. The question may be
answered by those who are better fitted to penetrate the
mystery of the artistic spirit which makes its habitation in such
fragile and apparently unpromising shrines. I can only say no
one loves and appreciates Glinka more than I do. I am no
indiscriminate worshipper of *Russlan*; on the contrary, I am
inclined to prefer *A Life for the Tsar*, although *Russlan* may
perhaps have greater musical worth. But the elemental force
is more perceptible in the earlier opera, as *Slavia* is overwhelming and gigantic. For this he used no model. Neither Gluck nor
Mozart composed anything similar. Astounding, inconceivable!
Kamarinskaya is also a work of remarkable inspiration. Without
intending to compose anything beyond a simple, humorous
trifle, he has left us a little masterpiece, every bar of which is
the outcome of enormous creative power. Half a century has
passed since then and many Russian symphonic works have
been composed; we may even speak of a symphonic school.
Well? The germ of all this lies in *Kamarinskaya* as the oak tree
lies in the acorn. For long years to come Russian composers
will drink at this source, for it will need much time and much
strength to exhaust its wealth of inspiration. Yes, Glinka was a
true creative genius.

(1888)

THE FIRST BAYREUTH FESTIVAL

I REACHED BAYREUTH ON August 12th, the day before the
first performance of the first part of the trilogy. The town was
in a state of great excitement. Crowds of people, natives and
strangers, were rushing to the railway station to witness the
arrival of the Emperor. I saw the spectacle from the window of
a house in the neighbourhood. First some brilliant uniforms
passed by, then the musicians of the Wagner theatre with their
conductor, Hans Richter, at their head; next followed the
interesting figure of the 'Abbé' Liszt with the fine, characteristic head I had so often admired in pictures. Lastly, in a
sumptuous carriage, the serene old man, Richard Wagner,

with his aquiline nose and the delicately ironical smile which gives such a characteristic expression to the face of the creator of this cosmopolitan and artistic festival. As the Emperor's train entered the station a rousing 'hurrah' resounded from thousands of throats. The old Emperor stepped into the carriage awaiting him and drove to the Palace. Wagner, who followed immediately in his wake, was greeted by the crowd with as much enthusiasm as the Emperor. What pride, what overflowing emotions must have filled at this moment the heart of that little man who, by his energetic will and great talent has defied all obstacles to the final realization of his artistic ideals and audacious views.

I made a little excursion through the streets of the town. They swarmed with people of all nationalities, who looked very much preoccupied as if in search of something. The reason of this search, I discovered but too soon myself. . . . All these restless people wandering through the town were seeking to satisfy the pangs of hunger which even the highest artistic enjoyment could not entirely assuage. The little town offers, it is true, sufficient shelter to strangers but it cannot feed its guests. So it happened that on the very day of my arrival I learnt what the 'struggle for existence' means. There are very few hotels in Bayreuth and the greater part of the visitors find accommodation in private houses. The tables d'hôtes of the inns are not sufficient for all the hungry people; one can only secure a piece of bread or a glass of beer with immense difficulty by dire struggle, cunning stratagem or iron endurance. Even when a modest place at the table has been secured, it is necessary to wait an eternity before the long-desired meal is served. Anarchy reigns, everyone is calling and shrieking while the exhausted waiters pay no heed to the rightful claims of the individual. Only by the merest chance does one get a taste of any of the dishes. In the neighbourhood of the theatre is a restaurant which advertises a good dinner at 2.0 o'clock. To enter and get hold of anything in that throng of hungry creatures is a feat worthy of a hero.

I have dwelt upon this matter at some length with the design of calling the attention of my readers to this prominent feature of Bayreuth 'melomania'. As a matter of fact, throughout the

whole duration of the Festival, food forms the chief interest of
the public; the artistic representations take a secondary place.
Cutlets, baked potatoes, omelettes, are discussed more eagerly
than Wagner's music.

I have mentioned that the representatives of all civilized
nations were assembled in Bayreuth. I perceived in the crowd
many leaders of the musical world in Europe and America. But
the greatest of them, the most famous—Verdi, Gounod,
Thomas, Brahms, Anton Rubinstein, Raff, Joachim, Bülow—
had not come.

(1876)

Nicholai Andreievich Rimsky-Korsakov

ON BALAKIREFF AS TEACHER

BALAKIREFF HAD NEVER had systematic training in harmony and counterpoint and believed such training unnecessary. Thanks to his talent and pianistic ability he yet became a first-rate practical musician. An excellent performer, incomparable improviser and sight-reader, endowed by nature with a feeling for correct harmony and part-writing, he easily acquired a vast amount of knowledge thanks to a keen and retentive memory. He was also a marvellous critic, especially of technical matters. He knew at once every mistake and whenever I played him my compositions he immediately pointed out errors of form or modulation; seating himself at the piano, he would then show me how the fault should be corrected. We obeyed him absolutely, for the spell of his personality was irresistible. Though appreciating talent in others he could not but make his higher accomplishments felt and his influence resembled an irresistible magnetic or mesmeric force.

With all his gifts and brilliance there was one thing he never understood: that what was good for him would be of little use to men who had grown up in different surroundings and whose temperament was entirely different from his own. He insisted on his pupil doing as he dictated; any departure from dogma was severely censured. He could take up a passage that had not pleased him and play it distorted and caricatured till the pupil, blushing with shame, recanted his error.

A gift for melody was looked upon with disfavour. Nearly all the thematic ideas of Beethoven's symphonies he considered weak; Chopin's melodies sweet and womanish; Mendelssohn's sour and bourgeois. Only the themes of Bach's fugues he held in respect. A composition was never examined as a whole but piecemeal. The pupil had to submit his work in embryo—a few bars at a time, which were praised or ridiculed—and the composition of a movement extended over a long period of time.

There was in Balakireff a strange contradiction. The man who could instantly find flaws in the work of others and correct a commonplace turn of phrase, improve a harmony or the arrangement of a sequence of chords, was yet himself a slow and deliberate worker. I must say, however, that at that time (he was twenty-four or twenty-five years of age) his self-criticism and manner of treating his pupils had not assumed the clear, tangible form that began in 1865 when other fledgelings appeared on the scene beside myself.

BERLIOZ'S CONDUCTING

HECTOR BERLIOZ CAME to us when he was already an old man. Though alert at rehearsal he was bowed down with illness and therefore utterly indifferent to Russian music and musicians. Most of his leisure was spent stretched on his back complaining of illness and seeing only Balakireff and the directors of the concerts. Once he was taken to a performance of *A Life for the Tsar* at the Mariinski theatre and left before the end of the second act. I imagine that it was not ill-health alone but the conceit of genius and the aloofness becoming genius that were responsible for his complete indifference to the musical life of Russia and St Petersburg. There was no talk of Mussorgsky, Borodin or myself meeting Berlioz, either because Balakireff, realizing Berlioz's unconcern, felt embarrassed and did not ask permission to effect the introduction, or because Berlioz himself asked to be spared the necessity of meeting Russia's young composers of promise.

At his six concerts Berlioz conducted *Harold in Italy*, the *Symphonie Fantastique*, several of his overtures, excerpts from *Faust* and from *Romeo and Juliet*, the Third, Fourth, Fifth and Sixth Symphonies of Beethoven and excerpts from Gluck's operas. In other words—Beethoven, Gluck and 'I'. Of course Mendelssohn, Schubert and Schumann were omitted—not to speak of Liszt and Wagner.

The execution was excellent; the spell of his famous personality did it all. Berlioz's beat was simple, clear, beautiful. No vagaries at all in shading. And yet, according to Balakireff, at rehearsal Berlioz lost himself in his own piece, beating three instead of two or vice versa. The orchestra, trying not to look at him, kept on playing and all went well. Berlioz, the great conductor of his time, came to us when his faculties were already on the decline owing to old age, illness and fatigue.[1] The public did not notice it; the orchestra forgave him. Conducting is a thing shrouded in mystery.

MUSSORGSKY

IN 1871 MUSSORGSKY and I agreed to live together and we shared rooms (or rather a room) on Pantyeleymonovskay Street. In the mornings until noon Mussorgsky used the piano while I did copying or scoring. By noon he went to his departmental duties leaving the piano to me. Moreover, twice a week I went to the conservatoire at 8.0 a.m. while Mussorgsky frequently dined out, so that the arrangement worked smoothly. That autumn and winter the two of us accomplished a good deal. Mussorgsky composed and orchestrated the Polish act of *Boris Godunoff* and the folk scene 'Near Kromy'. I finished and orchestrated my *Maid of Pskov*. The *Maid of Pskov* was performed for the first time on 1 January 1873, and favourably received. At the end of the season two scenes from *Boris Godunoff* were also given and scored a great success. Mussorgsky and all of us were delighted; after the performance Mussorgsky and other friends came to our house where we drank champagne, wishing an early performance and success to *Boris*. It was given in January 1874 and so well received that we were all jubilant. Mussorgsky was then already at work on *Khovanshtchina*. The original version of this opera had many details which have since disappeared. A whole tableau had been projected in the suburb of a German town and Mussorgsky played to us sketches of the scene composed in a quasi-Mozartian style to fit the bourgeois German scene. In Act I there was a rather long scene in which the people demolished the scrivener's booth. When, after Mussorgsky's death, I was preparing the opera for publication, I omitted this scene altogether as quite unmusical; it also delayed the action.

---

[1] *Berlioz was then sixty-four. He died in 1869.*

. . . There was some barbarous music of empty, perfect fourths intended for the choir of schismatics, which Mussorgsky fortunately altered later. There are now only odds and ends of the first sketch in the beautiful chorus of schismatics in the Phrygian mode.

After the production of *Boris Godunoff* Mussorgsky appeared in our midst less often; a marked change was seen in him. His conceit grew enormously and his involved manner of expression grew more marked; we could no longer understand his stories and sallies meant to be witty and amusing. At the same time he began to loiter in restaurants till the early hours drinking brandy. When he dined with us he refused wine, but after nightfall he would resort to the restaurant and drink heavily.

After his retirement from service Mussorgsky began to compose by fits and starts, going from one subject to another. . . . His mental and spiritual decline was largely due to the success and failure of *Boris*. The first success made him proud and conceited, but after a time the opera began to be cut about. The splendid scene 'Near Kromy' was omitted altogether and two years later, for some inexplicable reason, the work which had been most popular disappeared from the repertory. Every barman in St Petersburg knew *Boris* and *Khovanshtchina* and honoured their composer, but the Russian Musical Society, while treating him with great affability, denied him recognition. His friends still loved him and frankly admired his brilliant flashes of creative genius, but the press was continuously scolding him. In the circumstances his craving for brandy and the desire to lounge in taverns grew stronger every day. A drinking bout which may not have affected his companions at all was poison to a man of his morbidly nervous temperament. Though still keeping up friendly relations, he began to look upon me with suspicion. My studies in harmony and counterpoint did not please him; he seemed to think I was likely to become a pedant who would upbraid him for writing consecutive fifths. His relations with Balakireff had been strained for some time. Even in the old days Balakireff used to say that Mussorgsky had great natural talent but 'feeble brains' and a reprehensible fondness for wine.

The year 1874 may be considered the beginning of a decline which was gradual and continued to the day of Mussorgsky's death.

'BUREAUCRATIC' FITS

AT THAT TIME (1875) I was somewhat irascible when I came across negligence. I remember that during a rehearsal the errand-man who had forgotten to do something got such a tongue-lashing from me that the orchestra began to hiss. I calmed down as I did not want to irritate the orchestra. On another occasion I yelled at the librarian of the school who had not prepared the music in time and he (an amateur librarian) was offended. Such fits of temper, assuming the tone of a superior officer, seized me occasionally—possibly the result of my training in the navy.

That very season two talented pupils of mine, Lyadoff and G. O. Dutsch, grew lazy and ceased coming to my classes. After talking the matter over with the director, it was decided to expel them. Soon after their expulsion the two youngsters came to see me promising to work hard and asking to be re-admitted. I answered them with a blunt refusal. How could such inhuman passion for formality overmaster me? Of course they should have been re-admitted like the prodigals they were, and the fatted calf should have been killed for the occasion. Dutsch was very capable and Lyadoff extremely talented. But I did not do it. The only consolation is that everything is for the best in this world of ours. Later on both became my friends.

OPINION OF MASCAGNI AND LEONCAVALLO

MY OPERA *May Night* was given to full houses and was played night after night until displaced by Leoncavallo's *Pagliacci*. I did not like Leoncavallo's work. A cleverly handled subject of the 'realistic' style and true swindler's music of the type invented by that career-chaser, Mascagni, caused a furore. These gentlemen are as remote from old man Verdi as from a star in the heavens.

TCHAIKOVSKY'S LAST SYMPHONY
AND DEATH

TCHAIKOVSKY'S SUDDEN DEATH was a heavy blow to us all. Soon after the funeral the Sixth Symphony was repeated under Napravnik. This time the public greeted it rapturously. It was said that the symphony had been made clear by Napravnik which Tchaikovsky (when he conducted the first performance) had not been able to do. I think this is not true.

The symphony was finely played under Napravnik, but it had gone well also when conducted by its author. I imagine that the composer's sudden death (which gave rise to all kinds of rumours) and the stories of the presentiment of approaching end people discovered in the gloomy last movement of the symphony—all these tended to focus people's attention and sympathies on a work which soon became famous and fashionable.